Blood Gold Revenge

by Dave Wright

To all who have missing family members in the Australian Outback, may the answers become apparent for closure or justice.

Blood Gold Revenge

A copy of this publication can be found in the National Library of Australia.

ISBN: 978-0-646-95255-0 (paperback)
ISBN: 978-0-646-95324-3 (ebook)

Published by Blood Gold Publications and Productions Pty Ltd

This is a work of fiction, though various parts of this story were inspired by true events. All characters, names and places are fictitious, or fictionalized, dramatized or adapted from fact for the purpose of entertainment, {including the QLD Police Force}. Accordingly any similarities between characters contained within this story and any living or dead person should not be considered to be true and accurate reflection of that person.

Written by Dave Wright 22/06/2013. Email: bloodgold@bigpond.com
REGISTERED WITH-
US Copyright Office TXu 1-928-076
AWG JB009229
WGA 1667144 &1687127

AUTHORS BLURB

The author resides in sunny North Queensland, mostly raised in the outback with schooling done via correspondence. Finishing off grade 10 at age 15 in Redcliffe before starting work in the remote gold mines of Northern Australia 34 years ago. To this day the author has barely picked up a novel or put pen to paper before starting on this book. In real life when time permits he still rides the hills prospecting for gold with his mates and is currently part way through writing the sequel.

You Tube Channel - Goldhounds Nugget Recovery

PROLOGUE

Do not be complacent about its natural beauty; the Outback is unforgiving and must be given the respect it deserves. From our pioneers to the present, many have met with foul play, and the bush keeps its secrets well.

June 1985

A young girl aged 12 years, barefoot and dressed in nothing more than rags, stumbled over the rocky uneven ground towards two large burning ant hills, straining under the weight of timber she carried in her arms. Dropping the last bundle of wood heavily near the fires, the girl proceeded to fuel them with more timber. Sweat ran down the side of her dust-covered face.

A large-framed man with body language that exuded strength and authority sat upon a magnificent dark stallion standing well over 18 hands high. The animal had been reined in tight a short distance from the ant hills. His voice boomed harshly over the crackling of the fires. "Come on, child, we haven't got all day." The stallion had become skittish from the smell of the smoke, its nostrils flared and its eyes widened as the owner skilfully kept it under control.

The young girl finished off the chore assigned by her father. Exhausted she walked a short distance towards the mare that stood with its reins loosely draped over a tree branch. Lifting her tired arms up to grasp the pommel, she swung into the saddle with ease, glancing across at the towering figure for any sign of approval on his hard chiselled features. With none forthcoming, he pointed towards two saddled quarter horses grazing a good distance away. "Bring them home with you." With that said he sunk the spurs into the stallion. It responded instantly, galloping back towards the homestead, leaving a trail of dust in their wake. The sun started its downward path towards the horizon as the child followed well behind leading the other two animals.

PRESENT DAY March 2012

With the heat of the North Queensland outback quickly intensifying, an old prospector is making the most out of the morning cool, swinging his metal detector evenly from side to side 200 metres off the dirt road. He slowly works the gold machine around a small gully that had just produced a couple of nice nuggets. Sweat is starting to form quickly on Fred's forehead from the sheer exertion of swinging the pick to unearth the nuggets from the dry compact ground. On picking up the first few handfuls of dirt, he quickly feels the weight of another nugget in his palm before dropping it into an old leather pouch.

Two rough-looking men in a fawn 4x4 tray back are travelling along the dusty corrugated road when the larger of the two taps the driver's shoulder with the back of his hand. "There," he says in a gruff voice, pointing towards fresh motorbike tracks in the bull dust thrown to the road side. The driver nods and applies the brakes heavily. They let out a squeal of protest from the build-up of fine dust on the brake calipers. Coming to a stop, the men get out promptly.

The passenger adjusts his gun belt back above his hip line, unclipping the leather strap of the 357 Magnum sitting snuggly in its holster.

The men immediately pick up on the fresh tracks left by the bike tyres; the spindly dead grass is laid over, producing a definitive trail for them to follow. They move stealthily forward, weaving through the trees. They spot the old timer in a clearing 70 metres out in front.

The old prospector, having spent decades in the bush, had developed a sixth sense of knowing when he was not alone. Pausing with the detector, Fred turns, his clear blue eyes peering into the scattered scrub line for any sign of life while removing the headphones with a backward hand movement that left them sitting loosely around his neck. A combination of old age and years of machinery work had left him with diminished hearing; straining, he tries to confirm his suspicion that someone is close by.

On the edge of his peripheral vision, he notices a pair of squatter pigeons that had been well camouflaged in the dead grass startle and take flight. Within that same split second, Fred sees what had caused the birds' reaction; the advancing men. Realising their position has been given up, they make themselves visible and continue towards the prospector unperturbed. "How you fellas going?" Fred asks nervously.

The men, with snide smirks on their faces from the unanswered question, move closer; the thinner of the two, called Scrubber, bends down and picks up a rock twice the size of his hand. Both are now close enough for Fred to recognise who they are and, by their reputation, he knows he is in big trouble. Sensing that his number is up, Fred tries to run. His co-ordination not being what it used to be, he trips on a small anthill concealed in the grass and falls, forward into a cluster of exposed granite rocks. Trying in vain to regain his feet, the prospector goes down awkwardly.

Seizing on the moment, Scrubber moves in swiftly. A sickening thud is made as the rock connected with flesh and bone, splitting the old man's head like a ripe watermelon, with the spray of blood covering Scrubber's hands and forearms. The ferocity of the second blow caves in the side of his skull, leaving large blood splatters across the front of his well-worn dusty shirt.

Price, not wanting to be left out of the action, also moves in, placing a vicious kick to the old man's throat, completely crushing his windpipe. Fred's crumpled body lies twitching with muscle spasms on the ground as blood oozes out of the gaping head wound, quickly soaking into the dry thirsty dirt like a sponge; what is left congeals as the heat of the day increased rapidly. The detector continues to hum only metres away, with the name Fred clearly visible engraved on the side.

Satisfied the job is done, both men amble towards a small, clear running creek to wash the blood off themselves. Scrubber then sits on a large boulder beside the water's edge and, with a steady hand, rolls a smoke. Price follows suit. After looking down at his blood-stained shirt and taking a long draw on his smoke, he looks across at Scrubber. "He was a real bleeder that one."

Scrubber sneers back at him, "yeah, Max is going to be pissed off when we tell her."

Price replies after a minute's thought, "Maybe we shouldn't say anything. She goes from zero to bitch real quick. So what are we going to do with the body?"

Scrubber squints and tips his hat to cut out the majority of the glare as he watches a couple of crows landing in the large gum tree towering above the old prospector's body. Cocking their heads to one side to see if there is any movement from their new- found prey, they cry out, "Ark, ark." More arrive on the tree branches to find out what the gathering was about.

"Give it half an hour his eyes will be gone; in half a day, he will bloat, the scent will bring in the pigs and dingoes. They will scatter his splintered bones from asshole to breakfast all over the countryside. Leave him. Just find the bike and we will put it in the truck."

Price walks off in search of the bike and, within a matter of minutes, yells out, "Found it." Scrubber butts out his smoke on a rock, places the stub into his top pocket, gets up and walks past the body towards Price's voice. Once he is a comfortable distance away, the crows swoop from the trees to satisfy their hunger on the old timer's lifeless body, while the larger birds of prey start to circle effortlessly high above on the thermal currents.

The men pushed the motorbike back towards the truck, puffing slightly from the gradual uphill incline. Price drops the tailgate. Taking a deep breath, Scrubber says "On the count of three," and they heave the motor- bike onto the back with little effort, leaving it on its side.

Scrubber, despite being wiry in build and in his the early 50s, has the strength of someone half his age. A thick purple scar features prominently across one cheekbone, courtesy of a cantankerous scrubber bull that quickly taught him who was boss in the bush. That incident had occurred way back in his earlier ringer days but the nickname Scrubber has stuck with him from that day forward.

Price, on the other hand, is in his mid-30s. A large-framed man with substantial bush-toned muscles, he is slow in thought and speech from complications during his birth. His father, losing his wife shortly after, named him Price to serve as a constant reminder of the cost of his only son. During Price's tough upbringing on the station, his father had labelled him a useless simpleton and his elder sister was groomed for the job of running the station.

They swing the tailgate up, turning both handles to lock them into place then Scrubber spins the steering wheel, sending the four wheel drive back towards Hatchet River Station. They travel in silence, as Scrubber was never one to talk much unless necessary and idle chatter just irritated him. About twelve kilometres out from the homestead, Price speaks up. "So what are we going to do with the bike?"

Scrubber ponders on this thought and, after a few seconds, replies "We will dump it in one of the large water holes not far up the road here."

The vehicle swerves off the road, crashing a short distance through the bush to arrive on the high side of a permanent waterhole well known for the large salt water crocodiles that move upstream from the coast every year during the wet season; as river levels drop, the crocs settle back into the deeper holes like this one for a constant food source.

Price unloaded Fred's bike, pushes it a short distance through the bush towards a cliff face, giving the handle- bars a good shove just before the edge. It starts to cart- wheel, crashing down the rock face and making a huge splash when it finds the bottom and sending ripples across the entire water surface. As they watch the old motorbike rapidly sink out of sight into the murky depths, Scrubber, with a smug look on his face, states, "I've worked up an appetite. Let's go for lunch."

Rounding one last bend before the Hatchet River homestead, a trail of bull dust in their wake, the station dogs start to bark continuously until Price yells "Lay down." Price opens the gate for Scrubber to park in front of the homestead then the men walk inside to find Max emptying a few tins of baked beans into a pot. While giving it a stir, she turns from the gas stove. "So how was your morning? You get some food for the dogs?" Both men sit down at the table without replying, throwing a quick glance at each other.

Max, short for Maxine, has piercing green eyes and a very athletic build for a woman nudging 40. Having been raised as rough and tough as the environment she has lived in all her life, she has witnessed and assisted in many sinister and unsavoury events on the station from a young age that shows on her hardened face at a glance. Though letting her husband have a lot of say in the daily running of the station, Max has the final word on all matters. Scrubber is acutely conscious not to push his wife too far as she is easily superior to him with knife and gun and she has a wicked temper to match.

"You boys haven't answered my question, did you get dog food or have I got to do it myself?" Max brings over their plates of steaming hot beans and damper to the table.

Scrubber speaks up, "Price spotted some bike tracks so we went for a look." He then quickly shovels a spoonful of hot beans into his mouth so he can't answer the next question, knowing what is coming next.

Max's voice drops in tone. "And then what happened?" She glares over at her brother with a raking stare, knowing he will be first to buckle.

Price blurts out, "We beat his head in with a rock."

Max spins from the kitchen sink with a butcher's knife in hand, releasing it with expert timing. The blade buries deep into the timber table an inch from Scrubber's plate. In four swift steps, Max is by his side. "You ever leave me out of a hunt again, look the fuck out. You should have come back and got me."

Scrubber looks up from the plate to his wife's face. Her stare shows no emotion other than burning anger. Not wanting to escalate the situation further, Scrubber breaks eye contact, looking down at the butcher's knife still quivering in front of him. Diffusing the heated moment, he shrugs his shoulders. "Fair enough."

At 3am the alarm clock starts to crank up. John fumbles in the dark, finally turning it off and lies there, trying to wake up fully. He rolls towards his wife Meg, who is still snoring soundly, oblivious to the alarm clock going off. Thinking he would try his luck before heading bush, he slowly slides the palm of his hand over her silky, smooth thigh and runs it up towards her ample breasts.

Meg, startled out of her deep sleep, works out what John is intending. Letting out a groan from being woken up, she slaps his hand, shoving it away and saying, "You got Buckley's, mate!" then rolls to the outer edge of the bed and buries her head deep under the pillows. Realising he is getting nowhere fast, John gives up and climbs out of bed, whispering to himself, "It was worth a shot."

He loads the 80-litre bush freezer with frozen meat, fish, trays of sausages, and three-litre water bottles that keep the beer and other perishables cool in his esky for the duration of the prospecting trip. Filling the last space in the esky with milk, butter and orange juice, and having to apply the palm of one hand, John manages enough downward pressure on the lid to lock the hinges into place.

With the bike, swag, gas bottle, fuel, water and other essential equipment now on the back of the old but reliable 1988 model 4x4 tray back, John makes his way back towards the house with a rear patio light guiding the way. Moving as quietly as possible inside the office to the gun safe, he inputs the unlocking code and twists the handle. It swings open. Grabbing the 44-calibre rifle and a carton of twenty shells, he relocks the safe then tentatively walks back through the house and places them on the kitchen table.

John runs through his mental checklist. "Shit, nearly forgot the BBQ plate." He goes back into the shed and loads a heavy steel plate onto the truck. Satisfied that everything is packed, he returns to the bedroom and whispers "Good-bye" softly to Meg with a parting kiss as his lips barely touch her cheek.

John preheats the old diesel and flicks the key, firing it into life. Sitting in the morning cool patiently waiting while it warms up, he reaches over and turns on the two- way radio, glancing at the dashboard clock as he does so. 4.15am. Tim should be well on his way into town by now. Grabbing the hand piece of the two-way, he says, "You got a copy there, Tim?" adjusting the squelch knob slightly.

His prospecting partner's voice comes through loud and clear. "Yeah, roger mate, about five minutes away from the servo."

John slips the truck into gear, replied, "No worries, meet you there," and slowly moves his 4x4 down the driveway in first gear, not wanting to wake Meg or the neighbours. The vehicles pull up nearly simultaneously at the 24-hour servo and both men enter to grab a few last things. As John gets back in the truck with a pie and takeaway coffee, his two-way crackles to life. Tim's voice booms through. "You ready to get moving?"

John smiles, replying, "Yeah, bud, like a dingo shot up the arse. Let's get out of here."

The prospectors head off into the breaking dawn, each with different bands blaring from their stereos, showing the difference in their age and tastes in music. This is about the only thing that they don't have in common.

With spot lights overflowing off the bitumen, giving them more response time for kangaroos and cattle grazing on the fresh pick beside the road in the darkness, they drive towards their destination. Finally turning off the highway onto the dirt road, the vehicles leave a trail of bulldust up to a kilometre long in their tracks as they head along the well-worn track towards the Hatchet River.

Tim gives a running commentary on the two-way, pointing out spots where he had found gold over previous prospecting seasons as they drove along. Cautiously they swerve wide around stock near the road as they are well known to be indecisive when it came to which way to run from oncoming vehicles. After many hours on the track, Tim radios through, saying, "Not too far now."

Hitting it off from the first time they met, Tim had reignited John's love of the bush and passion for prospecting; they were now in their fourth year as prospecting partners and had covered numerous gold fields, with the Hatchet River being Tim's most productive.

They arrive at Jack and Sue's place, appropriately named the Oasis. It is a beautiful, lush, green lawn in the middle of a dry, rocky, parched land with gardens, a veggie patch and chickens along with numerous beautiful shade trees around the property. Jack had set the house up well over many years, with Tim always eager to lend a hand. The entire modern camp is run off large solar panels fixed to the roof that supply enough power to run every- thing from the deep freezers to the TV, and most importantly, the outback's rarest commodity, the abundant supply of drinking water being pumped from a bore nearby.

Jack and Sue both arrive out at the gate to give the dusty men a warm welcome, always happy to have some fresh conversation entering the camp. Jack is a huge man who stood close to seven foot tall, with hard sun weathering to his face from years of bush life. After fifteen years of living on the Hatchet River, he has become an accomplished bushman as well as a skilled prospector, and certainly is not one to back away from trouble.

Jack had also taught his sons from an early age the art of bush survival, though now both boys had moved into town to seek work. His wife Sue, a beautiful, bubbly, well- tanned bushie in her early 50s, slipped easily into the simplicity of bush life. She now cringes at the thought of leaving the Oasis to endure the bustle of town when shopping for supplies.

After a quick chat, John and Tim get to the business of unloading the trucks, starting with the bikes then the rest of their prospecting gear.

By the time their camp is finally sorted out, it is getting late into the afternoon so Tim makes a suggestion, "Let's go for a drink around the fire with Jack and Sue to find out what's been going on around the traps." He grabs a bottle of rum and a tin of cola. John follows suit and walks to his esky to pull out a mid-strength tin of beer. They stroll towards the unlit fire that is set on an old satellite dish surrounded by old timer's handmade clay bricks and settle into their chairs, taking in the serenity of their surroundings. Jack and Sue stroll over; Sue sits in her favourite chair as Jack bends over, flicking his lighter to start the dry timber.

Tim opens the conversation with, "So what's been going on?" The camp dog Bumpy starts nudging Tim's leg for some attention. "Hey, Bumpy" he adds patting the dog's head affectionately.

Jack starts with the run down on the news of his own gold finds and gossip from the area. "Yeah, the boys' camp has been finding a bit but nothing over the top. There have been some strange things going on though. I haven't seen Fred for a while; he normally pulls in for a yarn on the way home and shows us what gold he's found. Poor old bugger, he's got nobody else to talk to other than the dog. I was worried that he might be crook or something so today, after doing a dump run, I decided to make sure he was okay but get this bro," he switches his gaze between Tim and John.

"Fred hadn't been there for a while. His dog Plugger had knocked over the water container and died on the chain. I know sometimes he can go walk about for days, maybe even up to a week, but if he's not doing a day trip, he always takes Plugger in the milk crate on the back of the motorbike.

I hope he hasn't had a heart attack in the middle of nowhere. I wouldn't even know where to start looking. He used to cover a lot of country. Tomorrow I will go to the other miner's camps in the area and see if they have seen him."

Both Tim and John take this information on board, heads nodding.

Wanting to change the morbid subject, Sue, in her bubbly genuine smiling way, asks "So how's your art work going, Tim? Are the girls doing okay in town?"

Tim replies, smiling back, "Yeah, art work is going great, Danni's great" with John chiming in, "Yeah, all's good at home."

Polishing off her drink, Sue stands up from the recliner and announces, "I'll go and see where dinner's up to. It won't be too far away" and walks back towards the kitchen.

Tim says to Jack when Sue is out of earshot, "That doesn't sound good about Fred" as he stands to throw another log on the fire, sending sparks flying high into the air. "Got time for a quick drink before dinner," Tim darts off to get another tin of cola, yelling out "John, you want another tinnie while I'm out here?"

John looks at his slight beer gut sticking out of the shirt and declines the offer, "Na, bud."

Tim returns to the fire and flops onto his chair, "Ahhh, this is the life."

With a worried look etched over his face, Jack turns to Tim. "I know you do your own thing out there but I just had one of the miners call through yesterday. He run across three pig shooters who had done a fan belt while heading out on the road to town. He pulled up to see if they needed a hand and they got to talking. The pig shooters told him of an encounter they had with a station owner and two others; no need to guess which one it was. Guns were drawn in a Mexican stand-off between them. They had to backtrack, rifles still at the ready, to get out of the situation. All of them agreed that if they all hadn't had firearms or were not prepared to use them, they would all be in a shallow grave by now. Could be they are patrolling further up the river than they usually do, so keep an eye out while you are moving around."

Sue's raised voice breaks the silence. "Dinner's up in ten minutes!" After not eating a proper meal all day, they smartly polish off their drinks and move towards the kitchen.

The boys' camp is about twenty kilometres past the Oasis on another gold lease situated beside a large tributary of the Hatchet River. There is a huge swimming hole ten metres from the back door and numerous large shade trees with rope swings tied in the branches overhanging the water's edge. The trees had a dual purpose as they also spread shade over whole camp in the endless months of heat waves.

It is a very laid back spot run by an all-male prospecting team, with the majority of them from the younger generation. The boys' camp was always full, except for the annual wet season when it could be isolated for months with normally only a caretaker in residence. It had been well set up and boasted all the comforts of a town – a pub- sized pool table, a huge plasma TV with a large stereo system and an amplifier coupled to speakers placed around the camp cranking out the latest music.

A couple of the young prospectors went into town earlier in the week to replenish supplies for the camp. They decided to go out on the town for their last night to try to pick up a root before heading back out bush. By the night's end, things were looking promising. They had managed to persuade a group of single chicks to follow them back to the camp for a party and word quickly got around to other groups in the night club that a bush party was happening. Walking away from the club, the men could not believe their luck.

There were three crammed vehicles of half cut, unrestrained young women all aged between 18 and 23 years wanting to follow them home and with only one thing on their mind – to party hard! Driving one of the vehicles was a solitary male who had had a sexual encounter with one girl in the group the previous night. He was not overly impressed that he now had competition to contend with though he was still confident he could improve his tally.

After the newcomers' vehicles arrive at the camp, a few joints are passed around. Music pumps out of the speakers. Some girls, on a high from the weed and alcohol, run past the fire topless. Flaunting their bodies to a captive audience while throwing countless inviting smiles towards the young, hard-muscled prospectors sitting around the fire.

Nudging each other at the talent on display, the men are on their feet in an instant, scooping the girls up over their shoulders. They let out squeals of delight as they are carried away into the darkness effortlessly by the fit, bush-hardened men. Not wanting to be left out of the action, the rest of the young men waiting in the wings eye off a group of the young chicks sitting in a semi-circle; the girls return the looks, pairing each other off, laughing and swallowing cruisers like there is no tomorrow.

The next morning, Allan, the lead prospector and lease owner of the boy's camp, walks into the kitchen to light the gas stove. Now in his mid-30s, he is one tough man; being a bit on the alternative side he has a mane of well-plaited hair down to the middle of his back. Allan prefers not to wear a shirt or shoes whilst prospecting let alone a hat, and is bronzed from head to toe. He is extremely good at his profession of finding gold, having a reputation in the district for being the best operator on the surrounding gold field. Filling the kettle, he places it on the flame then turns to see Tonga, his right hand man, stumble into the kitchen after two hours of sleep.

"Boy, what a night!" says Tonga, slumping into a chair and looking worse for wear.

"So how did you go? Get a bit?" Allan asks.

Tonga replies, "I just pick out the ugliest one, bud. Never have any problems and they're always willing to please."

Allan laughs. "Go kick the others awake. We need to work out where we are going this week," he says as he spreads out a large unique map of the area brought for a bargain many years ago at a garage sale. It contains detailed markings of Chinese alluvial workings, and now includes where the boys have been and what they had found in the area. Hatchet River Station is marked out in red pen.

The rest of the boys arrive in the kitchen just before the kettle lets out a whistle. They grab seats around the table, all in various states of consciousness. Allan speaks up. "Right, where do you want to prospect this week?" He points to the map with a thin twig. "This area in the high ranges I only spent a day on and come out with half an ounce." He looks up from the map as nobody is voicing their opinion. Knowing his boys' reactions well, he says, "Righto, what is going on?"

Tonga gets up, clearing his throat. "Don't know if it was a good idea when they were full of piss but the boys all had a yarn last night and are tired of going to areas already done over, only picking up crumbs. They want to look in new country, virgin ground for the detectors."

Allan looks at his prospecting crew, realising where this conversation is heading. "So where are you suggesting?"

One of the boys, having done his homework, gets up to point to the red zone. "Red Claw Creek. As far as we know, no operators have been in the area; also in the research I have done, the old timers were finding nuggets in there the size of your fist. They named it the potato patch, with the largest nugget recorded in the area 135 ounces. We know the risk is high but also high are the chances of hitting it big." The young bloke sits down, with all the boys nodding their head in agreement.

Allan snaps back, "So you're all willing to risk the biscuit with no regard to yourself or a mate's life?"

Another of the boys chimes in. "Allan, it's a huge country. The chances of that station scum finding us would be like looking for a needle in a hay stack."

Allan shakes his head. "They are clued up and know their back yard well, no matter how large but if that's your unanimous decision, so be it."

All the prospectors leave the table to pack their gear. "What about the sheilas?" asks the youngest of the group. Allan, still not happy with the decision made, tersely replies, "Well, what do you think? They have been partying since they got here over 24 hours ago. They're out of grog, weed and food. Playtime is over, it's time for them to move on. We have work to do in organizing this run. You can go tell that bloke who came with them it's time to hit the road."

Grunting in disapproval, the young prospector leaves in search of the guy who had struck out badly with all the females last night and had slept uncomfortably in the driver's seat of his car.

At the Oasis, John is up early, brewing a good shot of coffee. Having rugged looks and standing 6 feet tall, he spent much of his childhood and teenage years on remote goldmines around the north though he was now used to his comforts. Town living for the last 25 years had made him soft with a middle-age spread, he is not the fit, seasoned prospector he once was.

On the other hand, Tim, a professional prospector, is bush hardened and in harmony with the wild country, able to adapt quickly to any situation. A skilled reptile handler with cat-like reflexes, he is very fit and has the ability to live off what Mother Nature supplies in this sometimes unwilling environment. Always up for the challenge of surviving the harsh conditions to earn a crust. If anyone could blow wind up Allan's arse for gun operator on this goldfield, it is Tim.

Jesting and carrying on with light-hearted banter, they set up their detecting gear, organise food and water and drinking coffee while discussing over a map where they were going for the day. Tim points to the map, commenting, "The closer you get towards the Hatchet River home- stead, the more gold; not that the area is any richer, just fewer operators venture down that way for obvious reasons."

John and Tim load on their backpacks with the detector shaft and coil sticking prominently out the top of their packs and mount their four-stroke 150s. Both bikes splutter to life after they hit the start button a couple of times, giving them a minute to warm up on choke. Both prospectors slip them into gear with a tap of the boot and they leave, following a side track taking them in a downstream direction.

After riding side by side for a good 25 minutes so neither was swallowing dust, Tim slows his bike to walking pace and studies the terrain on both sides of the dirt track. Pulling in the clutch, he comes to a stop, with John right behind him.

"This area looks pretty good." He points to features that contain mineralisation and faulting that could have shed gold in the past. "So which side of the road do you want to try, bud?" Tim asks.

John looks up and down the road and makes his decision. "I'll take this side" he says, pointing to the left. On that note he rides off the track out of sight and starts to set up his Minelab detector.

Tim, still sitting on his bike, turns at the hip towards John and yells out, "Channel 15, right?" Restarting the bike, he rides off in the opposite direction, swerving around saplings and anthills as he goes.

John is set up in minutes, working a few insignificant gutters a hundred metres or so from the bike. He manages to dig up a few nails within the first 20 minutes, swinging his coil over a third target that had a nice mellow drop tone to it. John's pick goes into action, striking the hard- packed earth repeatedly until he reveals what all prospectors live for, a glimmer of gold in the clay in front of him. He quickly picks up his first nugget of the trip in amongst the loose butter-coloured clay. Spitting on the nugget, he rubs it between his forefinger and thumb to reveal its golden lustre fully.

Sitting down for a blow under the shade of a nearby tree, John pulls out a water bottle and takes a few large mouthfuls then, removing a packet of cigarettes from his top pocket, slides the nugget in between the cellophane. Lighting a smoke, he calls Tim on the two-way. "Got one."

Tim replies, "Good on ya, bud. A good one or what?"

He looked at the nugget in the palm of his hand, it was close to the size of his pinkie fingernail, "Na, bout a three grammer."

Tim returned the call with news of his finds. "That's not a bad start. I've got an eight grammer and two one grammers."

John butts out his smoke and replies before picking up his detector, "Well done. Anyway, back to the grind."

They spend the rest of the day systemically detecting the surrounding gullies, with Tim picking up one more nugget late in the afternoon. Wiping the sweat from the forehead with the back of his dusty hand, he gives John a call. "Beer time, watcha reckon, bud? Meet you back on the track. I'm about 2km up from you." After a hard day in the relentless sun, the men join up and ride back towards the Oasis as the sun casts long shadows on the nearby hills.

Relaxing that night over drinks, they decide to set up a new camp downstream at the Croc Hole, which is what the locals call a large waterhole full of Barramundi and the odd large saltwater crocodile. Early the next morning, the men roll up their swags and load all their gear then pushed the bikes onto the trucks so they didn't wake Jack and Sue. By the time they are done, a light has flickered on over at the main camp kitchen. Tim spots it, "Time for a quick coffee with Jack and Sue then we are out of here, bud."

John says sleepily, "Yeah, I could do with a heart starter." After a hot brew with some light conversation thrown in, the prospectors are keen to hit the road.

Five hours later they arrive and start the same ritual of unloading and setting up camp. Nearing on lunch time with only coffee in their stomachs, John comment's "The grubs are starting to bite, mate. Could eat the arse out of a low flying duck at the moment!"

Laughing Tim replies, "Yeah, mate, I'm hearing you. There are tins of baked beans and tuna close handy in my tucker box, let's have lunch beside the river in the shade. Reckon we just do an afternoon stint within walking distance of the camp." Before departing, John flicks the locks on the bush freezer open, selected a frozen cryovac pack of curry beef for dinner and places it in his esky to slowly thaw out.

Geared up, the prospectors walk into the hills in the midday heat. It isn't the smartest decision to make and they go through their water quickly in the stifling heat, but they are keen to at least get wages for the day. The hills block any breeze from cooling the sweat that is running from their pores freely as they continue to dig deep targets in the gullies. The men's strength is sapped considerably.

John has one silver coin and a handful of Chinese coins for his efforts; being close to running out of water, he decides to head back. Misjudging the distance travelled, it takes longer than he thought and he finishes the last of his water at about the halfway mark. The thirsty prospector finally reaches camp and makes a beeline for his esky on the back of the 4x4. Grabbing a chilled bottle of water to quench his thirst, he takes small mouthfuls until the bottle is empty. Reaching for a mid-strength beer, John starts to gather wood for a fire before night fell, piling it into a heap, then decides to give his pard a call as darkness is not far off, "Hey, where are you, mate?"

"I'm about 10 minutes out from camp. Are you back there yet?"

John says, smirking, "Yeah, bud, with a coldie in my mitt as well."

John starts filling a large stainless steel pot for a hot shower then slides his solidly made BBQ plate off the truck. It had welded mesh on one end for the purpose of heating water with the rest ¾ inch steel plate for cooking. Extending the folded legs, he places it above some of the timber he'd collected. After scraping together some nearby dead leaves, John lights the fire and waits, crouching till the flames take hold properly while hearing Tim's approach from the downstream direction. He looks exhausted, trudging into the camp just as dark encompasses the entire landscape. Slinging the detector harness off, he places it under the truck to keep off the heavy dew that is guaranteed to fall overnight. Yarning with John, Tim reaches for his rum and a cold can of cola. "Boy, what an afternoon. Phew, bloody long way back. How did you go?"

John nods to the table where he had placed his finds earlier, replying, "Just some Chinese coins and this one silver coin. The rest were rubbish."

Tim shrugs. "True, mate. For my efforts all I got worthwhile was a ten grammer." Digging deep into his pocket, he flicks it onto the table where John had just sat down to remove his boots.

Picking up the nugget, he examines it. "Nice water- worn bit," he says, flipping it over to look at the other side.

"Yeah, the bloody thing was down in a bedrock crevice. My pick could only get part the way down the crack so I had to find a sturdy stick the right size to finish digging it out. Pain in the frigging arse; then I had to work it with the stick along the crevice until I could pick it up."

Both of them laugh then John says, "Good onya, mate." Handing the nugget back to Tim, he also passes over the silver coin he'd found.

After studying both sides, Tim exclaims, "Bloody hell, bud, that's a 1789 Spanish silver half dollar. I have never found anything like that up this way before. What a find, mate. That's impressive. Might be worth a bit too, bro."

John's spirits pick up considerably with Tim's excitement over the coin. "Cool. I reckon it'll become my lucky charm." He slips both feet into some thongs and gets up to organise dinner, emptying the now thawed curry into a pot to reheat. The men take turns bathing under the canvas shower bag hanging in a nearby tree then settle down for dinner followed by catch-up chat. John, feeling a bit off, says, "I must have got a bit dehydrated out there today. The few beers I've had have gone straight to my head. You miss being able to walk back to your bike for spare water when you run low."

Tim, concerned, says, "Yeah, bud I thought you were a bit quiet tonight. I went through a shit load of water myself. Have an early night, we have got a big day of exploring tomorrow."

John gets up from his chair. "Yeah, I think I will." Feeling lightheaded, he steadies himself and walks towards his swag. Slipping into the canvas covers, he is asleep within minutes. Tim stays up studying aerial photographs of the area for tomorrow.

Waking early the next morning, both men finished their coffees while organising supplies for the day. They are ready to leave on the bikes as soon as there is sufficient light to see in front of them. Tim suggests, "Throw your hand line and a few lures into your backpack; there's some good waterholes on the aerial photos that I have never been to."

Leaving just on daylight, the men ride through new country, looking for promising areas in their travels. It turn out to be disappointing other than a couple of grams each had found after digging up countless amounts of lead and other assorted junk.

They pull up on the bikes to confer. John shakes his head, "I don't know about you but I've has a gutful of digging shit targets all day. Where are the big nuggets?"

"You know what the saying is, mate; prospectors' fortunes can change on the next shovel of dirt."

John sighs, "Yeah, too true."

Tim, realising his partner's frustration after a hard day in the field for bugger all, announces, "Let's try to catch a Barra for dinner."

Tim follows the map on the top-of-the-range GPS mounted on his handlebars, with John not too far behind. A GPS was an essential piece of safety equipment in the bush, enabling them to retrace their tracks or to follow a new waypoint destination. As they approach a sandy creek crossing, Tim pulls in the clutch to study the GPS. "I plotted in the fishing holes last night. We have to get across this creek then down towards the mouth. This is also a shortcut to camp, or it's a long way around."

As it is getting closer to beer time after a long hot day, John replies, "What? We just got to get across this? It looks shallow enough to me!" Shrugging his shoulders, he says loudly, "Fuck it," and opens up the throttle of his motorbike before Tim can respond. Wheels spinning, John hits the creek crossing hard. He goes like a bat out of hell for the first 20 metres, a sheet of water spraying high into the air from both sides of the red rocket. Then it hits the quicksand, which abruptly stops any further advancement and nearly sending John completely over the handle bars. Both wheels sink out of sight nearly instantly and steam pours off as the red hot exhaust meets the cool water of the creek.

Tim, in fits of laughter nearly falls off his bike, yelling to John who is bogged to the eyeballs, "No, bro, I said we need to try and cross up there, you thick shit," pointing to a rock bar showing in the creek further upstream. Still chuckling to himself, he shakes his head while watching John struggle to get the bike out, finally making it back onto firm sand. Sweat running profusely down his face, he rides up to Tim. With a careless grin on his face, he says, "Nearly made it."

Tim, stifling his snigger, manages to get out, "Man, you crack me up." They cross up further where Tim had pointed out earlier without further incident.

Scrubber, Max and Price pick up on the prospectors' bike tracks in the bulldust and proceed to follow them, driving the fawn truck slowly through the bush to make sure they don't lose the tracks of their prey. Realising they are getting close to the creek, Scrubber turns off the vehicle and they sit in silence, listening for any foreign noises. "They can't have gone too far upstream, there's a breakaway gully." All three of them, knowing the country intimately, nod their heads in agreement then fall silent, again intently listening for the sounds of motorbikes or any noise not in tune with their bush surrounds.

Now on the opposite creek bank, Tim and John pull up on the bikes. Tim says, "Let's head down to the big holes around the mouth and we'll try to catch a Barra."

John replies after getting a second wind, "All right for some. You're way ahead on the gold tally this trip. I need to do a bit of catching up. I'll stay up this way and keep swinging."

Tim grins. "Righto, bud. Will give you a call when I've got dinner." He fires the trusty motorbike to life and moves off towards the creek mouth where it meets the main Hatchet River.

John dismounts then, out of habit, pushes the bike close to some shrubs before walking upstream. After about ten minutes on the high bank above flood level, he comes across the odd slate stone slabs telling the history of an established camp that had been at this point back in the gold rush days. This usually means the remnants of an old Chinese camp. Sweeping an eye over the area for previous detector holes and seeing no evidence that any other prospectors had already been here, satisfies John that this is as good as anywhere to start. With his forefinger pressed firmly on the start button, John fires up the detector. There is initially a high pitched noise from the speaker until the machine is ground balanced then it quietens down to a constant hum. Satisfied that the Minelab GPX detector had settled to the ground conditions, John goes on his way, swinging the coil of the machine low and evenly, consciously staying clear of the main camp to avoid hours of digging up junk, and before long starts to pick up a few Chinese coins.

Meanwhile Tim has found a promising fishing spot. Parking his bike under some shade on the bank, he is finally able to remove the heavy backpack. He lays it on the ground and unzips a pocket containing a handline and some favourite lures he had thrown in. Walking down the steep bank covered in soft, dark, rich flood silt, he steps over a line of timber debris from the last flood and makes his way down to some large boulders that had a deep waterhole running alongside them. Tim sets up the fishing line by tying on his most productive lure, throws it out as far as possible then retrieves it at a steady, even pace, making the lure work its wounded action through the water. He catches a glimpse of a large silver flash from a Barra that missed the lure by millimetres.

After ten minutes or more of standing beside the truck, Scrubber mutters to Price and Max, "They can't be far away. Let's go have some fun." Reaching in behind the seat of the truck, he pulls out a shotgun and offers it to Max. "You want this one?"

With a rare smile, she replies, "No, I am happy to watch this time around."

Knowing that the guns magazine is fully loaded, Scrubber opens the glove box, grabs out a handful of extra shells and shoves them in his top pocket. He points to a cattle pad winding in the general direction of the creek and moves off, with the other two falling in behind.

Arriving at the bank of the sandy creek with shotgun in hand, they come across the bike tracks. Scrubber points to the ground and turns to look at the others; they nod. Following the tracks to where John had ridden off the bank into the quicksand, Scrubber, frustrated, mutters, "Where the fuck have they gone?" Looking up and down the creek, he cannot see any evidence of bike tracks coming out on either side. He continues to slowly scan for any movement or noise.

Out of the corner of her eye, Max spots a lure being thrown into the water further downstream. Silently she signals, pointing towards a waterhole near the mouth. With stealth they walk towards the waterhole, with Scrubber feeding a shell into the chamber of the well-used shotgun.

Twenty minutes had elapsed when the shotgun breaks the bush tranquility surrounding Tim. "What the fuck!" he exclaims. The pellets from the first shot churn the water just in front of the large boulders he is standing beside; instinctively he dives behind them for cover. Landing heavily knocks the wind clean out of his lungs. Doing his best to recover from the impact, Tim immediately gulps in a couple of deep breaths and tries to inflate his screaming lungs in the thin mid-afternoon air. Quickly assessing the situation, Tim lies flat as possible on the rocks surrounding him, sweat pouring from every inch of his body as the heat absorbed throughout the day on the smooth water-worn rocks radiates back. He feels like he is being slowly roasted alive. With adrenalin now pumping through his entire body, the prospector has more on his plate to worry about than a few skin burns.

The second shot shreds the leaves of a small gum tree above where he had landed. A third shot rings out, the lead pellets ricocheting all around him. One pellet pierces his dilapidated old hat, leaving a flesh burn on his scalp. Tim decides against using the two-way to call John and turns it off, fearing it might give the gunman his exact position, even though the shots are already way too close for comfort.

Out of the silence, John hears Boom and then Boom Boom in quick succession. He turns off the detector to hear what is going on, thinking aloud, "That sounded like gun shots but Tim doesn't have a gun." He grabs the two-way and tries to make contact. "What the hell was that?" No reply.

After what seems like eternity but in actual time is a matter of minutes, the gunfire ceases. Tim cautiously slides towards the opposite end of the boulders. Moving his head partly around the boulder with his cheek hard pressed on the rock to avoid giving a clear target to peer across the creek, he can see Scrubber with the shotgun in hand trying to cross the quicksand.

His pulse starts racing and he mutters to himself, "The prick is trying to cross the creek to shoot me." He can hear his own heartbeat pounding in his chest; there is a dry lump in his throat that he cannot swallow. Weighing up the options left open to him, he decides to have another look before making a final decision, not knowing if it may be his last.

Peering back around the large granite boulder, he sees Scrubber struggling in the quicksand, now sinking up to his thighs. The further out he gets, the deeper he sinks. Price and Max are sitting on a log further up the bank, laughing loudly. Giving up while puffing hard from the extra exertion needed to get out that far, Scrubber finally admits defeat and turns his head and shoulders around to bark the orders for the other pair to come and help him out. Not knowing exactly what to do, they fruitlessly scout around for a large branch to rescue him with, smiling as they do so.

Scrubber, having been caught in this situation before, knows to get the weight off his feet. "Bloody useless," he mutters referring to his accomplices. Lying flat on his stomach, he manages to disperse his body mass and struggled to break free of the suction of the quicksand. Still clutching the shotgun in one hand, he crawls face first over the sand, eventually getting close enough to the bank to stand erect. He and the shotgun are now totally saturated by water and coated in wet sand. He throws the gun in disgust at Price, who catches it with one hand, trying his best to conceal his smile.

Scrubber, now in a foul mood, feels like he has come out second best from the encounter. A filthy scowl written right across his face, he looks down towards his boots, which squelch every time he takes a step. Wiping the sand off both hands down the side of his wet jeans, he reaches for the wet shotgun shells in the top pocket. His smokes and lighter are cactus too. Spitting some sand grit on the ground, he looks up at Max with a distinct look of pure evil in his eyes, "Let's go! Who ever that is will soon be dead, that I will promise you."

Fifteen minutes after the Scrubber gang walked back towards their truck, Tim hears the faint sound of their vehicle being started and driven off along a ridge above the creek. With a shaking hand, he turns the two-way back on to call John. "Scrubber has just shot at me! Get on your bike now! Meet you at the top bank."

John, shocked, replies, "You're joking. Thought it sounded like gun shots. Holy crap." He quickly packs up the detector, runs towards his bike and guns it off towards the top bank. Once there he turns off the ignition and waits silently. Within minutes, he hears the bike revving erratically towards him.

Emerging out of the tree line at speed, Tim applies the front brake a little too hard. With the front tyre digging into the soft sand nearly throwing him off balance, he comes to a sudden stop. His face is white with anger. He spits out, "The fucker tried to shoot me! He couldn't cross the creek though, thank Christ! But the track they're on does a big loop and ends up back where we are camped if they decide follow it all the way around. That's the only road in or out. We will have to shortcut across the bush. Best we move our arses; if they get there before us, sure as shit our trucks will be burnt to the ground."

Both men swiftly forge their bikes through the long spear grass across rock ledges, bouncing over hidden logs and ant hills. After a hell of a cross country trip taking well over an hour, they eventually end up back at their camp. As the crow flies, it is only 4km upstream from where the shots were fired on the Hatchet River tributary. Tim asks, "Got your rifle, hey Johnno?"

John stops, remembering he hadn't picked it up off the table and curses. "Shit. I left it at home. Looks like we are sitting ducks."

Tim responds, "If they're coming around the road, we can't get out anyway. Build up the fire and stack your clothes in the swag to look like you're sleeping. We need to find some weapons." Tim grabs a knife from the tucker box and John reaches for his detector pick. After setting up the decoy swags, they move out of the camp to hide in nearby bush. Both prospectors watch for any movement in the dwindling light, sitting in the rocks awkwardly, their eyes strained on the incoming track. The river breeze starts to pick up just after dark, sending a cool gust whistling through the leaves of the large river gums.

After a long, cold, sleepless night waiting for Scrubber and crew to walk into the camp, the prospectors move out of the rocks in the predawn light and return to camp, throwing some fresh wood onto the dying coals to warm up and make some much needed coffee.

Sitting around the newly ignited fire, Tim says, "We need to get out of this spot. I have never run across them this far up before."

He then tells John a story of when he was metal detecting off the road about 10 years ago. "I was wearing head- phones back in them days. Operating along a cliff face, swinging the detector close to the edge, I was hit forcefully from behind. I lost my balance and fell over the side, landing hard onto rocks about six metres down. I suffered a compound fracture in my leg, and smashed the bloody detector. I thought a cleanskin bull was the culprit, but I looked up and saw that arsehole Scrubber standing on the cliff edge looking down at me. The prick didn't say a word, just walked away, leaving me there; not sure why, maybe it was just a warning or he thought he had left me for dead, busted up and broken in such a remote location. After about 10 minutes of assessing the damage, I tried to splint the leg with a stick and my shirt sleeve. There was blood dripping onto the rocks everywhere and an exposed bone protruded out through the skin on my leg. Meat ants were starting to swarm all over the flesh wounds by the bloody hundreds. Trying to get out of the blaring sun and the heat from the rocks, I painstakingly crawled to the shade of a thin gum tree. I was thinking to myself, 'If I don't get the hell out of here soon, I will be eaten alive by meat ants.'

"After three painful hours of crawling and limping from tree to tree, I got back to my bike. Luckily the little 150 cc is an electric start 'cause my leg was totally buggered. I struggled to even climb onto the bike. I hit the start button and the engine came to life first go thankfully then I slowly weaved my way through the trees to get back onto the road and turned the bike towards the Oasis. I was knackered, bud, I can tell ya. Feeling very lightheaded from loss of blood and finding it very hard to control the motorbike, waves of nausea and pain started running through my body. I reckon about 1.5km from the house I started to lose consciousness. The bike speared off the road into the long grass. The last thing I could remember was getting my face planted into the dirt; the rest of the story Jack filled me in on after I got out of hospital."

"He was back at the Oasis. Having loaded up the tray of the 4 x 4 with rubbish for a dump run, he called Bumpy. The loyal dog's ears pricked up at the call from his owner. Realising his boss was going somewhere, he raced over and jumped in the back. Jack climbed into the cab and drove off along the dirt road towards their dump, which was about 2.5km away. Half way there, Bumpy started barking excitedly in the back, running from one end of tray to the other, trampling the bags of rubbish and tearing some open. Annoyed by the dog's behaviour, Jack stopped the vehicle and got out to see what the dog was barking at.

"Looking down the road, he noticed some irregular motorbike tracks weaving all over the place. Being an accomplished bush rider himself, he thought this is very unusual. By this time, Bumpy was whimpering with his front paws on the side boards of the truck, waiting for the command to jump off the tray. Within a split second of hearing the word, Bumpy was straight down, landing on all fours then taking off back up the road with his nose to the ground as he went. Disappearing into the long grass off the road, he started to bark very excitedly. Seeing this Jack jumped back into the vehicle, turned it around and drove about 100 metres back the way they'd come.

"Getting out, he could hear Bumpy still yapping continuously at his find. Walking into the long grass, he could see that a bike had been through there. Eyes darting all over the place, he spotted splatters of blood on some of the long, brown, parched grass. Now extremely concerned, he quickened pace and lengthened his stride. Another 20 metres in, he spotted the red mudguard of my bike. 'Holy shit, that's Tim's bike' ran through his head. Adrenalin kicking in, he ran over, smelling the petrol that had been slowly dripping out of the carbie overflow. Bumpy, now not far away, ran to Jack and raced around him in circles, barking excitedly. Following the dog, Jack could see that someone had starting crawling in the direction of the Oasis.

"He spotted my unconscious body and rolled me over to reveal my face, reckons it was a deathly pale white. He quickly felt for a pulse and was relieved to find a faint one. Thoughts of knowing that my life now lay in his hands and calculating how quickly he could get me to professional help were running through his head along with thoughts on what'd happened. 'Has someone done this to Tim?' Knowing that I couldn't answer any of these questions in my state, he swiftly scooped me up into his arms and started running towards the already idling truck. Placing me in the passenger's side as best he could, he jumped into his seat. Grabbing the two-way, he called Sue while crunching the truck in gear. 'Sue, it's urgent. Do you copy? Over.'

Sue walked over to the main radio at the camp from where she was preparing dinner, "Yes, my love, I have a copy, what's wrong?" Jack replied, "Ring the flying doctors NOW. I've just found Tim. He's injured and close to dead. We are ten minutes away." On hearing this, Sue started dialling the emergency number that was written on the wall beside the phone.

"Waking up four days later in the Cairns Base Hospital, my beautiful wife Danni by my side, a doctor came in to tell me that they had operated on the leg to clean out the wound and pinned it to reset the compound fracture as best they could but I could have a slight limp for the rest of my life. They explained that I was very lucky to be found when I was because the amount of blood loss was extremely dangerous. The Doc then left us alone, leaving Danni to fuss over me till I was on the mend."

Tim shows John the long scar where the bone came through the side of his leg then gets up, throwing the last of his coffee onto the fire. Fine ash spews into the air from the reaction. "The prick, he's hiding more on this property than just keeping prospectors out. Let's pack up and head back to the Oasis."

Scrubber is up early, leaving the station at 4am in the morning. The first stop when he hit town is the bank; after withdrawing cash, the next stop is a gas shop to buy six 100lb gas bottles. The shop attendant, trying to make small talk, remarks, "Stocking up for the wet season?"

Scrubber replies, "Yeah, something like that," smirking while he pays in cash. He ties down the load and starts driving back to the station, briefly stopping at a convenience store to stock up with a heap of tinned food as well. He pulls in to fuel up at the Huego servo. Paying for the fuel, he had a quick chat with the service attendant, who he seems to be very familiar with. Scrubber ends the conversation by telling him, "You can catch up with Price on my next run. I will bring him in with me." Climbing back into the vehicle, he continues towards the station.

The eight dogs chained all around the homestead go crazy half an hour before the fawn station truck stops at the front gate just before dark. Scrubber gets out and calls to the dogs

"Down." They shut up immediately and start whimpering. Walking over to the depilated shed, he enters and grabs a large leather type saddle; returning with it under his arm, he throws it into the back of the truck. Price walks out onto the porch. Scrubber asked, "Find anyone today?"

Price, being a bit simple, takes a while to answer. "Some bike tracks but couldn't follow them with the truck."

Scrubber swears under his breath and asks, "Did you hobble the horses in the top paddock?"

Price slowly replies, "Yep, they're all ready for tomorrow."

Scrubber issues his last order for the day, "Good, you just need to throw the rest of the saddles in the truck and we will leave at first light." They walk inside and the lights go out. Except for the sounds of the nocturnal wildlife, silence falls over Hatchet River.

In the grey of dawn, an array of bird species start their chorus, with the Kookaburras the loudest. Scrubber, Max and Price are all finishing off a breakfast of bacon, eggs, baked beans and toast. Scrubber says to Max, "Price told me you saw some tracks yesterday. Where do you think they were heading?"

Getting up from the table, she walks towards a large map on the wall with crosses all over it and says, "Well, looking at the direction they were moving and if they are navigating by GPS, they were most probably going towards the Red Claw Creek area."

"How many do you reckon?"

"I don't think it was the same blokes that managed to elude you the other day," she says with a smirk on her face. "Picked up on maybe three sets of tracks; they had different tread patterns as well."

Scrubber swears "Put that radio on scan, see if they are using two-way radios. Price and I will go do the drop off at the lab; when we get that sorted out, we will go check if your hunch is right." He cuffs Price, who was finishing his breakfast, on the back of the head. "Let's go. We have a big day ahead."

Price throws both saddles in the back of the truck and jumps in the front with Scrubber. They take off heading towards their airstrip; the strip itself they had covered in large logs strategically positioned to prevent any aircraft landing on the station unannounced. Swerving around some logs, the truck continues along this path until they came to a locked gate, Scrubber says to Price, "The keys are in the glove box."

Price fumbles looking through various calibre gun cartridges in search of the keys; finally with them in hand, he gets out and unlocks the gate. The 4x4 drives on, throwing a plume of bulldust over Price while he relocks the gate. "One down, two to go," he says, getting back into the truck. En route to the second gate, the country changes to a sandstone formation which is full of abandoned mine shafts, overhangs and caves, too numerous to count. Price unlocks the next gate.

Bulldust swirls around behind the truck in billowing clouds. They put the two-way on 'scan' to see if they can pick up anyone on the air. After opening gate number three, they drive over rough ground for 35 minutes. The Sandstone rock faces close in and looms over the vehicle. Pulling up in a small sandy creek crossing, Scrubber changes the radio channel to twenty and says, "Ten in 45" into the mic then he instructs Price to "Go get the horses."

Price shuffles off and after 25 minutes, returns leading the three animals. The men each lift a saddle from the back tray and place them upon the horses then tie them off to a nearby tree. Scrubber fits the unusual saddle on the third pack horse and walks the animalover to the side of the truck.

Simple Price heaves the 100lb gas bottles with ease, one on each side of the horse, and straps them in.

They mount up and head towards the towering sandstone escarpments.

Scrubber rides out in front followed by the pack horse and Price at the rear. They cross some rugged ground, with Scrubber saying to Price, "Just stay to the side of the cattle pad." Large caves loom on the face of the sandstones; they climb an embankment and end up in front of a dark entrance. Both men tether their horses to a tree outside the cave. Higher up, a small spring bubbles out of the sandstones to one side of the cave with a concrete dam and some poly pipe running down into the cave, all very well camouflaged with dark netting and branches from nearby saplings making it virtually invisible.

Scrubber and Price walk down the steep embankment into mouth of the cave, moving forward about 30 metres in pitch darkness before Scrubber calls out, "Open." A totally black sliding wall opens up to expose a bright, fully set-up meth lab. Semi-automatic weapons hang on the walls inside the entrance, there are bunks and a cooking area, and a huge exhaust fan feeds out of the cave ceiling. There is a two-way on the table set on channel 20; large banks of batteries that are charged by solar panels well concealed high in the rocks above the cave run all the bright LED lights the cooks needed to perform their job. This is a very well-established drug lab, one of the largest of its kind in the country, totally camouflaged for years in the vast remoteness of the north Queensland outback.

A formidable looking bikie, tattoos spread across his large body, rings adorning nearly every finger and wearing a black bandana, walks out. He looks Scrubber up and down, spits onto the ground, and says, "We're nearly out of gas."

Scrubber explains how many people are now coming onto the property by accessing the gazetted road; the bikie looks at one of his offsiders and laughs, pointing Scrubber firmly in the chest while saying, "It's your job, dickhead. That's why you get paid the big bucks for, is to keep prying eyes away and supply us with our needs. Our job is to cook or the big C will have us all buried alive."

Scrubber, fuming from being intimidated by the meathead biker, unloads the gas and tinned food then barks orders at Price, "Reload on the way out and get some of these useless pricks to help" as he strides out of the cave. The bikies start unscrewing the tops off some gas bottles stored against a wall of the cave and start shoving in kilo bags of amphetamines; the bottles are then loaded on the pack horses and transported back to the tray of the 4x4. After the exchange of gas bottles, Price returns with the last load of amphetamines. Scrubber, waiting in the truck, says, "I'd love to kill that fucker."

Price replies, "I will do it."

Scrubber retorts, "Price, you might get that chance yet. You drive the truck up a couple of kilometres while I sweep the tracks in the sand and unsaddle the horses." This was a tedious task that needed to be done properly. Scrubber had never trusted Price to do this job; keeping the lab's location unknown was paramount for all concerned if you wanted to keep breathing.

They drive back towards home, go through the gates and pull up at the homestead with all of the eight dogs going off. Scrubber yells out, "Down." They all go instantly quiet. Walking inside, he picks up the telephone and rings a mobile number. "Six Hours" is all that is said. Jumping back into the truck, he drives off towards Huego alone, leaving Price with his sister at the homestead, not being in the mood for any company after the confrontation with the head biker earlier.

The President on the other end of the phone puts it down without replying to the caller then turns and says, "Righto, boys, six bikes and the truck. Everyone use channel 25, let's hit it." The bikies start arguing as to who should go. "Ringo, your turn to dress as a ringer." The President goes to the cupboard and throws him a cowboy hat and shirt. "You got to look the part, a bushie coming in to fill up the gas bottles." They all laugh. The president yells out some names, including the sergeant at arms and instructs them, "You fellas are up today."

The rough crew assembles, all cursing and swearing they have better things to do. The President, hearing the grumbling, speaks up, "Just remember, boys, no mun, no fun." They leave the compound to load on the required mix from a safe house out of town for their next batch. With the six bikies packing guns, they ride off, three bikes well in front of the truck and three well behind so not to be noticed. Scrubber gets to Rice Creek just out of Dambulla, pulling up well away from the road and out of the sight of bypassing traffic. Half an hour later, the first three bikes come into sight. Checking out the area, they call on a hand- held two-way to the truck, "All good to come in."

The truck pulls up alongside Scrubber's station vehicle but out of sight to the rest of the world, the gas bottles are exchanged with the bikies' gas bottles full of ephedrine and pseudo-ephedrine that had been sourced by bikies state wide for the next cook. In return, a sports bag full of money retrieved from a hidden compartment under the bikies' truck is handed to Scrubber, who quickly unzips the bag to look at the rolls of money then towards the sergeant at arms.

He shrugs his shoulders. "Count it if you want to but big C is very clear with the split even thirds."

Scrubber nods, throws some ropes over his load to secure it well, climbs into the truck and heads off back towards Hatchet River. Having never met Mr C (which was no accident), Scrubber tries to profile him with what he knows about the man, when boiled down is very little so there was a lot of guesswork.

Mr C; a very elusive and discrete man with an extraordinary gift for organisation and attention to detail; thinking and acting on his feet had gotten him to where he is today. Scrubber had no clue to his identity; not even the bikers had met C, to them he was a voice. Ox, C's associate, was given the input and funding to set up the lab, run the sales and pick up his share of the profits. Everything else, now down to a minimum, was done by phone. This operation had been running like a well-oiled machine for a number of years now; the only people who know the true identity of Mr C are Ox, who runs his errands and tends to the dirty side of the business in conjunction with a corrupt cop named Marko.

C is a well-built, fit man in his mid-thirties, who has a habit of subconsciously twirling a thick gold band encrusted with blue sapphires on his ring finger when deep in thought. Ox was a straight out hit man who had been loyal to him and his dealings over the past decade. Both of them had an unsaid respect for each other's prowess in their mutual but totally different fields of the business spectrum.

The crew from the boy's camp had divided into two groups of four bikes, with the 4x4 ute following a back track part of the way. After that it was bush bashing by GPS, which was always a slow and tedious process for the first time, with Allan the lead prospector behind the wheel blazing a path towards the new location, fully loaded with all the camping gear and supplies needed for the duration of the trip.

Before leaving camp, Allan had given both crews the GPS location to all meet up at Red Claw Creek in two days' time. The boys had been roughing it, sleeping on the ground as there was no room on the bikes to carry their bulky swags. They could only manage a small amount of food, with the majority of the backpacks full of water bottles and their detectors.

Both groups, now in new country for them, had picked up nice gold along the way to the pre- organised camp 8km up from the mouth of the Hatchet River. Allan had decided to make it a base camp to work out of on a daily basis, covering a lot of gold-bearing country in the near vicinity while still keeping a wide berth from the Hatchet homestead.

Scrubber pulls up at the station after a long day, yelling at the dogs to lie down as usual. He throws the bag of money to Price, who had just come out of the shed, instructing him to "put it with the rest." Price shuffles off with the bag under his arm to an old excavator parked a couple of hundred metres from the station. He starts up the machine, letting it warm up while he rolls a smoke then lifts the bucket of the 12-ton excavator into the air.

In a dug-out compartment under the machine's bucket is a large tin box concealed under a couple of inches of dirt. Price wipes off the loose dirt on top and opens the tin box to reveal about 750,000 dollars in cash.

He throws in the bundles of money, carefree as he had never been to town to use this paper trade before, then shuts the lid, covers the loose soil back over the top, jumps back into the excavator and lowers its bucket back on top of the cash stash. When the large station man makes his way back towards the homestead, Scrubber instructs him to reverse the truck up to the shed and unload the gas bottles.

When they're all inside, Max declares, "We have pig livers for dinner tonight; shot a few boars up the dam while you were away today," and points to the sink where the fresh bloody livers are sitting in the sink with numerous blowflies buzzing around.

Price breaks into a big toothy smile that reveals his broken, badly tobacco-stained teeth and receding gums. "My favourite," he says, licking his lips.

"No, you mean your second favourite," Max replies and they all start laughing.

"Yeah," chuckles Price, reflecting back. "Nothing beats them blond, fair-skinned ones. Hopefully a few more come through."

Max finishes cooking dinner and while they sit around the table eating, Scrubber breaks the silence. "Anything been happening today?"

The reply is muffled as Max continues cutting through her half-cooked pig livers, blood oozing everywhere. With a mouth full of food, she does her best to reply. "A lot of broken ramble on channel 22. Must be just too far away to pick it up clearly but we checked out them bikes tracks that I was telling you about earlier. I reckon they're off towards Red Claw Creek." She finally swallowed her food.

"Righto," says Scrubber. "Now that drop off is done, tomorrow we go hunting." The others nod their approval. "Feed the dogs the leftovers but don't give them much; we want them mean and hungry for any stray visitors."

Price walks outside with one piece of liver for each dog. Snarling, barking and frothing at the mouth, they jump at the end of their chains, trying to get at Price while he stands in front of them, withholding their food as an act of dominance. He finally throws the Hatchet River Station guardians a bit each and they woof it down without chewing.

Meanwhile, over at the boy's new makeshift camp site on the bank of Red Claw Creek, music is blaring out of Allan's 4x4 stereo. Having been taught well, they all chip in, setting up the camp quickly and efficiently after many years of practice. Gathering enough firewood to last a week, they add some under the BBQ plate holding a large pot for boiling their shower water while they retrieve their chairs, swags and personal gear from the back of the truck. Once everything is set up, the young men start to chill out and settle in for the night.

"OK, boys, show us what you got," declares Allan

They all start emptying their pockets of gold from the last couple of days. Some nice nuggets are placed on the table in front of their finders; they all laugh and jest at who found what and how deep, then turn their attention to one of the newest prospectors who had found the least. He copped the brunt of harmless humour. They all have smiles on their faces at the end of another hard day. Everyone takes turns filling the canvas shower bag just out of main light of the camp with hot water, and enjoy hitting the shower, washing off a couple of days' dirt and sweat while the heat of the water soothes their aches and pains.

Allan raises his voice for all to hear. "We will change to channel 15 tomorrow; I don't want anyone listening in on 22." Reunited and refreshed they all start having a good time telling yarns, drinking and smoking. Allan throws some steaks on the BBQ, smiling in the dark as he listens to his crew's camaraderie.

Around the table as they are eating dinner Allan announces, "Boys, be very careful tomorrow. We are now deep inside the red circle, and a lot of things have happened down this way over the years. People have gone missing down here without a trace. It's got to be at least six missing persons that I have heard of; work in pairs, it will be safer, and remember channel 15. Also cover your tracks as best you can in obvious places, we don't want any other detecting crew picking up where we are or where we've been, or even worse, the station owners."

All the boys take the warning on board. After dinner and cleaning up, they start to bunk down, trying to get a good night's sleep before attacking the new area tomorrow. The fire dies to coals as Allan watches his crew hit the row. The fire dies to coals as Allan watches his crew hit the sack; deciding to do the same, he switches off the 12- volt led light and the car stereo.

Tim and John arrive back at the Oasis overnight and just throw their swags on the ground to sleep. Both wake up just before dawn. Over coffee, John says, "Tim, you really need to get that nose fixed, bud. You're bloody snoring kept me awake all night."

Tim's nose had been repeatedly broken in school yard fights, a fact unbeknown to him until a doctor's visit not so long ago for headaches. Tim replied with a smile on his face, "Yeah, I will have to find a few extra ounces for a nose job."

Jack strolls over from the main house not long after. "Got a hot coffee there for me, boys? Heard you come in last night."

Tim replies, "Yeah, no worries, bro."

Pouring an extra cup, Jack sits down while they tell him of how events unfolded down at the Croc Hole. "True?" he says in a deep voice, his huge calloused hand engulfing the coffee mug that was now barely visible. Raising it to his mouth and taking a sip, he says, "Boys, my thoughts are it's not just the gold prospectors of late, it's everybody. They are hiding something on the station that they don't want found. Old Fred is still missing from his lease, the bike's gone, his dog left there dead on the chain. I went to see the other miners yesterday and nobody knows where he is, also went back to his camp and buried the dog. I had a good look around while I was there, nothing unusual or out of place. So I called the police, listing him as a missing person.

I don't know exactly what Scrubber is doing down there but from what I have heard on the bush telegraph, they have become very active in keeping everybody away, even more so than the past. It's only a grass lease on the property off the government. It is not freehold land and they certainly don't own what gold is underneath. It was a goldfield 140 years ago, well before it was a cattle station. There is a gazetted road through the property that anyone can legally drive on if they're game enough, but now there seems to be a lot more traffic from tourists and campers who don't have a clue about the danger.

"The crew upkeeping the road have had the police out to smash down locked gates, with Scrubber, Max and Price all with their rifles at the ready. A truck driver nearly died because of the spikes that have been purposely placed across the road. That's classed as a man trap. Also, shots have reportedly been fired at choppers just for flying over the place, for Christ's sake. A bush walking party of ten were pulled up by Scrubber and co. at gun point and told to leave;

that incident was reported to police as soon as they got back to town.

Bakerstown Police have a list a mile long on what's been going on out here, and the man is still running around. I was told he doesn't even have a gun license. So, boys, you read between the lines. Nobody can get away with what he has done without higher help. We know the gold is down that way but only the desperate prospectors or ones with gold fever ever venture down towards Hatchet River homestead. There are caves, mine shafts and saltwater crocs in permanant waterholes that you would never be found.

We've been here 15 years now and Hatchet River Station hasn't been mustered for at least 10 years. So where's the money coming from to run that station and patrol it like a maxi-mum security prison?"

The conversation is broken by Sue's "Boy's, brekkie is on" as she walks past to let the chooks out and Bumpy off the chain. Jack continues, "I will tell Sue what happened at the Croc Hole later; you know how she worries. Just go swinging locally and we will catch up around the fire later tonight."

John says to Jack, "Got to head out this morning, I have work tomorrow. Give me a ring on anything you need brought in." Walking over for breakfast, John says to Tim, "Don't head down that way by yourself."

Tim replies, "Don't worry, bro. I'm fit and fast, Scrub-ber won't know where to turn," and he laughs.

John, with a serious face, very firmly says, "No, bro, not by yourself. It's too dangerous!" Finishing breakfast, John says his goodbyes and drives off towards town, pulling up at home in the mid-afternoon, tired and covered in bulldust that had dried into a slight mud because of his sweat.

At Red Claw Creek, the sunrise sets off a beautiful picture of the northern outback. The boys roll out of swags that are covered in dew; the air was sharp and thin overnight, with the temperature reading close to 10 degrees. Everyone in the camp is blowing vapour from the cold out of their mouths. The young men sit close around the rekindled fire for warmth while patiently waiting for a hot coffee. Nebo, one of the more experienced operators, says, "It's cold enough to freeze the balls of a brass mon-key."

Allan replies, "Make the most of it. The hotter the days get, the deeper the gold becomes."

Matt, one of the new additions to the crew, says, "What do you mean, Allan?"

"Well," he explains, "the hotter the ground gets, the noisier the coils are, especially with the bigger coils. So the rule is the colder the better. Night time is prime for detecting, especially in this country," he says as he throws the coffee in the billy.

At Hatchet River Station, they start packing the fawn 4x4 for their day of hunting prospectors. The 30-30 magazine is loaded and put behind the passenger's seat while Max places the fully loaded shot gun in between the front seats for quick access. Scrubber says to Price, "I was thinking on it last night, there's too much traffic now they've opened the road up. We need you to stay at the station and keep an eye out."

Price, with a look of total disappointment, slumps his huge shoulders. "We will be on channel 20 if anything happens here, but where we are going we could be out of range for some time."

"Righto," he mutters, feeling rejected. He looks down and starts kicking the floorboards with his boot.

Max, overhearing the conversation, could see her brother was upset at being left out of the hunt and she tries to cheer him up. "Price, Trixie the brood mare is coming on heat. You can round her up and put her in the barn. Let her settle, give her a feed and you can have your way with her tomorrow."

Price brightens up instantly and his face breaks into a toothy smile. Scrubber and Max climb into the truck, laughing at his delight. They warm it up and drive off, leaving a slight trail of bull dust. Price watches them drive off and sits on the steps of the homestead, pondering how to fill his day. He rolls a smoke and shuffles off to saddle up the stallion in the yards not far from the homestead. After picking up the brood mare and stabling her, Price looks satisfied.

Meanwhile Scrubber and Max are now many miles up the dirt road. Short cutting through a fenced paddock off the gazetted road, the 4x4 bounces across some rough country. "They headed this way," Max says to her husband as they cross the Hatchet River for the first time in years. Maneuvering through some jack knife gullies, the station truck catches up on the bull-bar then the tail end. As the cruiser creeps towards their conquest, Max turns on the two-way and presses the scan button, hoping to pick up on anyone using a radio close by.

Back at Hatchet River Station, the dogs around the homestead prick their ears up and listen intently; the hairs start to rise on the dogs' backs as they start to growl. Coming along the gazetted road, bouncing through the corrugations, bulldust and large pot holes, is a hippie camper-van hired out of Cairns. A beautiful blonde Swedish chick is sitting in the passenger's seat with a map on her lap. The driver, a brown-haired, large- framed Swedish guy, says, "Kris, where the bloody hell are we, babe?"

She replies, "Axel, we should be coming up to Hatchet River Station, but on the map it does not show a road towards Claytown. How can that be? The guy at the servo in Huego says the road is good all the way to Claytown." They continue talking as other dirt tracks heading in all directions appear. Instead of becoming more lost, they decide to pull up at Hatchet Station to ask for help.

By this time the sound of their vehicle has the dogs surrounding the house going crazy. Price briskly walks inside, reaches for the two-way mic and tries to call his sister and Scrubber. "There's a van at our front gate, what do you want me to do?" The radio crackles with only broken words coming over the two-way.

The van pulls up at the first gate. Krisa says to Axel, "I can't see anybody coming out."

He scans the situation, saying, "Don't worry, at least all the dogs are on chains."

The dogs in the meantime are becoming more de-ranged, hitting the end of their leashes with no reserve. Price, not being able to get a hold of his sister or Scrubber on the radio, gives up and throws the hand set onto the ground in frustration. Axel gets out before they open the last gate into the yard and yells out, "Hello." Price re-sponds by giving a wave from the homestead door; by this time all dogs are foaming at the mouth. "There," says Axel, "someone is over at the house."

He drives forward, pulling up about 40 metres from the homestead. They both get out and Krisa yells out, "Hi, how are you going? We are a bit lost."

Price, seeing the sexy looking blonde, licks his lips and breaks into a stupid grin. Now standing near the home-stead stairs, he waves them across. Axel turns before walking away from their van, pulling out the keys then, after pressing the central locking, slid them into his shorts pocket. Krisa looks at him and asks, "What are you doing?"

He shrugs, replying, "Just a habit from home." Before they make their way to the homestead, Krisa stops to check her hair in the side mirror on the van; Axel, only 25 metres away from Price, waves the map around while Krisa starts walking towards the men. Price strolls over, lets two dogs off the chain, and mutters, "Get him."

Not needing any more incentive, the first dog hits Axel in his hamstring, tearing out a large chunk of muscle and sinew. A deep growl comes from the dog that was now leaning back on its haunches, trying its best to topple his prey. Axel pivots at the hips, trying to grab hold of the dog by the head as the second dog latches onto his thigh muscle, shaking its head wildly. Axel lets out a grunt of pain, having been taken by surprise in the attack, spinning around in time to see a third dog launch itself in the air towards his head. Axel manages to brush the dog to one side in mid-flight then turns his attention to the dog that is locked onto his thigh muscle, belting it repeatedly in the head with his closed fist as the dog showed no signs of releasing its grip.

Krisa sees what is unfolding as she walks towards her boyfriend and screams in horror, yelling, "Run" to Axel, while taking her own advice and running back towards the van. The third dog that was thrown to one side came back with a vengeance, latching itself onto the Swede's forearm. With three dogs now in tow, Axel turns, trying to make it back to the van.

Price, enjoying the attack, releases another two dogs that were going off their heads at the smell of blood, also wanting a piece of the action. Taking off like guided missiles, they hit

Axel from behind, bringing the large man to his knees. Now that their prey was on the ground, the first two dogs change position and go for the kill as they all start tearing him apart. The sound of bones getting crunched and flesh getting torn off the bone is sickening. Axel tries to yell but can only get a gurgled groan out as one dog tears out his throat. His shredded body starts convulsing as the dogs throw up dust dragging him around the yard.

Krisa runs to the car then remembers the keys are in her boyfriend's pocket, and he is now being devoured by Scrubber's dogs. She panics, trying to pull open the door handle on the van and looking around as two of the dogs start running towards her. Krisa starts to slide down the side of the van, resigned to the fact that she is now dog food. Just before passing out, she faintly hears a commanding voice call, "Here."

As Price walks towards the van, he pats one of dogs on the head then picks the Swedish chick up. Slinging the prize effortlessly over his shoulder, he starts whistling while he carries her unconscious body towards the shed. Gently laying her down onto the work bench, he shuffles around the shed to find some rope. Price strokes her fine blonde hair, smiling at his trophy. Pulling the cord of an old-fashioned light bulb to illuminate the shed, he ties the ropes tightly to the legs of the work bench then knots her hands and legs thoroughly so any attempt at escape is futile. Turning, Price pulls the cord to the light and the shed falls back into darkness.

Walking back out into the sunlight, he calls the dogs off the large Swedish male's remains. There are only torn bits of flesh left on a torso that is nearly ripped in half. By the time Price gets the dogs back on the chain, Krisa has started to come around; at first delirious until it dawns on her that she is tied fast. Her mind quickly flashes back to Axel being eaten by the dogs and her running to the locked van. She has no idea how long it has been since the attack on Axel. She tries in vain to loosen the ropes that tightly bind her hands and legs; using the only option left, Krisa starts to yell, "Help! Please help."

Hearing the calls for help excites Price. Rubbing his scrotum, he shuffles quickly over to open the shed and turn on the light. Krisa's eyes take a few seconds to adjust and refocus. With Price now in full view, she recognizes the look on his face, immediately reading what's on his mind. "Please don't hurt me," she pleads.

Price grabs the pocketknife from his belt and opening the blade, cuts off her denim shorts to reveal a tiny, red, lacy G-string. Licking both lips, he quickly pulls down his own pants while reaching for the flimsy white top and ripping it straight off, exposing Krisa's firm, perky breasts. Price's excitement heightens. Breathing heavily he roughly tears off the G-string. Now hysterical, Krisa lets out a blood-curdling scream that is absorbed by the huge expanse of bushland surrounding the station.

Meanwhile Scrubber and Max have been following tracks all day and as night starts to fall, they are about 4km up from the mouth of Red Claw Creek. Max says, "They are up there somewhere." The moon has started to rise, throwing enough light on the creek bed for them to slowly navigate upstream. At about 9pm in the silence of the night, they can hear faint music from the boys' camp. They pause to give each other confirmation of the noise and proceed up stream with purpose. After 30 minutes of walking, they can spot the campfire through the trees.

Sticking to the shadows thrown by the moonlight, they climb out of the creek to overlook the camp. "Let's shoot the lot of them," whispers Scrubber, raising his rifle.

Max grabs him by the arm and in a quiet but firm voice, says, "I count seven, maybe eight of them. It's too many to go missing at once. We will have more trouble at our doorstep if we do this now."

Scrubber pauses, lowers the gun and rubs the stubble on his chin. "Yeah, you're right. Too many bikes, including the vehicle, to try and get out of here and bury. Got me buggered how they even got a truck in this far."

She cocks her rifle, saying to Scrubber, "Let's go down there and tell them to fuck off. If we have problems at all, might just have to shoot them all anyway."

Allan had just finished cooking a meagre amount of eggs and baked beans and all eight boys were sitting around the fire when Scrubber and Max boldly walk into the camp. "What the fuck?" says Allan as he jumps to his feet.

Scrubber replies, "Move one more foot and your guts will be all over the ground," and levels the shot gun at him. Allan stops in his tracks while Max has the 30/30 trained on the rest of the boys, slowly moving the rifle from one to the other.

"What's going on?" asks Allan.

Scrubber spits out, "I want you out of here, now!"

Worried, Allan looks at his boys. "Look, Scrubber, most of these men don't have headlights on their bikes, it would be suicidal to try and get out of here at night time."

Max responds in a gravelly voice, "Leave now. Just get on your bikes and piss off or we will shoot you where you stand."

The boys look at each other; Nebo walks over to roll up his swag. Scrubber growls loud enough for everyone to hear, "Leave everything, just fuck off now!" Allan and the boys swear and carry on but do as they are directed. The 4x4 starts up. Flicking on the headlights, Allan says, "Boys, ride the best you can out in front."

Twelve hours later, they arrive bruised and grazed back at their main camp, leaving the truck well behind once they had enough light to make their own way home, all of them eager to put their 10-cents-worth in on what had happened.

Allan arrives into camp many hours later and calls them all together. "Whose bright idea was that?" The boys drop their heads in guilt. "The gold we found down there probably won't even cover all the camping gear that we had to leave behind. It's getting way too dangerous to stay around. I've been thinking of heading to Western Australia for a change; big nuggets and lots of ground. Anyone who wants to come is welcome but it must be under your own steam, and that includes throwing in some coin for more camping gear. I don't have the money to prop you all up till you find something, so those of you who want to come and have some gold to sell now, I am going to head into town in two days' time. Make up your minds and let me know tomorrow. I'm going for a few hours' sleep."

He walks off towards his caravan. The boys around the table start to work out what gold they have stashed and, more importantly, who had found enough to get to Western Australia. Before long they work out there are three who don't have the gold to leave camp.

By the time Scrubber and Max trudge back to the vehicle, they are exhausted. Scrubber pulls a lukewarm water bottle out of the back of the truck, has a long guzzle and passes the bottle to Max. Opening the door, he digs around under the seat and produces a plastic container of amphetamines and passes her two of the pills. "Got to keep ahead of everything that's going on," he says, throwing two pills down his throat. They jump in the truck and head back towards Hatchet River Station.

Just as the dim light of morning appears on the horizon and the truck nears the homestead, they notice the Swedes' van. They look at each other puzzled. Scrubber guns the diesel tray back towards the homestead, Max cocks her rifle at the ready. The truck pulls up in a huge cloud of bulldust and they both jump out. Scrubber walks straight to the van and tries the door handles. They are locked.

Max starts walking then breaks into a half jog towards the homestead steps, noticing the dogs are unusually quiet and content. She spots the crows over towards the fence line, to the side of the homestead. The dogs had dragged the remains of the male Swede over that way in the height of the attack before Price managed to put them all back on the chain. She swears. Thinking the worst, she screams, "Price." The remains are unrecognisable.

At this time Price is lying on the ground beside the work bench, naked from the waist down, covered with only a thin, worn blanket. Sleeping lightly, he hears his name being screamed and, jumping up, he quickly pulls his pants back on then pushes opens the shed door.

Scrubber spins around at the squeak of the shed door and points the shot gun in that direction. Realising it is Price, he lowers the shotgun. "What the fuck is going on?"

Price shrugs his shoulders, blurting out, "They just turned up. I couldn't get you on the two-way, and stuff just happened."

Scrubber swore, back-handing Price across the face. It rang out, leaving a huge red welt but Price took the punishment, not even flinching or blinking an eye. "It's not like it used to be," spat Scrubber. "We have a main road going right through the goddam property now. Cars are coming through more frequently, anyone going past would have easily spotted the van."

Max is standing beside her husband. "What's done is done. Let's get this mess cleaned up."

Scrubber says to Price, "Bury the van with the rest of them. I will get rid of what is left of the body."

In the shed Krisa regains consciousness. Remembering what happened to her before she passed out for the second time and once again trying to free her arms and legs with no success, she can hear raised voices outside. Sucking in as deep a breath as she can muster, she yells out, "Help." Scrubber turns, "What the hell?" Lifting the gun, he strides towards the shed.

The blood drains from Price's face as he runs past Scrubber and makes it to the shed door first. "Can I keep her? She's pretty." Just as the words come out of his mouth, Scrubber's gun butt smashes across Price's chin, both eyes roll back into his head and he slumps to the ground, out cold.

Max and Scrubber open the shed door to see the naked female tied to the table. "Thank god," Krisa says. "Help me."

Max says, "I will fix this one," while cocking her rifle.

"No," yells Scrubber. "It will be a bigger mess to clean up." He walks over to pick up some rope hanging on the shed wall. By this time Krisa realises that they are not here to help but are debating the cleanest way to end her life. Now resigned to what is about to happen, she starts to sob uncontrollably. Scrubber cuts the rope to the right length and wraps it tightly around her throat. The screams are soon a strangled, gurgling noise, with a soft wheeze coming from deep within her chest. Once again the shed falls airily silent.

Scrubber releases the rope and looks across at Max. "See, no mess," he says calmly "Wake up your stupid prick of a brother and get the tarp; you know where to put them. I will take care of the van."

Scrubber walks over to the backhoe parked near the old excavator. Starting the machine, he drives down towards one of the many large flood silt terraces of the Hatchet River and quickly digs a large enough hole in the soft sand. Caving in on one side, the door of another vehicle buried previously is exposed. Satisfied the hole is deep enough, Scrubber drives the machine over to the van. Pulling a chain out of the tool box and hooking it around the axle, he lifts the front wheels of the van off the ground slightly and starts towing it towards the river terrace. Once the van is close enough to the hole, he unchains it. Reversing the backhoe around to the rear of the vehicle, he starts pushing it into the hole with the bucket of the machine.

Back filling of sand over the van takes only a couple of minutes. Finishing off, Scrubber back blades the soft sand with the bucket, smoothing out where the machine had been. Continuing this all the way back to where he originally started, he covered over all visible tracks.

Back at the shed, Max kicks Price. "Wake up," she yells. He stirs, moaning and holding his swollen chin. "Help me throw them in the truck." Price spots the girl's lifeless body and lets out a cry of anguish. "You'll cut that shit out if you know what is good for you. Come on, let's go." They throw Krisa's body and what is left of her boyfriend's remains onto a heavy tarpaulin in the back and drive off towards the gates at the end of the airstrip. Unlocking the gate, they continue on.

Scrubber parks up the backhoe then walks over to the station's second old, beat-up 4x4. He throws in two large tyres cut in half and drives towards the shed to retrieve a drum of molasses. Moving on to where the van is buried, he drops off a tyre after filling it with molasses. He places the last tyre halfway between the stationary backhoe and the freshly covered hole. Satisfied that by morning, with the stock drawn to the molasses like a magnet, there would be scores of cattle prints everywhere, naturally covering all signs of his handiwork. He turns the truck around and drives back to the homestead.

First thought on his mind is a long hot shower and he heads over to light the donkey to heat the water. Beside the donkey lies the blood-stained shirt he was wearing when they had their run in with the old timer. Picking it up, he throws it into the flames that are now flicking up around the side of the 44 gallon drum

While John is in town working, Tim decides to head in the opposite direction of the Hatchet River homestead, looking for new ground to detect. Finding close to half an ounce on the first day out, he is quietly content with that. Calling it a day, he puts the detector into his back pack for the last time, and finding neutral on the motorbike, Tim hits the start button and heads back towards the Oasis. A bit short of half way back, he runs across Allan on the road to town, his vehicle all packed up with two of the boys sitting cramped in the front, ready to hit Western Australia. Tim parks up on the bike while Allan pulls the 4x4 to a stop. They nod to each other. "How's it going, fellas?"

Allan replies, "Fuck me dead, Tim. We had a run in with Scrubber two days ago, lucky to get out of there without being maggot food." Allan fills Tim in on the encounter. A second vehicle pulls up behind Allan's, it had been travelling a distance behind to avoid filling the air cleaner with bull dust.

Tim glances at the second vehicle, quickly doing a head count. "So where the rest of the boys?"

Allan shrugs his shoulders. "Well, they couldn't get enough coin together to come over to WA with us. They got some tucker there and about a month's fuel for the generator but other than that, they have to fend for themselves."

Tim asks, "How long you going for, bud?"

Allan lifts his hands off the steering wheel, palms up. "Not sure but I'm out of this joint for a while. Look, bloke, I've got to keep moving. We have a long way to go." Anxious to get out of the place, he puts the truck in gear and slowly starts moving forward, with a parting word to Tim, "Watch your back, bud, and if you get time, call in and see how the boys are travelling." Allan gives a wave goodbye as he pushes the accelerator towards the floor. The motor responds and they take off up the dusty road.

Tim lifts his arm up with fingers out stretched as a wave to the second 4x4 packed with three men in the front as it slowly goes past, with Tim saying, "Good luck, boys." They wave back in the same manner and then they too are gone.

Tim sits on the bike, thinking about what Allan has just told him. Reaching into the top pocket for his tobacco, he automatically rolls a cigarette. Without any thought or attention, he puts it to his lips and flicks the lighter to life. Taking a couple of heavy drags, he turns around to see the sun starting to sink towards the western horizon. Slipping the well-worn toe of his Composite boots under the gear leaver to select second gear, he lets out the clutch slowly and evenly so the bike does not stall. Heading towards home, the only thing on Tim's mind now is an ice cold rum and cola, a hot shower and a good feed after a long day.

Arriving just before dark, he wearily climbs off the bike. Bumpy, hearing the motor stop, knows the owner of that particular bike and makes his way to the gate to greet him. Now ten years older since he had saved Tim's life, the old dog had developed arthritis in his hips but still makes the effort to meet Tim every evening when he comes out of the hills. Walking in, Tim gives Bumpy an affectionate rub from his head down to his coat, which is also showing signs of age.

Sue and Jack are already sitting around the fire with freshly opened beverages. They smile warmly as Tim walks towards the fire with cold rum in hand. "How did you go, bro?" asked Jack.

"Yeah, made wages," replies Tim. Sue, with a smile, puts her hand out. On seeing this, Tim digs into his pocket to pull out three well-worn gold nuggets. She then passes them on to Jack who, in the fading light, turns on the torch beside his chair for better inspection. Sue hears the phone ringing and walks quickly back to the kitchen to grab the cordless phone as Jack and Tim talk in earnest over details of the what, where and how deep the nuggets were found.

Sue arrives back with the phone; talking and laughing, she interrupts the men's conversation. "Tim, it's Danni" and passes the phone to him. Filling Danni in on his day and the finds is followed by what happened to the boys, and that most of them were heading off to Western Australia.

Danni, concerned about the news she has just heard, instructs Tim, "I don't want you going down that way at all. It's just not worth the risk!"

Tim stands and nods continually as he cops an ear-bashing. Finishing off the conversation, he passes the phone back to Sue and shakes his head. "Bloody women," is all that was said. Tim climbs into his swag after a hot shower and a big feed of crumbed steak, chips and salad, and within ten minutes, he is snoring loudly, even waking the dog up from his sound sleep.

Back in town John has knocked off for the day and is doing his homework. Topographical maps are laid out in sequence over the outdoor table, the laptop is also close by with Google Earth on the screen. Working with one then the other, cross-referencing information, finding areas of interest.

After extensive years of work in the gold fields, he knows exactly what he is looking for. John works the mouse, zooming in and out on Google Earth and taking snapshots of areas while making up a short list, numbering all the prints and marking north, south, east and west in the areas of most interest to him. Late into the night, Meg comes out and puts her arm over his shoulder and onto his chest. "Give it up for the night, babe," she whispers into his ear. "Let's go to bed."

On hearing this, John turns to see Meg in a see-through negligee that reveals her stunning, curvaceous body. Not needing any more encouragement, he stands up, turns off the light and follows her inside the bedroom.

The next day after work, John has all the information he needs to access the areas of interest with GPS co-ordinates, map details and distances from the road. He gives Tim a call at 7.30pm at the Oasis, knowing that he would have gotten back, had a shower and finished his first drink. Tim answers the phone as he had just finished talking to Danni. After John tells him of his research, he replies, "Hey, bro, all's good. Danni's got two weeks off work; a man's not a camel, if you know what I mean," laughing into the phone. "I'm heading in first thing in the morning to pick her up."

John says, smiling, "No worries, bud. You have a good time and I will catch up when your mind's back on work." The two weeks fly past for Tim and Danni while John is biting at the bit to get back out, fuelled by his new found research. Having had Tim as his mentor for the previous three years, John is now an accomplished operator in his own right. He had learnt a lot over the years from Tim's experience and wealth of local knowledge; everything from vegetation, rocks, different soil types, fault lines, the list continued on to where and how Tim had found gold before, being on top of his game in this particular field.

Tim turns up at John's place at a reasonable 11.30am after dropping Danni back home and shopping to replenish supplies for a prospecting run. Meg puts on a coffee for the men as they go through the maps and photos that John has complied.

After discussing at length while also planning the best way to attack the new area, they start heading back out towards the Hatchet River. It had been a long day for Tim since he had started his morning from the Oasis in the early hours. The decision had been made to camp out as they were getting too far away from the Oasis, losing three hours a day in travel instead of detecting.

Arriving at the GPS co-ordinates for the shortest track towards the location, they pull up the vehicles to start looking for a way down the steep hillside, preferring to set up camp beside water. After about half an hour, they work out a self-made track to the creek bed. The 4x4s crawl down the steep hill in low gear, with Tim on the two-way, advising John of timber spikes and razor sharp slate rocks that can flatten a brand new tyre before you could blink an eye. Using low gear while riding the brakes, they finally make it to the bottom. Tim comes over the two-way, "Here we are, bud. Let's unload and set up."

Hearing the approaching vehicles, a large boar pig wallowing in the mud on the side of the creek gets up, snorts, and trots away, leaving its tell-tale stale stench heavy in the air. The men get out of their trucks and can smell the boar, indicating that it has only just left. Tim points to the muddy puddle beside the creek; John nods, acknowledging Tim's observations.

While they are setting up camp a Kingfisher perches itself on a branch overhanging the creek. Its stunning colour gleaming in the late afternoon sun, it eyes off its prey swimming around in the stagnant waterhole directly beneath him.

As it is getting on by the time camp is set up, they decide to start fresh in the morning and empty a stew Meg had pecooked into the pot. The prospectors hastily eat dinner early, knowing a big day is ahead. Both men settle in their swags for the night, within 15 minutes Tim is snoring loudly. John, this time round, is prepared. Pulling out a pack of PK chewing gum, he starts chewing vigorously. Once it is down to a bland taste, he breaks it in half, wraps it in toilet paper and pokes it in both ears. He enjoys the best night sleep on the Hatchet River gold fields to date.

Tim's alarm starts going off at 4am; he rolls over to backhand the top of the alarm clock, which was now gathering momentum. It goes silent. John, oblivious to it all because of the gum in both ears, does not wake until Tim has started the fire up to boil the water for coffee. Bouncing out of bed after a great night's sleep, John starts getting his gear together for the day's proceedings. After two cups of Tim's super strength plunger coffee, they are ready to move out of camp just before sunrise when they have enough light to ride into the unknown. Riding along saddles and ridges and following the GPS location marked from John's research,

Tim leads the way, skilfully manoeuvring the bike down a rocky spur towards a small creek.

Stopping on an alluvial bank, he spots a large, rusted out gold pan in the long grass. It had been left by the old timers. Still sitting on the bike, Tim sticks his boot through the rusted hole in the bottom and lifts his leg to show John, commenting, "Old timers have been here, that's a good sign." Both men dismount and go through the motions of setting up the detectors out of their backpacks, firing them up then ground balancing before heading off in different directions, each swinging their machine coils low and slow with two-ways in their pockets, keeping a good distance between them so the detectors didn't interfere with each other. They run across broken bottles from the Hatchet River heyday. "This must be an old timer's township," Tim claims over the two-way.

"Yeah," replies John, "old timers' stuff everywhere. Haven't seen any detector holes yet."

Tim presses the button on his radio, replying, "Neither have I," while zigzagging with his detector towards the creek, a twinge of excitement in his voice. The detectors respond on maximum settings while still in the morning cool. The 4500 detector blares out targets left, right and centre. Tim listens to his machine's response and digs a few of the more mellow sounding targets to retrieve brass belt buckles. Realising he is too close to the huge camp, he changes his trajectory away from that direction. "There's rubbish everywhere," says Tim over the radio.

"Yeah, same over here, bud. I'm going to try a bit further out," replies John.

Walking 30 metres since the last two-way message, Tim spots some coins lying on top of the ground beside an old timer's clay brick oven. Bending over to pick them up, he recognises the markings of gold sovereigns. Not believing his luck, he looks at the coins in his hand again. Two gold sovereigns and numerous Chinese coins. He thinks, "We're on it here."

At the same time, John, who is working well away from the camp, gets a strong signal. After three strikes of the pick, he scoops a handful of dirt out of the hole. Waving it over the coil, he feels the weight of the target in his hand and prays it is not a lump of lead. He lets out a "Yee-ha." While trying to compose himself after looking at his find for at least five minutes, he gets on his two-way. "How you going, Tim? Just pulled out a two-ouncer over here," he says proudly.

There is a moment of silence before Tim comes back on. "Good onya, bro, best you pull your finger out; already got two gold sovereigns, a three-ouncer and two four- ouncers."

John's jaw drops, "You're kidding me."

Tim quickly responds, "No, bro, this area hasn't ever been found. It's like going back 100 years. Everything is as they left it before moving to the next rush in the area."

Pumped from their finds, they hit the area hard, methodically working the thick patches of gold one after another, unearthing numerous gleaming gold nuggets, all in unique shapes and sizes, throughout the morning session. Dipping with sweat and hands covered in blisters, Tim calls John on the two-way. "Hey, bro, how much water you got left?" "About a litre and a half. Why?"

"Well, bud, I've been digging this hole to China for the last hour or so, I'm up to my chest in depth and run out of bloody water ages ago. Can you bring me some over? This target is big and getting very loud, it's not far from coming out now."

John replies, "No worries, mate. Which direction are you?" Given Tim's rough position, John plots his own co-ordinates into the GPS and leaves the detector on the ground, also having a sweet target to unearth. Walking towards the bike, he rides towards Tim's rough position, eventually finding him lathered in sweat. Climbing out of the huge hole, he gulps down some of the warm water remaining in John's plastic milk bottle, which was frozen solid when they left camp that morning.

Tim's face is smeared in mud from wiping the sweat away with dirty hands, his shirt is wringing wet from the physical effort of trying to reveal this target. They find the nearest shady tree to sit down under and have a smoke as they talk in detail about their finds so far and what might be at the bottom of this huge hole. They both have grins on their faces that go from ear to ear. John says, "Righto, Tim, I will sit in the shade here and watch you dig that sucker out."

Tim stubs out the smoke butt, gives a slight groan as he lifts himself to his feet, and turns the detector back on. He sighs deeply as he walks back towards the unknown target. Climbing back in to swing over the bottom of the hole, the detector screams over the target. Tim ducks out of sight once again, wearily throwing out dirt while his partner sits in the shade, knackered himself from digging targets all day.

Eventually locating the target with a yell of triumph along with a groan of relief that it is over, Tim's head finally pops up into sight. He is holding up a nugget larger than the palm of his hand. John walks over from the shade of the tree, with Tim exclaiming, "You little ripper" and flinging the flat piece of gold with brown quartz imbedded in it towards John. Still in the hole, he swings the coil around again making sure that it is the only target.

John, catching the nugget, exclaims, "Good onya, bud." Looking at the piece while juggling the weight in his hands, he says, "It's got to be 10 to 12 ounces easy." The 4500 screams again from the hole. "Fuck me dead," John says out loud. Tim pulls out another one from the side of the hole; this time about six ounces but looking identical to the first.

After making sure nothing is left in the hole, Tim climbs out, exhausted but on a high. Giving John a smile from ear to ear, he says, "Two peas in a pod" and passes the second nugget to John as well. Both prospectors examine the pieces under the scant shade of an iron bark. They are identical, other than size. "That's nearly a pure gold leader," says Tim, "heading towards the hill where the old timers dug out the reef."

After sitting down and taking on board the direction of the rich leader, the men discuss the logistics of the find, knowing it cannot be dug out by hand and machinery will be needed. This meant pegging a lease on the area, submitting an environmental plan and bond money along with lodging paperwork at the Mines Department and waiting a minimum of a year for approval. The cost of all this would be way more than they could afford. Tim decides, "Bugger it. We will have to conceal it and come back when we find enough gold for this venture."

John starts feeling that his own finds are insignificant to Tim's and heads back on the bike towards his detector and the target yet to be unearthed. The sun is now throwing long shadows on the trees and, after adding on travelling time, they both realised that they would have to make a move back to camp shortly. John gets back to his spot and quickly hooks up the 4000, digging for twenty minutes to retrieve the target. Holding a large slug of lead between his fingers in the end, "Fuck me dead," he mutters to himself. "Time to head back to camp for a cold beer."

Arriving back just before darkness falls, they slip on their head lamps to scout for more firewood. They are both looking forward to a hot shower. They kick down small ant hills to use around the camp fire so it doesn't escape while they slept. Finishing the few jobs that needed doing around the camp, they get to sit around the fire to relax after a hard day. After a few drinks, John says, "Let's weigh it all." Walking to the back of his truck, he selects one of the plastic boxes that had the old style hanging scales, a gift from his mother-in-law years earlier. John sets the scales up on the table, saying, "Come on, Tim, show me what you got."

Tim walks over to the backpack beside his bike. He had to give up on filling his short's pockets earlier in the day because the weight of gold was constantly sending his strides down around both ankles. Rummaging through the pack, he starts placing nuggets on the scales; every weight they had on the scales was still not enough. They have to settle on weighing in the larger nuggets individually. A total of 52 ounces for the day. Both men are on an extreme high and have problems eating dinner that night, but have no worries hitting the grog to celebrate.

John startles to the sound of the alarm clock at 4am, having forgotten the gum-in-the-ear trick after too many drinks last night. Tim had conveniently put the alarm under his bed and it vibrates randomly around in the dust until John, on his hands and knees, fumbles in the dark, locates it then throws the alarm towards Tim's swag.

Muttering something crude under his breath, he staggers to the tray of the truck where the primus gas ring is set up. Igniting the gas, he fills the kettle and puts it on to boil. John then picks up his chair and moves it near the previous night's fire, throwing some small sticks onto the all but dead coals. The kindling starts to smoke then all of a sudden it bursts into flames. Adding on some larger logs, John sits down and waits for the kettle to boil.

Tim, hearing the alarm going off somewhere close near his bed, smiles and waits snug in the warmth of his swag for the kettle to sound out before venturing into the cool of the morning. As the whistling sound increases, John walks over and grabs it off the gas, then fills the stainless steel coffee plunger full of steaming water. Tim climbs out of his swag, cheery and jesting at John, who replies, "It's bloody too early. Don't talk to me until I've had at least two cups of coffee" Tim laughs, continuing on regardless. After the second cup is nearly empty, the caffeine starts to kick in and John slings back as much shit as Tim dishes out. Laughing and carrying on, they get their gear ready for another day in their newfound hot spot.

John finishes unloading the frozen water bottles from the 80-litre freezer into his backpack and they climb onto their bikes just as dawn is breaking to follow a well-worn cattle pad away from the camp. Deciding to have a better look around before heading back over to where they were picking up gold yesterday, they come across an old timer's track that heads up into the steep hills, leading away from their spot. Tim pulls up on his bike and turns to John. "That old timer's track could lead to more unfound townships."

John looks at the faint track up the extremely steep hill and shakes his head. "It's amazing where they went. We would be flat out getting our bikes up there."

Tim replies, "Yeah, they were bloody tough men back then and we think we do it hard. Let's go get some more gold." Riding on for some time, they stop adjacent to the creek where they started smashing the gold yesterday.

Studying the area more intensively, John says, "I might head out a bit further and see if I can pick up on the run of gold."

"Righto, bud," Tim replies. "Make sure the two-way is on." He heads off towards some small hills to the north as his detector screams with its first target for the day.

Riding about 1.5km away, John picks a likely spot and starts to set up the 4000, ground balancing the machine then heading off up a little side feeder creek. After swinging for half an hour, his tally is only two lumps of lead, including a few boot tacks from the gold rush days. Deciding to change direction, he heads over to the next feeder and starts working back towards where the main gold was found.

Climbing out of the gully to start the next, his foot rolls on an exposed tree root in the grass and he hears the muscle in the ankle tear as he falls to the ground. Cursing, he sits there, tenderly rubbing his ankle and dreading the thought of taking off his boot. After a ten-minute break, he manages to regain his feet and tentatively tries to put some weight on the left foot. With the flash of pain, he quickly reverts back to his right foot. John continues on, heavily favouring that side. Now moving a lot slower down the gully, he can feel the ankle swelling up inside the boot. Having to keep all of his weight completely off the injured foot, he starts to fully limp.

John has difficulty negotiating the terrain ridden with unstable rocks of every shape and size on one foot. His ankle is like a balloon by the time he gets back on his bike. He calls Tim on the two-way and informs him of the situation. Tim replies, "Shit, bro. Come back to the water hole in the main creek, I will meet you there." John starts the bike, thanking God for the electric start. Not being able to change gears with his foot and having to lean down to change the bike into second gear by hand, he slowly rides off towards the water hole.

Finally arriving with the bike still in second gear, John hits the kill switch, takes off his detecting gear and limps towards the shade of a tree 100 metres from the water hole. Tim turns up. "Shit, bud. Best you get that boot off and soak it in the cool of the creek to get that swelling down." John does as Tim instructed, leaning on his prospecting partner for support down to the creek. They both sit down, and Tim informs John that he is up another six ounces for the morning. After close to half an hour of soaking the ankle and trying to reduce the swelling, Tim pulls a sticky bandage from one of the pockets in his detecting belt (kept handy for snake bites). He starts wrapping it around John's ankle in a crisscross fashion for the best support. About to finish it off, Tim asks, "Mate, where's your pocketknife?"

John answers, "On my detector belt up at the bike."

He shrugs. "Yeah, mine is there too. Here, I'll just burn it" and without further thought, he flicks the lighter to life. Having burned half way through the width of the bandage, it catches on fire. Tim's first reaction is to put out the fire. He immediately starts hitting John's ankle with open palms, trying to put out the flames.

John's face goes a shade of grey and he lets out a "Fuck me" that could be heard for miles.

Tim, still feverously trying to put out flames, realises what he has just done. "Shit, bud, sorry" and instantly plunges John's foot into the water to extinguish the bandage. If John wasn't in so much pain, he would have laughed at the turn of events.

Arriving back at camp way earlier than anticipated, they indulge in a few stiff rums, which start to dull the pain in John's ankle. After a throbbing, sleepless night, John decides, "Bud, I am going to head back to town. No good trying to prospect in this country on one foot, it's hopeless, and is only going to slow you down."

Tim agrees. "No worries, mate. I will load everything, make sure you get out alright and sweep your tracks. We don't want any other operators picking up where we are. I might take a ride to see if Jack wants to have a swing while your foot's mending."

"No worries, mate. Can do bugger all in this condition," says John.

He climbs into the 4x4 as Tim loads the last of his partner's gear onto the back. Jumping on the bike, Tim leads the way up the steep hill. At the top, just before entering onto the main road, they say good bye. Gritting his teeth every time he applies pressure to push in the clutch to change gears, John leaves in a trail of dust while Tim breaks a bushy sapling branch and starts sweeping the tracks of the truck, then proceeds to stand the grass back up from where the tyre marks were visible. Looking back and inspecting his handiwork, Tim is content that all signs of activity have been concealed then rides off towards the Oasis to see if Jack is keen to come out for a swing and pick up some gold.

Over at the boys' camp, the remaining operators are all a bit down from being left out of the WA trip. The parties were all over, the chicks had gone, and now they were detached from the main crew to gouge out a living from the harsh Hatchet River gold field. All had their own thoughts on how they were going to achieve this, with the best operators, who were also their mentors, having left for WA, as they sit down for a small meal of mince balls with tinned spaghetti and bread. Tonga, the eldest and most experienced of the operators left in the camp, had certainly found enough gold to leave with the rest of the crew, but having to send half of what he had found to his ex-wife to support his kids left him short.

"Well, boys," says Tonga, "the only way I can see for you two to catch up with the rest in WA is to head deep into the red zone." He points to the map. "Someone has to stay as caretaker for the camp so I will if you guys want to get over there that bad. That's where I would go. High risk, high reward."

The other two boys left in camp are relative newbies to the game compared to the rest and they discuss this in depth. Especially after what had happened last time they ventured down that way, by night's end they decide that's the plan and voice their decision. "Tonga, it's on. We just got to duck and weave and go in commando style." They plan to do a day run, leaving the bikes and opting to walk for miles so the noise would not travel, no two-ways so they could not be tracked on the air waves and meet back at the bikes before 4pm. With that plan firmly in place, they leave at daybreak towards the Hatchet River home-stead.

Following a back track that Tonga had drawn them on a mud map, they pull up on the bikes and unpack their gear. "Meet you back here at 4pm" is the last communication for the day as they move off in different directions with one goal in mind, to succeed in finding big gold. Slipping into the long grass made them virtually invisible as they are wearing khaki clothes and blend in with the dying surrounds of the bush.

A slight breeze slowly changes direction over the morning and sends the unaware prospectors' odour towards the dogs chained at the homestead. Picking up on the slight human scent, they get agitated and bounce around on their chains, their noses high in the air trying to confirm the brief smell that is fractionally too distant from the dogs for them to zero in on.

By midmorning, the two young prospectors have changed their detectors from loud speaker to headphones. They are working their way closer to the homestead and do not want to make any unwanted noise on targets they come across. Both operators swing their detectors rhythmically from side to side as they walk through rough uneven ground with relative ease.

The first young prospector arrives back at the bikes 15 minutes before his partner, shrugs off the backpack then seeks out a shade tree. He kicks a few sharp rocks out of the way before he sits down and reaches into his backpack for a joint, ready rolled for the end of the day. Lighting it up, he can faintly hear his partner approach. Being dressed in camouflage gear, it is difficult to visually pick up on his mate until he is 30 metres away. He walks in with a huge smile on his face. "How did you go?" asks the first young guy, passing the tail end of the joint to his mate.

"Four and a half ounces at a guess." He reaches into his weighted down pocket to produce a handful of nuggets and slumps down beside his friend, exhausted.

"Yeah, well, you just piped me I reckon. I've got about four ounces, but man, that was like walking the gauntlet. I could hear their dogs going off downstream. The hairs on the back of my neck were up most of the day, I reckon. Anyway, we found our Western Australia money so now we can catch up with the rest of the crew."

His mate agrees, adding, "Let's piss off out of here. This place gives me the creeps."

At the homestead, Scrubber walks out onto the porch and leans over the hand rail, pulls out a packet of tobacco, and rolls a smoke. He scans the opposite side of the river bank for any signs of dust, contently looking towards the cattle licks where at least 50 head were now meandering and grazing on the small new shoots of grass in the area, covering all signs of where numerous vehicles were now buried. Max strolls out of the homestead and sidles up beside her husband. He glances at her then returns his stare almost trance-like to the bush surrounds. In silence Max turns her head in the same direction, transfixing on nothing in particular at all with not a single word spoken between them.

Stooping to get out of the chicken coop, Price shuffles towards the homestead with fresh eggs in hand, finishing off his regular chores. Max finally breaks the silence. "He's still pretty down over that last girl."

Scrubber looks her way and replies, "That simple idiot is going to get us into more trouble than he's worth one day."

Max nods, replying, "Nothing we can do. He knows too much and he is my brother. We'll just have to take him with us on our trips and let all the dogs off while we're away. Least no one will get in the yard gate."

Scrubber grunts in agreement, mumbling, "Yeah, I suppose," and flicks the dumper of his smoke out into the yard in front of him.

Price arrives at the steps of the homestead. "Eight eggs this morning," he says, proudly holding four eggs in each of his huge hands.

Scrubber says, "Put them away and grab the truck. We will all go for a run. Those bloody dogs have been acting up all morning, something is stirring them up."

Price's eyes lit up instantly. "Righto" he says as he hastily moves towards the kitchen. Returning with the truck, he gets out and jumps straight into the back as the others climb into the front. Price checks the 357 Magnum pistol strapped tight on his hip. They head off upstream towards where the two young men from the boys' camp had been swinging their detectors, missing them by twenty minutes.

Tim arrives back at the Oasis, with Bumpy meeting him at the gate as usual. Patting him on the head, he says to the dog, "Where's Dad, Bumpy?" Turning his head, the dog trots off towards his owner, who was down moving some earth with the excavator for a new toilet block.

On seeing Tim, Jack idles the machine down and jumps off onto the tracks then down to the ground, pulling out the earplugs, his face and hair covered in dust. "How's it been going, bud?"

Tim returns the grin with a smile. "Yeah, good, bro."

Jack's huge arm curves around Tim's neck. "Let's go back to camp so you can tell me all about it. Where's John?"

"Fucked his ankle so he decided to head into town early," replies Tim.

"True? That's no good," Jack comments with concern. Walking into the cool of the camp, he moves towards the fridge and grabs out a cold water jug. They sit at the table, with Tim pulling out some of the nuggets he had found.

Jack's eyes light up at the beautiful gold being passed towards him. "Far out, bud. You guys have been onto it!"

Tim, still with a smirk, says, "That's nothing." Returning from the bike with his backpack, Jack looks at Tim.

"You're goddam kidding me" and starts laughing as Tim piles the nuggets onto the table. "Hang on, mate. I'll just go and turn the excavator off. That's it for the day now. Are you hungry, bud? I could eat a horse and chase the rider at the moment then we will celebrate the find."

Tim laughs. "Yeah, bro. No worries. I'll be in that. Where's Sue?"

"She's headed into town to get some supplies and catch up with the kids. She'll be another couple of days yet," Jack says.

"Righto," Tim replies, "so you can come for a swing then?"

Jack, removing leftovers out of the fridge from last night's dinner along with some homemade bread from another plate, eagerly replies, "Too bloody right, mate."

As the afternoon wears on, the number of empty beer tins pile up on the table with nearly a story for every nugget. They celebrate long into the night, with Tim marking the spots on a toppo map as both men discuss the area at length.

Waking up a little bit rusty in the morning, they fuel up their bikes and load up the backpacks with dry sup- plies, including enough drinking water for a couple of days then they head back towards the bush camp Tim and John had prepared. They spent a good 20 minutes covering their tracks, including riding through the bush half a kilometre from the actual turn off to conceal their movements from any other shifty operators in the area who might try to pick up on any fresh tracks to follow.

During the previous night's discussions, they had roughly worked out there were four separate patches of gold that had been found, along with a thick gold leader heading towards the reef that runs too deep for using hand tools. Concentrating close around the patches that had already unearthed good gold, it isn't long before they start picking up again; not as much as previously found but eight ounces between them for the day was not too shabby. Working the area for another two days, they start picking up less and less each day until the last morning both men are down to finds of grams not ounces. Deciding to call it quits, the men pack up and head back towards the Oasis as Sue is also expected in that day as well.

They are not back fifteen minutes before Bumpy starts barking to the sound of an oncoming motorbike and Tonga slowly rides into the camp. Out of instinct the men quickly hide their gold finds and welcome him in for coffee. They all sit around yarning on who's doing what. In one of the many conversations, Tonga mentions that the last two remaining boys had headed towards the Hatchet home- stead and had done very well, picking up eleven ounces for the day. The gold finds gave them enough to head to WA to meet up with Allan and the other boys, adding that the pair would have left a shit load behind as they were nowhere near experienced operators and were still learning the ropes.

After about two hours of talking idly, Bumpy starts barking as Sue's vehicle comes over the hill into the view of the Oasis. Tonga, picking this as his cue to leave, says goodbye and rides out just as Sue pulls in. They wave to each other in passing. Sue drives right up to the house to unload the supplies, happy that Tim and Jack are around to give her a hand. "Many hands make light work." Chatting as they put away the supplies, Sue says to Jack, "The kids have a couple of weeks off work and are bringing some mates up to go camping, do a bit of detecting and Barra fishing."

Jack replies, "That's great news. I went for a quick fish down the Croc Hole the day you left for town on the motorbike and picked up a few good fish in about half an hour. They're on the chew at the moment. When are they due in?"

Sue says, "In two days' time. So we will be OK at the Croc Hole? I don't want anyone to be in danger from them scum."

Jack replies, "We have been going down there for the last 15 years and have never run across him; besides, he never crosses the river. If it puts your mind at ease, I will throw in the rifle, OK?"

Sue answers, "Thank you. So you will have to pull out the swags and camping gear from the shed and get it sorted out."

Tim, running low on supplies after a four-week stint, decides to head into town to have a bit of a break and Tim, running low on supplies after a four-week stint, decides to head into town to have a bit of a break andspend some time with Danni. Tim informs Jack and Sue and, being still fully loaded, he points the truck towards town and disappears in a cloud of bulldust.

Jack walks over to the padlocked shipping container beside the shed and starts rummaging through an array of camping and fishing gear, ready to pack into the 4x4. He is pleased that both sons, Rick, the eldest, and Rob, were coming in at the same time as he had not seen them in six months or longer. Two days flew by and on their sons' arrival, he has the truck ready to go. After a quick hand-shake, they are back on the road before the dust settles. Jack winds down the window and yells out, "Channel 20, let's hit the toe."

He is keen to get going, knowing the bush track to the Croc Hole is extremely rough with a few tricky washouts and gullies thrown into the mix. Most of the way is in low gear 4x4 with the hubs locked in. This kind of track sorts out the experienced 4x4 drivers from others quick smart. Only being 14km downstream as the crow flies, it was at least a four-hour drive, without having to winch the less experienced drivers through parts of the track. Jack's vehicle, along with his sons' trucks, have the least problem getting through but by the time all five vehicles finally get to the Croc Hole, five and a half hours have lapsed.

The spot they picked out became a hive of activity of setting up camp, collecting firewood, organising the tables, chairs and the like. Jack, being in the know, pulls up near a large tree, for its shade as well as its firm, level surface, which was covered in short green spindly grass that looked like it had been mowed but actually had been cropped by passing cattle. As the sun is flicking its last rays before slowly dying on the horizon, the camp is fairly well organised. The campers all congregate towards the eskiesand their chairs to chillax after a long day of travel. They share many stories around the campfire and laughter rings out well into the night, with a good time being had by all.

Just before dawn, a chorus of different bird species all sing out, giving their own version of the morning anthem. Some of the larger Barra in the Croc Hole start chopping at the top of the water, hitting the small perch they had cornered into the shallows of the water hole, leaving large swirls on the water surface. Most of the men are up, with Jack stoking the fire and boiling water for a much needed coffee while two of the young men are going over their four-wheel drives for dints and scratches from the previous day's trek. To their horror, they are numerous as both of them had got hung up on rocks. One side step is not looking too healthy and they are both swearing under their breath over the damage inflicted on their trucks.

Jack strolls over with a hot mug of coffee in hand and inspects the trucks. He tries to smooth things over by saying, "Don't worry, fellas. Most of it is cosmetic, that side step we might have to Cob & Co it to get back into town." Shaking his head, he talks to himself as he walks away, "Why the bloody hell would you bring a $75000 4x4 out here and think you are not going to get a scratch on it is beyond me."

Jack turns and yells back over his shoulder, "Hot water over there for coffee, fellas" as he walks over to start rigging up his fishing gear. Both sons have already started on setting up their lines so they can get to their preferred spots, a large snag downstream where they had picked up some nice Barra from previous trips. Jack, realising what is going on, smiles and quickens the pace to organise his own fishing gear.

The locals call it the Croc Hole but it is actually a series of deep holes with rapids about knee deep. The water is crystal clear in the shallows, with one hole that is shallow enough to see the entire bottom. This was the chosen swimming hole as you could check for crocs before entering. Shallow rapids flowed into it from the start so while you were in wading, a croc's approach would be easily noticed. Jack said to his sons as they took off like a bitches on heat just let off the chain, "Boys, last time I was down here, I had to hide behind a tree to bait my hook they were that hungry."

The boys laugh as they shoot off with a handful of spare lures to their favourite locations. Rob yells out to Rick, "Same deal as last time round. The loser has to get the firewood." Both young men are happy to be back in their bush element, familiar from childhood, with the family. Jack chuckles as he listens in on the bet being organised. Searching into his own gear, he retrieves a little hand reel with a tiny hook attached then grabs a bit of bacon out of the esky.

Thinking it's like the young bull and the old bull story, he walks back to his extensive array of fishing gear, selects a 60lb line with a 8o size hook tied fast then heads up towards the shallow rapids to catch a small perch for live bait. Jack glances downstream to the first fishing hole. Seeing some of the visitors are already in strife, fighting to get their lures out of the overhanging branches and into the water, he returns his concentration to the job at hand. After two little nibbles, he has his first live bait.

Just down from the rapids where he caught the Perch, Jack is eyeing off a nice snag down deep into the bank with a reasonable structure to it; the water had a nice back eddy for the float as well. Sinking his hook through the Perch's backbone, Jack re-adjusts the float to the right depth for the snag and throws in the 60lb line. Sitting with his back resting on an old paperback tree, he starts to relax and listen to the whisper of the river. It is not long before a huge silver flash comes out from under the bank to nail his bait, instantly snapping him out of the trance that had engrossed him. The float disappears out of sight, with Jack letting the fish run just enough before pulling back tightly on the line to set the hook.

Underestimating the size of the Barramundi, 60lb line cuts straight into his fingers and draws blood. Cursing, he stands to tackle this large fish before it spits the hook. Leaping out of the water, the Barra shows off its true size. Blood pumping, Jack has problems keeping his footing on the slippery moss-covered bank that slopes steeply towards the water's edge. At one stage he is nearly pulled into the water hole. He regains a solid footing and manages to turn the large Barra, knowing he is now on top off the contest. Jack slowly wears the fish down, yelling for Sue to bring the landing net as it would be nearly impossible to lift up the 1.2m Barra on the 60lb line up the steep bank.

Sue arrives with the landing net and exclaims with excitement, "Holy snapping duck shit!" This is as close to Sue gets to swearing.

The large fish was now exhausted, lying on its side beside the bank. Jack replies, "Yeah, a bloody beauty, hey honey." He grabs the landing net with one hand and slowly manoeuvres it over the head of the Barra as his prize fish gives a last-ditch effort, thrashing its tail in a bid for freedom. The massive Barra only half fits in the net as Jack lifts the 23kg fish out of the water with little effort, bending the landing net's handle in the procedure. An hour after throwing in his small line to catch the bait, Jack is back at camp with a gilled and gutted fish measuring one metre plus and mused to himself, ''Yeah old bull, young bull alright.''

Meanwhile, downstream his two sons are in a battle of their own with a 75cm Barra by Rob and another 78cm caught by Rick. While the rest of the visitors were floundering to even get a lure into the water properly. One of the young men, first time ever Barra fishing, flexes the rod until it nearly snapped, trying to retrieve his lure. Stuck fast in the overhanging paper bark branches, the soft bark gives way under the pressure from the tension on the line with the lure burying itself deep in his arm with the recoil.

Being extremely embarrassed over the predicament, and not wanting the attention that would be directed towards him back at camp while also dreading the jokes over drinks that night, he decides to try and remove the hooks by himself with the help of a folding multi tool strapped to his belt. He digs deep into the soft flesh with the pliers and after a lot of swearing and pain, finally removes the hooks. Yelling, "Fuck the fish," he heads back towards camp with blood running down his arm.

He walks around the outside off the camp not wanting anyone to see all the blood, he spots Jack sitting down talking to all the women in the camp with his esky half open and a massive Barra tail hanging out of it. All he can do is shake his head. He goes to the first aid kit in his 4x4 and bandages the wound after splashing a generous amount of antiseptic on the raw, torn flesh.

The two sons decide to head back to camp with their catch as their worms are starting to bite and they are in need of a good feed; both boys are quietly confident that they would be up on Dad. They trudge back towards the camp through the loose sand, both making jokes. "There's a nice piece of firewood up there; we'll have to let Dad know." The boys have always been very close and they laugh out loud at each other's slinging off.

On arriving into the camp, a nice catch of Barramundi slung over their shoulders, they have smiles on their faces like cats that have just eaten the canary. Rick smugly says, "Well, Dad, there's a nice couple of lumps of firewood about four to five hundred metres downstream" and they both break into laughter.

Jack, sitting back on his chair with a cold beer, also joins in, laughing loudly. "Well done boys, they are nice fish no doubt." The brothers are looking around for high fives from their mates, slightly puzzled by the lack of response. Their old mate, with his arm now heavily bandaged, nods towards Jack's catch. They glance over at the esky in the shade beside his 4x4, the smiles quickly retracted from their faces as they look upon the largest Barramundi they have ever seen come out of the Croc Hole. On seeing his sons' facial expressions, Jack strikes while the iron is hot. "So boys, where is that firewood you were talking about?"

The brothers sit quickly and scoff down some sangas the girls had prepared earlier, both deciding to head back downstream, changing lures before they left. Jack turns to the other men and women in the camp and says, "Let's go for a swim. It's heating up." All in agreement they head towards the shallow swimming hole in Indian file, with

Jack leading the way. The group are pleased to be cooling off while the brothers are feverishly casting lures to catch a larger Barramundi than their father, but without luck.

Meanwhile, Scrubber and co have found nobody in two days of searching but had discovered fresh tracks where people had been. Scrubber is livid and decides to sweep out further than usual to include the Croc Hole. Driving in from the opposite side of the river, they pull up on the high river bank overlooking the waterhole. Turning off the vehicle, a stiff north easterly breeze swiftly carries away any noise of their presence, with no one below being any the wiser that they are being watched.

All three get out and sit high on the ridge above the sequence of deep water holes. Max states, "Bingo. Five vehicles in total; not sure how many people but at maximum two in a 4x4 gives a total of ten people."

Scrubber grunts in agreement with Price chiming in, "You see any girls down there?" licking his cracked, windburnt lips.

"Let's go down and find out," replies Max as she lifts up off her haunches effortlessly and walks towards the vehicle Price clambers into the back excitedly while his sister instructs, "Put one shell up the spout of your pistol; you will have the best shot from the back." Price nods and does as instructed before grabbing a hold of the headboard of the truck with one hand. Scrubber starts the diesel 4x4 and slowly climbs down a steep old mine haul road towards the Croc Hole.

They drive near as possible to the waterhole, Price spots through the trees people splashing and wading around, cooling down in the refreshing river. He sharply thuds his palm on the roof of the truck. Instantly Scrubber stops the vehicle and turns off the ignition. They get out, leaving the car doors open. Price jumps from the back, and Scrubber leads the way towards the laughing and squealing coming from the water. Standing on the bank, Scrubberyells out to the mob of people mucking around in the river. Jack is first to pick up on the yelling through the other carry on around him. He looks up to see two men and a woman on the opposite bank. Jack, telling his crew to quieten down, walks through the thigh-deep water towards the other side only to be met with abuse. "Get the fuck off my property," Scrubber screams at him. Realising that it is Scrubber and his wife, Jack spins quickly to see where his mob are as instincts kick in immediately and he feels the need to protect his family and those around him.

The young men that were in the water had made their way over to see what all the commotion is about, totally oblivious to how dangerous these people are. The girls, now standing up in their wet bikinis, had caught the full attention of Price, who was eyeing them off like pieces of meat, a strange look coming over his face.

Recognizing the stare makes Jack's blood boil. Going from being totally surprised to building anger, the big man clenches both fists. His cheeks redden, his eyes are now just slits. He cuts off Scrubber's yelling and ranting about them leaving by taking a few steps forward and starting his own tirade, with his deep voice bellowing over the top of all, "Listen, I don't give a fuck who you are or what the fuck you think you own. We have lived out here for over fifteen years. I know my rights and this is a river; nobody owns the river so get in your fucking piece of shit and fuck off!"

Scrubber and Max, not accustomed to this, are taken back by the blunt verbal assault while Price's gaze burning with desire had not left the bikini-clad women. Drool is now running down the side of his jaw and he wipes it away with the back of his hand. Max turns. "Is that so?" Her temper has started to rise as well and she walkstowards the truck and reaches in behind the seat, her hand resting on the butt of her 30/30 rifle.

Jack, having a fair idea of what she is going to grab, quickly takes the couple of lengthy strides needed to get within reach of the door at the same time, yelling, "What you going to do? Shoot at me like you did my nephew down at the creek crossing?"

Jack's sons arrive out of the trees from the water line after hearing raised voices originating upstream from their fishing spot. "What the hell's going on?"

Price, being surprised by the arrival of another two men coming out of the bush, snaps back to reality and takes some steps backwards, his hand hovering over the pistol.

Jack quickly thinks 'If she goes to bring that rifle out, I will jam her in that car door before she gets a chance to take aim,' but at the mention of the previous shooting, Max lets the rifle drop back behind the seat.

Realising this man, even though unarmed is not about to back down, and there are five men in front of them now, including witnesses watching intently from across the river. Max quickly calculates the odds and yells at Scrubber, "Let's go!" Scrubber and Price heed the call and back track towards the vehicle. With Scrubber still screaming threats and obscenities, the 4x4 roars away, heading back up the old mine road they had come down.

Sue meets Jack at the water's edge, his temper still simmering. "We should leave," she says.

Jack fires back, "Stuff him. We have just as much right to be here as him. No, seriously, I have had a gutful of tiptoeing around this prick like we have been for bloody too many years. He's a gutless piece of shit shooting at unarmed men, holding women at gun point; who the helldoes he thinks he is? Wyatt Earp? No, we are staying and going to enjoy ourselves not run and hide. Enough is enough."

Sue replies, "Don't know about you but from what I heard and saw, the wife is calling the shots, not Scrubber."

Jack's family and friends stay on for another week without incident, catching some nice Barramundi before they head home to the Oasis. The young men, once back to familiar ground, waste no time in heading back to town as for most of them it was work the following morning. Jack and Sue, though enjoying the company of their sons and their friends, were also looking forward to a quiet couple of days at home alone.

The next day one of the miners in the area calls in on the way past the Oasis for a catch up before heading out to town to sell some gold and get supplies. Over coffee Jack relays the run in with Scrubber. The miner, taking in the story, falls quiet then shakes his head and says to Jack, "He will not let that go, you know."

Sue looks at Jack and can see the hardening in his eyes. Knowing him too well, she quickly changes the subject to light chat. Once coffee is finished, the miner bids them farewell and leaves towards town.

Jack and Sue enjoy nearly a week alone before Tim rocks up with his vehicle loaded to the hilt. Bouncing out of the truck, he pats Bumpy on the head while strolling down to the house. No one is there though he can hear the excavator working further down the gold lease. Sick of sitting down from the drive in from town, Tim decides to stretch his legs and follows the dust drifting into the air on a thin breeze.

Jack is doing a dish of dirt while Sue watches from a nearby shady tree. Tim walks over to Sue; they sit and chat about what he has missed while in town. Five minutes later Jack walks up to them with the gold dish in one hand. "Four small bits and ten colours." He passes the dish to Tim, who swirls the small amount of water left in the dish to reveal the specks of gold that Jack is referring to.

"That looks alright."

Jack replies, "Yeah, bro. That's about my tenth dish from here and they all look pretty consistent. I think we will start carting from here when the bloody parts finally arrive for the gold plant."

"Any idea when that will happen?" Tim asks.

"They sent the wrong frigging parts last time so I'm guessing maybe a week," responds Jack.

"Where's John?" Sue asks.

"Work's got him a bit bogged down but he should be good to go towards the end of the week now his ankle has healed," Tim replies.

Sue suggests they go back for a cold drink. Climbing onto the quad, Jack asks Tim, "Do you want a lift?"

"No, it's all good. I'll catch you back up there." Tim follows the quad, heading back towards the house on foot.

On arrival back at camp, Bumpy starts barking, signalling the approach of a visitor. A quad comes into view over the hill and steadily makes its way to the fence beside the house. Jack's face breaks into a grin when he recognizes Ray and his dog Buddy on the back.

Ray is a miner as well but a relatively new chum on the block. Ray and Jack had hit it off from the first meeting several months ago; they had a lot in common and each enjoyed the other's company. Greeting each other with a warm hand shake, they walk towards the kitchen just as Tim comes out of the gully and walks into the kitchen behind them. Tim and Ray had met on several occasions and had also hit it off, having both swung detectors in the same areas over different goldfields across the north there was never a shortage of conversation.

Tim and Ray exchange "Gidday's" and Jack grabs some cold colas out of the fridge. He asks Ray, "You getting a bit of colour up there on the lease, bud?"

Ray shakes his head in disappointment. "I was starting to get everything sorted but blew a bloody hydraulic hose on the excavator this morning. I've got all the standard hoses at the camp but Murphy's Law comes into play."

"What one?" Jack asks. "I might have one here."

Ray shrugs. "I doubt it, mate." He takes a long guzzle out of his tin of cola then continues, "It's a small hose from the hydraulic pump."

"No, I've got nothing like that lying around. Sorry, bud."

Ray replies, "Yeah, I didn't think so. It looks like I'm going to be down for a week or so. Anyway, I've got a mate up from the Tablelands so looks like I'm going for a swing with the detectors while we wait for the hose to arrive."

Jack looks at Ray saying, "Well mate, I'm broken down too. The gold plant shit itself so I'm waiting on parts to arrive as well." Tim adds, "Well, why don't we all go for a swing together? We can show you around."

The men make plans for the trip, deciding to head into the rugged ranges by bike for a day run to show Ray and his mate Sam some of the old mines, including the extensive array of Aboriginal art in the area, and hopefully pick up some gold. Ray, who had never been up that way, is as keen as mustard. Heading off towards the quad, he says, "Well, I will see you fellas at my place at sparrow's fart."

"No worries, we will be there," is the men's response.

It was an early night at the Oasis and both men are up before dawn. They swill a quick coffee, load on their back packs and leave on the motorbikes towards Ray's place with just enough light to see the road. Arriving at the camp, they shake hands with Sam while Ray puts Buddy the Red Cattle dog on the chain. In protest, the dog starts barking. Ray gives him an affectionate pat on the head, saying to the other men when walking to his bike, "He really doesn't like being left behind. Normally he goes everywhere with me."

Jack replies, "Yeah mate, but it's a pretty hairy ride where we are going. You are flat out getting up there yourself let alone with a dog on board. He would have to run a lot of the way, his paw pads would be raw in an hour."

Ray agreed. "Righto Buddy, be back tonight." They ride off with the dog left whimpering on the chain.

After two and a half hours of challenging riding, they finally arrive at the end of a long ridge. Ray and Sam, who have never been up that way before, are in awe. Sheer cliff faces surround the prospectors as they basically had to climb down into one of the gorges, coming across Aboriginal art in nearly all the sandstone caves and overhangs along the way. On the way down, they run across many old timers' shafts that went straight into the sandstone cliffs, with one even having a small railway line to carry ore out in carts, the majority of it erected only a foot or so from a sheer drop off. The men pause for a rest and take some video footage. "Isn't it amazing where and what those old timers did?" Ray says to the group in admiration. "They were tough as boot nails them blokes. We have had to virtually climb down here and then you look around and there's a bloody stamper (to crush the gold ore). It must weigh tonnes upon tonnes and it is hanging on a little ledge. How did they even get it down here?"

Eventually arriving at the bottom of the gorge, they are met by Chinese rock stacking's towering above their heads. The Chinese, working in large crews, used to pull out the oversize rocks and stack them by hand to extract the gold-rich alluvial dirt out of the creeks and gullies.

Tim sits down and rolls a smoke before setting up his detector. "This is it, fellas," he says, loud enough for all to hear. "I have picked up some nice pieces through here but haven't had a proper look around. I was by myself last time around, it's a huge amount of ground to cover with one detector. Bear in mind we can't operate close together as the machines interfere with each other so space your- selves 40-60 metres apart." They each choose a direction and go their separate ways.

By mid-afternoon Ray has eight grams; one was a six grammer while the other nugget weighed two. Tim has a three grammar, after collecting two death adders by removing the top layer of slate that the snakes were concealed under to dig his targets. The other boys have both come up empty handed, with Ray and Tim both slinging shit in friendly camaraderie at the other pair for their fruitless efforts. Tim looks up in the general direction of where the bikes are parked and says, "Now for the fun part. We got to get back out of here."

They all grunt in unity. With sweat now profusely exiting their bodies because of the extreme prospecting experience, the exhausting climb back up takes its toll on all the men; some more than others depending on their fitness level. After a tiring ride back, they arrive at Ray's camp for a cold drink, and make the unanimous decision that tomorrow they would follow the gazetted road to have a look in the main Hatchet River. Leaving the sheer cliffs to the young and fit bush-hardened prospectors to explore, Ray says, "We will take my truck tomorrow," before walking off to let Buddy off the chain. The Red Cattle dog bounces around him, excited he is back home.

Tim says, "Well, if you're bringing the truck down empty, I will throw my bike on in the morning when you get to Jack's place."

Ray replies, "No problems. I will take Buddy for a run with us if we are going for a couple of days." As all are in agreement with the plan, Tim and Jack head for home in the quickly diminishing daylight, arriving back just on dark.

Tim places the detector battery on to charge and grabs a couple of tins of cola along with a bottle of rum before moving over to the fire that Sue had organised. Jack dives straight in for a hot shower while Tim just mellows out around the fire with Bumpy, enjoying the quiet. Jack yells out, "Shower's free" to Tim. Over dinner the men decide not to take their two-ways, knowing Scrubber scans all channels.

Back at Hatchet River homestead, Scrubber and co are still smarting from the Croc Hole run-in, even though that was days ago. The phone rings. It is left for the answering machine to pick up. A male voice says, "It's C, pick up." Scrubber dives over like a shot and picks up the phone. The conversation is short. "I've told the crew to work 24/7 day shift and night shift. We need to keep ahead of the New Year high demand period. So your pick up will be five days earlier than normal, and delete the message bank," followed by a click before Scrubber can reply.

"Fuck me dead, like we haven't got enough to do," states Scrubber. It irks him to take orders from someone he has never laid eyes on who basically has the run of the station, with them as his puppets. Over the years, all deals and organising of the lab, including the initial set up, was done by the head bikers on behalf of C. When originally approached, Max agreed as large amounts money were being offered for something they'd already enjoyed doing for many years, keeping people off their property. Scrubber, now feeling like everything was getting well out of their control, concludes he is being pushed into a position that he resents more each day.

Just before dawn, Bumpy lets Jack know a vehicle is approaching. Tim wheels his bike out the front then returns for his bike ramp while Ray parks his truck, with Buddy in the back. He drops the tail gate and secures the ramp in place; the motorbike easily scales the ramp onto the back though there is barely enough light to see. Jumping down off the back to find the tie downs for the bike in his early morning daze, Tim barely remembers to yell, "Morning, fellas" before returning for the rest of his gear. Jack has also had to readjust as he normally took his own vehicle for camping out.

With everything loaded, they hit the road leading to-wards Hatchet River Station, a total of three in the front and Tim in the back standing beside Buddy. Tim can hear the laughter drifting from the front when the truck slows down enough to cross gullies. After about an hour's drive, they come to the main Hatchet River and decide to travel about four to five hundred metres downstream to put the truck out of sight from any passers-by. Ray pulls the vehicle up under some shady paperbarks with a beautiful waterhole in front of them.

Jack swings open the passenger's side door to climb out of the cramped front, commenting, "They need to bring back the bench seat, I reckon." All of them had been squeezed in like sardines because of his large frame. "Well at least we are a bit off the road. We can leave some of our gear without the worry of it being flogged, while we are all out swinging."

They unload and set up camp, all biting at the bit to get started. Everyone heads off in different directions, trying their luck to find the first bit of gold. As the day nears an end, they all trudge back into the camp. Buddy is glad to see his boss return after being left on guard duty at the camp all day and becomes overly excited when Ray lets him off the chain. He runs around smelling everybody for a hint of anything he had missed.

As darkness falls, the fire is lit and the men sit around a wobbly collapsible table. They all have drinks in hand and after a bit of banter between them, they start putting their gold on the table. Tim lets the other three go first, and a couple of two and three grammers appear on the table top. When they are done, he then pulls out nearly two ounces, with the largest nugget being at least half an ounce. The rest of the men are impressed. "We will head your way in the morning," they say in unison.

Tim, not being a greedy person by any means, says, "No worries, fellas."

Sam, who is a bit on the quiet side, asks, "What if this Scrubber fella is about?"

Tim responds, "We are on a public road and camped in the main river bed, which nobody owns. It is crown land."

Jack adds, "I've had a gutful of his intimidation tactics, the gutless prick, hiding behind a rifle." He is still seething from their run in at the Croc Hole. All having had a good feed, it is time to roll out the swags and catch up on some shut eye before a big day tomorrow.

Sam moves his brown sleeping bag closer to the fire for more warmth; being dog tired, he doesn't even bother removing his boots before turning in. During the night, an ember from the fire lands on the end of his nylon sleeping bag and it starts to smoulder; as luck would have it, the dew is so heavy, the ember is short lived and only partially melts his bag.

Tim is up and about at dawn and adding some wood to the fire when he notices Sam's boots are sticking out the end of his now burnt sleeping bag. Having quite a chuckle to himself, he walks over and wakes up Jack and Ray. When they emerge from their swags, Tim points at Sam and they all start laughing loudly. Sam wakes to the laughter; on standing up, he realises the plastic coating on the sleeping bag has melted to his boots. He hops around with the bag stuck fast, holding the top under his arm pits. "Come on, fellas, help me out here, will ya?" he pleads.

All laughing, Tim replies, "Damn, bud, you're the ugliest kangaroo I've ever run across." With that, all three men roar with laughter and are barely able to stand. Finally Ray walks over and cuts the melted plastic off his mate, leaving a burnt reminder on Sam's hiking boots.

Once everyone has finished their coffee, they all suit up in their harnesses. Ray says to Buddy, "You can come for a walk today instead of being left on the chain."

Jack and Tim look at each other, with Jack speaking up, "Do you think that's a good idea, mate? We don't want to go chasing dogs that take off looking for cattle or chasing wallabies."

Ray replies, "No, Jack, he does not leave my side while prospecting. Buddy comes swinging with me all the time." Both men shrug their shoulders, figuring that Ray's mind is set so fair enough.

Tim leads the way downstream, crossing the river at some shallow rapids below the camp because all the waterholes further down, running consecutively for a couple of kilometres, were too deep. Tim points out where he found the gold the previous day, reminding them all to keep a good distance between themselves so there was no machine interference. The men separated.

After a sleepless night, Scrubber gets up and scoffs down some baked beans that Max has ready. He is keen to get out. "Come on, let's get going," he barks at Max, who is just finishing her coffee.

"OK" she says, reading his mood. "What about Price?" "Leave him, he can have the morning off," he replies as he gets up from the table and walks outside towards the truck. His pace is so brisk that Max is flat out trying to keep up with him. They jump in and take off upstream.

The morning is heating up quickly as the men work their coils carefully around rock bars, hoping to pick up a sweet target. Moving up a little gully, Tim is the first to hear the oncoming vehicle. He turns his machine off and walks towards the high bank, trying to work out which direction the vehicle is coming from. Jack has also heard the truck and has done the same, heading to higher ground as it sounds to him like it is moving closer towards their location. Ray, who has his headphones on, is oblivious to what is going on around him and concentrating on the job at hand, with Buddy just a few steps behind. At that point in time, neither Tim nor Jack have any idea of Sam's or Ray's exact location.

Scrubber's truck comes into view from where Tim is standing. "Fuck" is all he can say as he ducks instinctively behind a large old metal gold jig that had been left there from a previous era. The hairs rising on the back of his neck, he watches as Scrubber drives slowly past, his head moving from side to side, surveying the bush for any signs of prospectors. Jack happens to be on the ridge opposite Tim and is also able to view the station vehicle, with Max in the passenger's side. Concealed behind a small pile of oversized rocks, Jack crouches, motionless. The 4x4 goes along at a slow pace until, all of a sudden, Buddy, hearing the vehicle, barks. Hearing the bark clearly himself, Jack swears and looks around the rock pile to see Max pointing down in a gully. The truck pulls up instantly and Max jumps out of the passenger's side and pulls the 30/30 from behind the seat. Max and Scrubber, not spotting anyone else around, assume he is a lone prospector with his dog and act swiftly.

Down in the gully, Buddy moved forward as the station vehicle headed towards them, letting out another bark at the truck as it drew closer. Ray, this time seeing his dog bark, pulls off the earphones. "What's up, Bud?" He looks up and sees two people on the bank; within a matter of seconds, a rifle shot rings out, shattering the ambience of the bush. The other prospectors immediately duck low out of instinct on hearing the sound of the gunshot so close.

The station 4x4 starts up and drives down the old road about 50 metres before pulling up again. A second shot echoes through the Hatchet River hills. Frozen by the shots, not wanting to move and not knowing where the others are, the men all laid low. After about twenty minutes, Jack can hear something heavy being thrown into the back of their truck. The muffled voices are fractionally too far away for Jack to make out what is being said, then Scrubber and Max drive off back in the direction of the station.

Once the vehicle is on the move, Tim takes off, run-ning in a half crouch through the bush; Jack also heads in the same direction. They run into each other on the bank of the Hatchet River. "Where are the other boys?" Tim asks Jack as they draw nearer to each other.

"Don't know, bro, but I saw that bitch pointing down into the gully and heard Buddy bark just before the gun shots."

"You wait here," Tim says as he hastily pulls off his detecting gear, "and give me a cooee if the boys come out of the bush. I will head up that gully where the shots were fired. I might be able to spot them." With adrenalin pumping through his entire body, Tim takes off like a light-footed mountain goat, bouncing from rock to rock as he goes up the gully at a surprising pace considering the terrain.

He pauses every now and again to yell out their names, his ears straining for any faint reply. Getting over half a kilometre further upstream from where he had first heard the truck, he is becoming more concerned that he has not seen or heard the other men. Wiping the sweat from his face with his shirt sleeve, he thinks aloud, "Well, they could have cut for it over the hills and are heading back to camp."

Climbing out of the gully, Tim jogs back down along the ridge. It is a lot quicker than going back the way he came, "Any sign of them?"

Jack replies, "No, mate. They could have headed back to camp but fucked if I know. I definitely heard something heavy getting thrown into the back of the truck before they left."

"You're kidding?" Tim replies. "Let's get back to camp; hopefully they are already there." He picks up his detecting outfit before taking a long pull from his water bottle.

Trudging back through the last 150 metres of loose sand with protesting muscles, Tim and Jack look intensely at the camp for any sign of movement. As they approach, Buddy, recognising them, comes running over. Both men let out a sigh of relief. Jack calls out, "Hey Ray, it's us, bud." No reply. The men's faces soon change from relief to worry as there is no one to be found in the camp and Ray's truck is still locked. Both men sit in their camp chairs, running through all the different scenarios of what could have happened and discussing what they should do next. Tim decides to head back down and run all the gullies heading towards Hatchet River homestead. Before he leaves, Jack says, "If Ray was hiding in the bush or injured at all, his dog would be by his side."

Tim nods in agreement but adds, "A lot of dogs bolt after a rifle shot; only Ray would know how Buddy would react." Tim refills his water and organises a lighter back- pack then sets off again, totally oblivious to fatigue, back towards where the shots were fired.

Scrubber and Max, getting back to the homestead, hit the brakes hard out front of the gate where Price is waiting to open it. "Heard the gun shots, what's going on?" he asks.

"We got ourselves a lone prospector. Get in the back and give us a hand." Price does as instructed and they head off towards the locked gates past the end of the airstrip.

Tim has been running himself ragged, scouring gullies for hours, looking for Ray, Sam, blood or anything to give a clue of their whereabouts but has still come up empty handed. Seething with rage, he is now in clear view of the Hatchet River homestead, still calling out for both men. The station is silent and there is no sign of movement other than the dogs going off their heads at the noise and smell of an intruder. "Where the hell are they?" Tim yells as the rage overcomes thoughts of his own safety.

The station truck is nowhere to be seen. With no response or activity from within the homestead, Tim decides to walk the ridges a different way back to camp in the fading hope of finding the men. Finally arriving back at camp exhausted, one look at Jack's face tells him that nobody has returned. Slumping into his chair in despair and disbelief at the day's events and holding his head in his hands, he is barely able to speak. "What now?"

Buddy, now on his chain, barks. Both men swivel their heads around. In stumbles Sam. "What the fuck, where have you been? Where's Ray?" asks Jack, firing a hundred questions at him.

Sam shakes his head. "He's not with me." Falling into his chair, buggered, Sam tells them of the gun shots, even the smell of the gun powder, then he ran for the hills, exhausting himself in the process and passing out due to a genetic heart condition. When he came to, he got his bearings and walked back towards camp. It dawns on Tim that Ray also has the keys for the locked truck on him, so their only means of transport is his bike. In all the confusion since the gun shots, he remembers the satellite phone in his backpack. Grabbing it out of the case, he says, "Crap, forgot I had this. I will ring an old prospecting mate, Wazza. He will have the Hatchet River Station number for sure."

Jack replies, "Well, I will ride your bike back to my place and return with my truck." Jack jumps on the small 150; it groans under his weight as he takes off towards the Oasis. Tim calls his old mate, briefly tells him what had happened then scrawls the station number into the sand with a stick. As soon as Tim is off the line, he starts punching in the numbers for Hatchet River Station. It goes to the answering machine after four rings. Tim leaves a message, "Scrubber, if you have my mate held hostage or have hurt him in any way, I want him released now or I'm calling the cops," and hangs up.

Price jumps out of the back of the truck and landing flat footed, he grunts slightly in discomfort as the impact shoots up through his legs. Opening the last locked gate, he lets them through then swings the gate shut. He throws the keys through the window to Max. Scrubber gives a very rare smile as Max catches them in her left hand out of reflex. They sit in the front of the cruiser, content with the day's outcome, not needing any amphetamines for a high with the victim fresh in their minds from the thrill of the kill. To them the best kill of all was prospectors.

When they arrive back at the station, Price jumps out of the back and Scrubber says, "Hey, you need to feed the dogs, and give them a bit more than usual. I'm in a generous mood."

"Righto," answers Price as he trundles off to do the thankless chore, thinking, "While he is in a rare good mood, I will hit him up to do my own hunt for a girl and get to keep her." The more he thought about the idea, the clearer it formed in his mind.

Scrubber even pats one of the dogs chained beside the steps of the veranda as he walks past. The dog, not used to any attention, goes from a savage dog to a tail-wagging puppy instantly.

Bounding up the stairs, Scrubber asks Max, "What's for dinner?"

Reading her husband like a book in this favourable mood, she replies, "You can have me for dinner tonight," with a grin on her face.

Scrubber cracks a thin smile as he touches Max's thigh for the first time in months. Price walks into the kitchen, also asking, "What's for dinner?"

Max turns, smiling. "Tinned spaghetti on damper; something quick and easy tonight."

None of them had seen that there was a message waiting to be heard on the answering machine.

They sit down to their meal. Price, finishing off a mouth full of food, raises his eyes to look directly at Scrubber. "I need a girl," he says out loud, his bottom lip trembling slightly.

Scrubber looks up from his meal then across at Max. Returning his gaze, she shrugs her slim but muscular shoulders in consent. Scrubber then directs his eyes back to Price and without blinking holds Price's stare. Still chewing, he slowly nods his head and replies, "Yeah maybe, see how things pan out." Price, happy with it not being a straight out no, is satisfied with the response.

Scrubber changes the conversation. "Were there any car or bike keys on that prospector?"

Price acknowledges the question by tapping his palm on his trouser pocket, "Yeah, car keys."

Scrubber states, "Righto, first thing in the morning we need to find the truck and dispose of it. Can't be too far off the road, we should be able to follow the fresh tracks easily enough."

Having finished dinner, Max gets up, saying, "Bird bath for me, no one was home to light the donkey today." This didn't worry Scrubber or Price in the slightest as they would go days without a shower. Max slips out briefly to clean herself and grabs Scrubber's arm on her way back in. Walking towards the bedroom, she says to Price in pass-ing, "You can clean up." She enters the bedroom, with Scrubber close behind.

With Jack gone to get his truck from the Oasis, Tim and Sam sit pondering what they might have overlooked in the heat of the moment. Tim, churning things through in his mind, finally says aloud, "Ray's an experienced bushman, there's no way he could be lost. All the creeks and gullies run into the main river, even a novice couldn't get lost." He turns to Sam. "That's it, I am ringing the cops. Ray's had more than enough time to make his way back."

Tim grabs the sate phone and calls the Windum Police Station, telling the officer that his mate had gone missing after shots were fired and gives a brief description of the day's events. It being about eight hours since the shots occurred, Tim is only now realising the quick passage of time.

Jack arrives back with his 4x4 as the day is nearing its end. "Anything, boys?" They both shake their heads.

Tim says, "No but I've reported it to the police and not to the station; that seems to fall on deaf ears. They will be here first thing in the morning."

"Good," replies Jack. "Well, fellas, we can't search for Ray in the dark and Scrubber will now know that there was more than one prospector after the call to his station. They could turn up here anytime and we have nothing to protect ourselves with. I think it's a good idea to leave and come back before daylight tomorrow."

Tim agrees, adding, "We can leave some food, drinks, swag and my sate phone with the Oasis number programmed just in case Ray turns up. We should also set up a large fire in the sand close to the river bed as a guiding light and landmark in case he is trying to make his way back to camp in the dark." All in agreement with this plan, the men get stuck into it. Just on dark they leave in Jack's truck, with Buddy and Tim in the back.

Sue is pacing out the front of the Oasis with a very concerned look on her face when the 4x4 headlights shine over the hill and into the yard. As the men get out of the truck, Sue asks, "Anything?"

All in unison, they say, "No." Jack goes straight to the landline phone to ring the police and confirm with them the information on Tim's call and to leave his home details. He was advised to meet up with the police on the main Hatchet River Road leading towards the homestead. The Sergeant informed Jack that after getting the initial phone call from Tim, he had contacted Cairns headquarters to inform them of the incident and they were relaying the information of a possible homicide to Brisbane Head Office. Two four-wheel-drives were being dispatched from Cairns to arrive at the Hatchet River before daylight.

Mr C is two mouth-watering bites into his meal of T-bone and chips covered in peppercorn sauce when the phone rings. Annoyed at being disturbed, he glances over to his phone and recognizes the incoming caller's number as his cop employee Marko. "WTF." Knowing that the only time he rings is when something is up, he quickly scoffs another mouthful before getting up from the table. He picks up the phone, saying, "Yeah, what's going on?"

On the other end of the line, the cop replies, "We got big trouble, C. Just got off the phone with a mate letting me know that shots have been reported near Hatchet River Station and there is a prospector missing. All this infor-mation has gone around me and was directed to headquar-ters; there's no way I can stop the ball rolling now. Two troopies of cops are en route and will be onsite around day break. A search party is getting organised as we speak."

C's expression does not change as he takes in all the information. When there is a pause on the line, C replies, "Right. I want you to get me in there pronto. I will take care of the rest."

He hangs up on the cop while he was in the middle of saying, "I will try my best."

C's mind is racing at the turn of events. He pushes a number on speed dial. His associate Ox, the hit man, picks up the mobile. Never one for small talk, he says, "Speak."

Recognising C's voice, he immediately puts down his razor in mid-shave.

"Get a hold of the President and tell him to contact the factory and shut it down as a precaution. The shit has hit the fan out at the station. I very much doubt that they would find it but I don't want to take any chances. Tell them to bring what product they can squeeze in and cover up the solar panels with the hessian bags. Sweep their outgoing tracks and I will have a chopper pick them up first thing in the morning. They know where to go," he said, referring to an area that had been inconspicuously cleared about a kilometre from the factory for emergency evacuations like this. "Get a hold of that chopper pilot, what's his name? Yeah, Frank; drag him out of bed if you have to. Tell him we want that jet ranger up there first thing before search aircraft get involved. I will text you Hawkeye's numbers to pass on, tell him to come in from the North West for the pickup. It's a waste from that direction, there's no way the chopper will be heard from the station."

Hanging up the phone, C starts twirling the ring on his finger out of habit as he goes through the complications of the situation facing him once again in his mind. He swears. This could put their product output well behind for the festive season after having gone to extraordinary lengths to plan and get ahead of his competition and setting up one of the best organised and most productive factories in the country.

The factory exit plan had been worked out years previously for quick and discrete pick-ups or drop offs by chopper, the GPS co-ordinates had been programmed into C's phone under the name of Hawkeye. Frank the chopper pilot had done previous work for C; he knew how to keep his mouth shut as it was in his best interest to do so both physically and financially.

Scrubber had been very effective up until now at keeping outsiders from nosing around their operation but C is now starting to wonder if he had passed his use-by date. Their careless actions could trigger a full-scale search. Not wanting to draw attention to himself, he refrains from picking up the phone and calling the Hatchet Station direct, but he knows now he will have to take matters into his own hands. Deciding on Scrubber and co's fate would come at a later date. Picking up his unfinished dinner, he drops the plate into the bin before walking into his bedroom, switching off the light on the way past, to break down today's events into segments.

Getting up in the early hours of the morning for a piss, Scrubber fumbles his way in the dark towards the veranda, relieves himself, gives it one extra shake for good luck then continues back on the same path towards his bedroom. Getting near the kitchen, he spots a faint red light softly illuminating one corner of the room. Realising it is an unread message on the answering machine, he walks over and pushes down on the message button.

Tim's voice comes through on the speaker. The blood drains from Scrubber's face. When the brief message had finished, Scrubber lets out an almighty "FUCK." Picking up the nearest thing to him, which happens to be a chop-ping board, he sends it straight through the kitchen window. Glass shatters into the sink and fine fragments spray onto the outside veranda.

Max comes running out of the bedroom, torch in one hand and a shotgun in the other. "What's going on?" Swinging the torch light around the kitchen, Max stops at the smashed window.

"Listen to this," Scrubber says, his fingers fumbling to rewind the answering machine. Max listens intently to the message while Scrubber is pacing and talking. "The prick was not alone so how many of them were there? What did they see?" he says, throwing questions at Max that he knew she could not answer. "We didn't see anybody else, just that dog."

"Maybe they saw nothing," Max suggests. Scrubber does not agree with Max's hopeful assumption.

"If that was the case, why would they be fucking ringing me?" he spits out. "It's 2am, the cops will be here by sunrise for sure. Delete the message and burn that bloody map on the wall while I start the generator and wake up boofhead," he orders. Walking the 40 odd metres to Price's quarters gives him time to clear his head and quickly work out what needed to be done on or just before dawn.

He kicks in the door, Price jumps up, startled. "What the-" is as far as Price gets.

"The prospector wasn't alone, there are witnesses. Get dressed and start the generator, we got a lot of work to do before the sun rises." He turns and retraces his steps as the generator comes to life and lights up the homestead by the time he got to the veranda. Max is standing at the sink with a lighter in one hand and the incriminating map in the other, with all the X marks now well and truly on fire. Once it is ash, she turns on the tap and all evidence of their kills runs down the drain.

"What about the factory?" she asks.

Scrubber retorts, "Nobody will find that unless someone shows them. Max, I want you to jump in the truck, grab those pills from under the seat, and ditch them down the sink then head out to the Nine Mile Dam. There's always a heap of pigs around it first thing in the morning, bowl over three or four then load them up; make sure you cut all their throats in the back of the truck to cover any slight chance of blood splatters being left from yesterday. When you get back, we will chop them up for dog food."

Scrubber instructs Price, "Saddle up the stallion then go open gate two along the river. I want you to run a good mob of cattle into there and up around the old gold plant. There should be a good heard on that green pick near the river bank. Shut the gate on the way out, that should cover any tracks, then I want you back here quick."

Max leaves in the opposite direction to Price, who is having some trouble saddling up the stallion by torch light. Scrubber looks at the clock on the wall and realises they are running out of time with it being only one hour until dawn. Turning on the two-way, he tries to pick up on any chatter from the cops as he goes through the house looking for anything left that might be incriminating. Coming up empty handed, Scrubber is satisfied everything is in order.

Max arrives at the homestead with blood from one end of the tray to the other; the sun is starting to rise and they can hear vehicles approaching in the distance. Max looks around and states the obvious. "Price's not back yet."

Scrubber grunts. "Well, he'd want to hurry up, them vehicles are getting closer. I'll grab a couple of butcher's knives, you want to make us a coffee?"

Max is crossing the yard with a coffee in each hand when Price rides up out of the river at full gallop on the stallion. Scrubber points to the horse yards and yells, "Get the saddle in the shed and get over here."

Price quickly joins his mentors near the station truck and proudly announces, "All done."

"Good," Scrubber replies. "If you talk, we are as good as dead so keep your mouth shut," he says, looking directly at Price. "Just act dumb, which should not be too hard for you. Big C and the bikers will be livid when they find out about this." They can hear the four-wheel drives distinctly changing down gears as they approached the opposite side bank and crossed the river to the station homestead.

The dogs start going off around the house before Scrubber barks the command to lay down; immediately the dogs obey as six fully-armed police jump out of the troop carrier wearing bullet-proof vests. There were originally eight officers but two had been left with the prospectors at Ray's vehicle, which was still in the position he'd left it. The officer's approach with their guns drawn walking towards the couple who have their backs turned and are casually cutting up feral pigs on the tray of the truck. Price is walking around throwing lumps of bloodied pork to the dogs that now had no concern over the intruders, only the fresh meat being thrown to them. Used to being underfed, they were all woofing it down, taking only a couple of chews.

"Where is the prospector?" the Senior Sergeant in charge of the investigation yells at Scrubber who casually turns around while sharpening the butcher's knife on a steel.

He shrugs his shoulders and replies with a blank look on his face, "What prospector?"

On seeing the knife in Scrubber's hand, the officer yells, "Drop the knives now!" Max looks at Scrubber; she drops hers to the ground first, closely followed by her husband. "Handcuff them," orders the head cop, "and him as well," he says, pointing towards the house at Price. Once the suspects are secured, the questioning continues.

In the meantime, the jet ranger is leaving fully loaded from the lab, with none of them being the wiser.

A tirade of questions gets fired at all three; they hold their ground, denying ever laying eyes on the prospector.

Back at Ray's truck, Tim, Jack and Sam are also being questioned by heavily armed officers but their line of questioning is vastly different to those being directed at Scrubber's gang.

At the homestead, two of the officers start walking around the station vehicle. Max has left the driver's side door open. Peering over the back of the seat, one officer calls out, "Sarg, got two firearms here"; the other cop chimes in, "There's also a box of bullet shells on the seat." The Senior Sergeant looks at Max for any signs of worry or concern in her features. From his previous experience, the females always cave in first. Expecting some kind of flicker of emotion to cross her face but not seeing any, he quickly categorises Max as a very cold, calm and resourceful woman. Studying her body language, he asks himself the question, "Is she capable of being involved in such a crime?" The answer is yes.

Max says, "The guns are out because we have been shooting pigs for tucker and dog food."

With no attention being paid to the half cut-up pigs lying on the tray, blow flies start to turn up in numbers.

"You don't mind if we have a look around the homestead then?" the Sergeant asks.

Scrubber sneers, "Not without a search warrant. I know my rights!"

On this refusal the Sergeant walks back to his vehicle and calls base. "The station owners are admitting to nothing and are not cooperating; we are going to need a search warrant for the homestead and the whole property."

The head officer at base replies, "We have a chopper coming out of Cairns with the warrants and to join the search there are also 25 officers with quad runners on the way, including the stock squad on horseback. We are also hiring a second chopper, who should arrive in the morning.

By then we need to have a command base set up and search patterns worked out. I want the three witnesses brought to town for questioning and statements, including gun residue testing, finger printing and mug shots."

There is a briefing from the initial officers when the homicide detectives arrived at Ray's locked 4x4 on the questions that had been asked and the witness response given. All officers agree that the men's accounts of the incident are identical. The three men are asked to show the detectives where the gunshot incident had happened and their positions in relation to where the shots were fired. The detective assigned to Tim is a very fit looking man with muscles rippling under his shirt and thighs as thick as tree trunks. He was the top in his unit for fitness when applying for a position in the Police's Elite Tactical Unit and also the Specialist Response Unit.

Tim gives him the once-over while shaking his hand, and says, "You be able to keep up all right, mate?"

Steve gives Tim the once-over and smirks back. "No problem."

They all proceed downstream from the original camp, with Tim and Steve well out in front setting a cracking pace. Jack and Sam, along with their detectives, soon lose sight of them. Tim, being the fittest of the other prospectors, would cover at least three times more area in a day with his detector.

Retracing his steps from that day, he points out to Steve where he had detected that morning, including the spot where he'd hidden from the oncoming station vehicle and all the areas he had covered looking for Ray. About three hours in, Steve was starting to fall behind noticeably, pulling up more frequently for water, his shirt wringing wet with sweat. Tim scales yet another steep-sided gully, glancing over his shoulder to see Steve struggling to negotiate the boulder-strewn gully. Perching on a rock, Tim rolls a smoke and waits for Steve to catch up. When most of his rollie is gone, Steve emerges out of the gully with sweat streaming down his face while sucking in the big ones.

Tim pulls out his water bottle, which is still full, takes two mouthfuls then offers it to Steve, who declines out of pride even though his own is empty. Shrugging, Tim replaces the lid, quickly rolls another smoke, stands up and says, "Not going to get much done sitting here." Steve, who has practically only just taken the weight off his feet, groans inwardly. His heels are starting to blister and both calves are starting to cramp. He looked across at Tim who still has a smoke in his mouth and only a little show of perspiration around his armpits. Tim starts off down along the ridge, raising his voice for Steve to hear, "You're pretty fit for a copper." Steve lifts himself off the ground and shakes his head, almost every muscle in his body screaming for a rest.

About half an hour on, Steve spots some of the stock squad on horseback over towards his left. Doing his best to gain their attention, he tries to whistle but his mouth is to dry. Waving continuously, he catches the eye of one of the mounted officers, who gallops over. Tim, hearing the horse, turns to see them in discussion, and decides to sit down under the shade of a tree at some distance and wait. The Stock Squad Officer pulls the horse up with a questioning look on his face. All Steve can get out through his parched throat is the word, "Water."

The Stock Squad Officer, looking concerned, says, "Sure, mate," and hands over his flask. Watching Steve gulp it down, he says, "Slow up a bit, mate. In this heat your gut will just swell up and you will start getting stitches." Having spent a few years in the stock division, he had racked up numerous bush hours, learning by personal experience what he was talking about.

Steve finally gives back the flask, now empty, and, wiping the last dribble from his mouth in a backhand swipe, is now able to string a sentence together. "I can't believe this bloke. He hasn't stopped all day. His water bottle is still nearly full, he walks around with a bloody fag in his mouth and he's hardly raised a goddam sweat! He's like a mountain goat." They both look over towards Tim simultaneously; noticing their stare, Tim throws up his arm in a wave, not knowing they were talking about him.

The Stock Squad Officer chuckles. "Yeah, mate. To carve a living out of this country you got to be tough as nails."

Tim finishes showing Steve around and says, "See you back at camp, mate." Realising that the man is in physical pain, he adds, "Take your time, you got heaps of light left before it gets dark."

Nodding, Steve replies, "No worries. Which way back to camp?"

Tim smiles and points. "That way, bud." Leaving Steve to it, Tim leaves at the same pace he started with that morning. Steve hobbled his way back towards camp like a man three times his age, trying his best to salvage some pride in the last 50 metres. Under the scrutiny of all camp members, the young detective adjusts his gait, trying to walk in a normal fashion.

After spending all day with their respective detectives, the three witnesses are instructed to go into the Bankston Police Station to complete their formal statements.

Arriving just on the outskirts of town at about 8.30pm, Tim asks Jack, "You got your mobile phone, bud? I will give John a quick call to let him know what's going on and see if we can crash at his place tonight. It's going to be late by the time we get out of the cop shop." Tim quickly makes the call and hands the phone back to Jack. "All good to stay there."

Arriving at the police station, they are separated into different rooms, each with a new detective to conduct the interviews and record their statements followed by residue tests, fingerprinting then mug shots. They walk out of the station at about 1am. Tim and Jack make their way to John's place, mentally and physically exhausted from having had no sleep in 48 hours or even longer. Sam, having organised a lift back to his Tableland property, waits out the front of the cop shop for his ride.

Getting up early, John has the jug boiling for coffee, ready to catch up with the guys on all that had happened the day before. "Where's Tim? Still asleep?" he asks as Jack strolls out.

"No, bud. He headed back to his place after an hour's sleep to catch up with Danni for a bit. He's planning to head back out today to help look for Ray and I'm keen to join in the search as well"

"Well, mate, my ankle's come good so I will pack up my gear and come back to help in the search."

"Haven't you got work on, bud?" Jack asks.

"Looking for Ray is more important. Work will have to wait."

Tim arrives back at John's at about 10am, saying, "The cops want me to go back in for more questions, it won't take long. I'm keen to get back out there to look for Ray." They agree that Jack would head off first in Tim's truck while Tim would jump in with John for the trip back after he finishes at the cop shop.

Back at Hatchet River Station, the detectives are not making any headway with Scrubber and co. From the descriptions given by the witnesses, the cops know that Price was not one of the two there at the time of the shooting. Scrubber and Max are put in separate police vehicles, to be transported into Bankston via Huego for further questioning.

An area close to the homestead is now a hive of activity as a command post is established; all types of electronic equipment are being set up and portable radio towers erected. Tents are pitched and a rough camp kitchen/eatery area is also set up. Portable generators come to life as darkness falls.

An hour after sunrise, a chopper circles above to let them know he is ready to land. Head of Ops looks up. "Can't be one of ours, they only left half an hour ago." Turning to an officer close by, he says, "Go see what they want. If it's a camera crew, tell them to piss off out of the search area."

The pilot is met by a cop soon after landing nearby and introduces himself. "The name's Chris." The pilot stretches out his gloved hand in the Aussie outback gesture, shaking hands with a firm grip.

The cop replies, "My name's Fred. We are conducting a search on this station, I am going to have ask you to leave."

Chris replies, "I know. I heard the other choppers on the VHF radio while passing through the area and have two days before my next paying job if you want another chopper to hire?"

Fred shrugs. "I will ask the boss." Grabbing his radio, the young constable moves away and returns after a couple of minutes. "He said that due to budget cuts, he cannot afford to pay for flight hours but can supply the Avgas and food if you're still interested."

Chris responds casually, "Anything to help, mate. That's what we do up this end of the country. So someone is missing; what was he pig hunting or something?"

"No," replies Fred as they ride back to camp, "it's a prospector, under suspicious circumstances."

"Shit, that's no good," says the chopper pilot, concerned.

The quad pulls up where the search co- ordination team is now fully established, with maps covering every inch of the tables. Chris is introduced, and shakes hands with the Head of Operations. "Welcome aboard. Working through the north, you would know the country a lot better than us so we will appreciate any input. Or ideas that will benefit the search."

Chris is shown on a map where the shots were fired, and the area where they had the SES and Stock Squad currently searching. "Where are the other choppers working?" asks Chris.

The Head of Ops replies, "They are concentrating along the river, hoping that the prospector is still alive and, having found water, is staying there."

"Righto, well, I will head over towards these grid sections," pointing to the map, "so we don't cross paths with the other choppers. Are you supplying a spotter?" Chris asks.

"Yes, mate. Fred, come over here. This young consta-ble here will be with you, mark off the grids in highlighter when you're done. OK, I'll let you get to it then." He turns back to the maps.

"So we meet again," Fred says to the chopper pilot.

"Let's go. We are not going to find him down here." He fires up the chopper and asks, "Ever been in a chopper before?" "No," replies the Constable as he anchors on his seat harness.

Back in Bankston, Tim's interview at the police station is taking way longer than he had expected, he was getting anxious to get back out there to help in the search. When he is finally leaving the cop shop, he runs into Ray's family, on their way in to find out what is happening with the search. Tim's heart goes out to them, they are visibly upset and searching for answers. Ray's wife is trying to hold a brave face beside Ray's two burly brothers who, with one look, Tim could see they were certainly not men to upset. He figured that if Ray wasn't found safe, some bush justice could be in order.

Tim starts to tell them what he knows but before he can get too far, a detective spots the congregation just outside the glass front door. He walks outside and firmly explains that witnesses cannot discuss the investigation with family members of the victim. Tim, not getting out anything near what he wants the family to know, quietly says to one of the brothers, "We'll catch up later." The brother nods with piercing steely eyes.

Tim jumps into John's truck and they move off to- wards the Hatchet. Arriving just before dark, both men agree to stay at the Oasis and head down to the search area early in the morning. Over coffee well before daybreak the next morning, Sue is telling the men how many phone calls offering help she'd received in the 24-hour period they were away. "I got a visit from Tonga yesterday, he wants to help in the search too. Shouldn't be far away, so he may as well go down with you guys."

Half way through their coffee, Bumpy and Buddy start barking as Tonga pulls in on his motorbike. Solemn greetings are exchanged. Knowing they are in for a long, hard day, they fill their back packs with water and the sandwiches Sue had made the night before. Also, Rob, one of Jack and Sue's sons, had arrived during the night to give support to his family and help in the search.

They head off, three on bikes, and Jack driving the 4x4 accompanied by son Rob at his side. Arriving at the original camp site where Ray's car had been, they notice it is gone. A bit higher up on the bank, a couple of police vehicles with quads and tents have been set up. Jack and Tim recognise one of the detectives and walk over. Jack asks, "Where's Ray's truck?"

The Detective answers, "It, along with one of the station vehicles, has been put on a body truck and sent to Cairns for forensic testing."

"Have you found anything yet?" Jack asks.

"No."

"Well, we have brought down some blokes who have good bush knowledge to help out; they can handle the heat and know the country," says Jack.

Tim asks, "Did you find anything in the area we suggested?"

The Detective looks at him before replying, "Yeah, nothing. We had the chopper go through."

"What? No bikes? Nobody on horseback? You're not going see fresh tyre marks from a bloody chopper. We told you the station truck headed back towards the station after the shots were fired, so that decreases your search area by 50 percent."

The Detective, slightly embarrassed, knows they are out of their depth in this inhospitable landscape, as were most officers in these extremely hot conditions. Some of them had never been off a bitumen road before. "We did try and go down that way by quad but the report came back that there were locked gates."

"Well why are they locked? There has got to be a good reason," says Jack.

"That's where we are heading for a look," says Tim.

"Sorry," replies the Detective. "The order has come through from headquarters that nobody is allowed across the river as it is now classed as a crime scene. We have stopped the media and all other volunteers coming in from the Huego side."

Tim shakes his head in disbelief. "You're bloody well kidding, aren't you? We have come back to help look for our mate, and have the best people here for the job and we can't even cross the river."

Jack butts in. "My missus heard on the two-way that you had twelve coppers and SES flown out from heat stroke on their second day out here." As a chopper flies overhead, Jack continues, "The SES has their heart in the right place but look at them; most of them are over 50 and are not used to this heat or the hills. Where's the army? That's who you need in here, bud. They would have the training surely to be fit for these types of conditions."

The Detective is nodding his head in agreement, silently empathising with the motley bush crew, seeing the desperation and rejection on their faces. "The reason you can't cross is because we can't let you find any evidence. We need to find it and follow through with the chain of protocol. If it ends up in court, the Defence could say that you planted it. Jack and Tim, you can come over with us on quads to the map tent and show us again where you think we should be looking. The rest of you fellas will have to wait here or head home. The Captain has made it very clear that if you don't have a badge or clearance, you don't get access to anywhere near the Hatchet River homestead."

With that the two prospectors cross the river being doubled on the quads, leaving four cops in the camp. Another detective comes over to introduce himself to John, Tonga and Rob; with a hand-held recorder, he takes all of their details and their whereabouts on the day of the alleged shooting. The quads arrive at the command centre after introductions are done and Tim and Jack engage in discussion with the senior ranking officers in charge of the search.

Thirty minutes later, they emerge, with Head of Ops throwing new orders around. "Right, get them choppers on the radio. I want that new bloke to take Tim for a surveillance run along the sandstone formations past the gates, and the mustering chopper can come back and pick up Jack to take him over to his place to get a metal detector." Taking another glance at Jack's large frame, he changes his mind. "No, cancel that. Send back the jet ranger for Jack and two of the spotters can take an early lunch."

Many hours later, Jack returns on the quad. "Where's Tim?" John asks.

"Well," says Jack, "we suggested using a detector in the area Ray was shot. Let's be honest about it, that's what has happened, pure and simple. So I got a lift in a chopper to my place to get Tim's 4500. One of the coppers does a bit of detecting but hasn't used a GPX so Tim's going to show him the basics and let him go for it." Jack turns his two- way in the truck to channel 15 and calls the makeshift operations centre. "Can you let Tim know when he gets back that we have headed home. He will be hours away yet after showing your guy how to use his detector."

The return call is "Roger."

Tim flies overhead in the chopper as Tonga and John leave on their bikes first to try to beat the dust from Jack's truck. "Now this is the only way to prospect," Tim says, looking down at the hilly terrain and hundreds of gullies that feed into the creeks. "You see many Chinese stacking's as you're flying around?"

"Yeah, every now and again, a lot you wouldn't even attempt to get at other than in this," Chris says as he pats the joystick.

"Now there's a spot I'd like to get to," says Tim, pointing out the side of the chopper. "What do you charge an hour?" Tim was glad to have his mind off the whole goings on beneath them even for a short period as they travelled towards the sandstone cliff faces.

"Well," says Chris, "we might be able to work something out with a percentage of the gold you find."

Tim looks across at Chris. "Sounds bloody good to me. You live around here?"

The pilot responds, "Na mate, but within flying distance."

The prospector turns his concentration back towards the ground again as the sandstone formations loom in front of them. They spend a good hour flying over the area.

Yarning about various topics on the way back, both men having spent so many years in the bush, find they have a lot in common. "So where did it happen, mate?" asks Chris curiously as he had only been looking in the wide search area, not ground zero.

Tim, knowing what he was referring to, says, "Just downstream a bit on your side."

"So you reckon the station owner shot him?"

Tim is pointing to a red patch of dirt. "It was just down in there. Too bloody right. They did it, I was there and saw it happen. The pair of them drove straight past me in the truck."

"True?" Chris replies, a bit red in the face. "Every station owner I have met out bush are great people, salt of the earth. What would he do that for?"

"Drugs," replies Tim. "That's what it's all about."

Chris shrugs, saying, "Well, if it's drugs, there have been choppers flying over this station for days now. You think they would have found a crop."

Tim shakes his head. "Na, not dope, mate. There's got to be a speed lab set up here somewhere we reckon."

Chris, gob smacked, says, "Fair dinkum, ya think so?"

"Yep, sure of it," Tim says confidently as the chopper comes in to land. "Thanks for the ride, mate, that was great. Still reckon that area needs a good ground search."

Chris hands Tim a business card, saying, "Here's my number. Give me a call when you are back finding some yellow stuff."

"No worries," replies Tim. "I will keep you to that, you got a pen? I will give you my satellite phone number in case you get a few days spare and I'm camped out here somewhere prospecting." After giving the details, he shoots off towards a waiting quad.

Tim takes the time to run through the metal detector with his new pupil Constable Reeves; once confident the cop had a gist of the basics, he gets a lift back to his bike on the other side of the river. He arrives back at the Oasis after dark with a head lamp on. Dismounting, he walks towards the open fire where everybody is seated. They all look at Tim as he enters the circle without response. Everybody is quite. Tim sits down with his bottle of rum and cola then breaks the silence. "Righto, what's going on?" he says to the group in general.

Sue looks at Jack and tears start to swell up in her eyes. Jack raises his voice through gritted teeth, "Scrubber and his wife were taken in for questioning. They are refusing to speak a word in their interviews. For police to hold them longer than 24 hours by law, they had to supply them with how many witnesses there were, including our names!"

"What?" exclaims Tim. "They know our fucking names!"

Jack nods. "Yep. It's not going to be safe here or for that matter even in our home towns. If Scrubber is as well connected as we assume, it will take no time for whoever is working with him to have our addresses. No witnesses, no case. It's a bloody joke. No wonder witnesses go missing all the time before cases get to court."

Sue raises her voice loud enough for all to hear. "We are packing up and leaving first thing in the morning. Tim, best you ring Danni and tell her to get out of the house and go to a friend's place or something. We have no idea if or how quick they could move on this." Sue passes Tim the cordless phone; he doesn't hesitate. He grabs the phone and walks a short distance from the fire to talk to Danni in private.

After about 15 minutes, he returns to the light of the fire, telling the others that "Danni has just heard on the radio that the couple brought in for questioning about the missing prospector have just been released. They are not allowed anywhere near the station and have to report to the police daily."

"Root a roo," John says aloud. "How can they be released when there are three goddam witnesses that have already given statements? This is getting worse by the minute."

"Are they allowed around here?" Rob asks, directing the question at his father.

"Well mate, do you reckon that mob are going to be told where they can and can't go? We will have to lock up everything in the shipping containers, shut up the house and see if Tonga can keep an eye on the place for us."

Tim interrupts. "Oh and I forgot to mention an anonymous phone call to Crime Stoppers stating they know where Ray is, so the search is being moved further up- stream."

"That can't be right," says Jack, puzzled. "No vehicle passed us heading upstream after the shooting."

"Probably a prank call," adds John. "There are a lot of wankers out there that call shit like that fun."

Tim goes on, "Well, police are now appealing for the caller to ring back, Danni was telling me." Pulling a business card from his pocket, Tim goes on to say, "I will ring the detective that took my statement in the morning and see what she can tell me."

Rob adds to the conversation. "Who's to say it's an anonymous caller? Wouldn't Scrubber or his wife try and put the search in the wrong direction?" All agreeing that could be possible, after a few more hours of deliberation, they move in different directions to hopefully get some shut eye.

As morning approaches, the birds start their daily ritual, all singing out different notes, welcoming in the new day and the camp begins to stir with the natural alarm clock. Sue and Jack are already up, packing personal items into cartons for the trip to town. About half an hour later, the rest are up, helping themselves to coffee and toast. The dogs start barking minutes before anyone in the camp can pick out the noise of the approaching vehicle. Slowly driving into the yard is an old, short-wheel base 4x4 that had seen better days, driven by an old miner. "Oh great, it's Brass," says Jack.

Sue rolls her eyes while Tim says out loud, "What's he bloody want?"

John and Rob, not knowing the man at all, pick up on the vibe that he is not very welcome here. "Who is he, Mum?" Rob asks.

Sue replies, "He lives in a tent under a tarp in the bush. He has a lease of his own but has done nothing with it since we have lived here. Call it women's intuition but there's something about that man that doesn't sit well with me. But I can't put my finger on what exactly."

Old Brass slowly climbs out of the 4x4, and is met by Jack and co before he can get anywhere near the house. Picking up that he is not going to be invited in for a cuppa, he takes a couple of steps backwards to lean on the bonnet of his vehicle. After a nod acknowledging each other, Brass lifts the brim of his oily, sweat- stained hat to sit higher above his forehead and starts to speak. "We have had choppers up our way and they're going through Ray's camp. I think I will move down there just to keep an eye on his gear and stuff; already been down there a couple of times to check on things."

Jack recalled a previous conversation with Ray saying that he had suspicions Brass had been going into his camp while he was away, with alcohol, food and other small things missing from around the camp. Snapping back into the conversation, he says to Brass, "I don't think that's a good idea, I'm sure his family would like to see how things were left by Ray and pack up his personal stuff."

Brass just dismisses Jack as his eyes rest on Buddy lying under a tree not far away. "Which makes that dog my property," he says, pointing to Buddy.

Jack, with anger now starting to build, replies, "How do you work that out?"

"Well, I have contacted Ray's wife, a lovely lady I might add, and she has given me permission to stay at Ray's camp and keep an eye on the place for them. We all have to help the best we can," he says, giving a sly smirk and a wink to the men in front of him.

Jack is about to give Brass a mouthful but is stopped by Tim's hand on his shoulder. "Bud," says Tim quietly, "you have enough on your plate as it stands, you don't need this extra shit on top. Anyway who's going to look after the dog in town? You're packing up and by the sounds, we will all be ducking and weaving. We have got nowhere for the dog to go."

Jack sighed in agreement as his better judgement surpassed his anger. Lowering his voice, he says to Brass, "Take the bloody dog then."

Brass's smirk breaks into a wide smile; he knows he has won. He calls Buddy, who comes obediently and jumps into the back when Brass taps the side of the old 4x4. Brass had picked up on Tim's soft tone while reasoning with Jack to calm down and he thought he would have one last stir. "By the looks of things, you're packing up. I can call in and check on the place for you."

Jack in his current stressed out state rebuts very quickly "Pig's arse you will. Don't come on my property again. I will have someone keeping an eye on it for me so keep the hell out!"

Brass gives them a wink as he drives slowly back the way he came. "Leech," is all Jack says as he returns to help Sue pack up.

John goes over to the camp to let them know that he may as well head back to town also. "The cops won't let us in to search and I am now way behind with work."

Tim tells his prospecting partner, "No worries, bud. I will help them finish off packing up and be back in town myself to get stuff sorted out from my end. That reminds me, I have to give that D a call." John says his goodbyes to Jack, Sue and Rob, reminding them to keep in touch and let him know what was going on. They wave a farewell as he heads towards town.

Coming back from the phone, Tim announces to the others, "They are now looking into other missing person cases in the area and are calling for anybody that has had a run in with Scrubber over the last 20 years to come forward and give statements."

"They will be swamped with calls on that one, no doubt," Jack says as he tapes up a box of personal items and places it in the back of the truck.

"True," says Sue, "but how many will come forward and make a statement for fear of retribution? The rumours about the bikie links have been around for a long time now."

Tim replies, "I don't give a shit. Them pair of pricks have shot one of our mates in bloody cold blood. We have to do what we can, not only for Ray and his family, but also anybody else who will run across those murdering scum when they are allowed back at the station."

Rob returns with, "Surely the cops would have a tail on them in town?" leaving the question open for somebody to respond.

"We hope so," Sue quietly says, giving him a half hug across the shoulders, adding, "Don't know if it's me but every time I walk outside to put something in the truck, it feels like I've got a target on my back."

Jack, appreciating his wife's sixth sense as it had proven right many times over the years, replies, "Let's get this finished and get out of here. You can't second guess a deranged man; no one can." With the idea now festering in their minds that there might be someone perched in the hills looking though the scope of a high-powered rifle, after all there had been no mention of where Price was, the four of them pick up pace to get it finished. All of them now feel exposed out in the open. From the Oasis they can hear the choppers working a search pattern not far downstream but knowing the SES and police are walking the hills and creeks nearby is of little comfort.

Scrubber and Max were released from the Bankston cop shop after questioning, finger printing, photos and gun residue tests, and are trying to work out what to do now. Scrubber feels in the rear pocket for his bulging wallet that held a considerable wad of cash, which had also led to extra questions being asked by police. He gives Max a $50 to go grab a couple of soft drinks and some change for the public phone. Only taking minutes to do this, she is soon back with a handful of gold coins. They walk towards the public phones. Scrubber gives her back some coins and instructs, "Max, I need you to put an anonymous call into Crime Stoppers with information to send them in the opposite direction while I call the barrister to fill him in on what's going on, then we will book into a pub for the night and get some sleep."

Max's phone call is brief while Scrubber's takes a considerable time longer and he keeps feeding the gold coins into the slot. When he finally hangs up, Max asks, "Listen ing to your side of that call didn't sound good. What did he say?"

Scrubber, still trying to get his head around it, says, "Fuck, he won't represent us in this case. They do not want the pigs to link his firm with us because of all the work they do on bikies' cases. It's too much publicity."

Max replies, "Well, my call went better than yours; they took it hook, line and sinker. Don't worry, we could hire a tin pot solicitor just out of law school and it wouldn't matter. They can't prove anything without a body."

Scrubber comments, "C would know by now for sure. I haven't even got a number for him; he always rings me and the number is always blocked."

"Oh well," says Max, "nothing we can do about that. We will just have to find a place in town until they give up on the search then we can go home. Anyway, Price is there to keep an eye on things."

Scrubber grunts, "Well, that's not a great comfort. Yeah, I have to get onto C. I've got the names of the three witnesses for him to track down. I know where one lives, that's the asshole we ran across at the Croc Hole that day. I might just start with him myself."

As the couple walk down the street looking for a rental car business, they see a teenager aged about sixteen walking towards them. He is dressed pretty scruffy and is wearing his baseball cap on backwards; he is busily texting away on his phone and not looking where he is going. He is about to walk right into Max and she is going to give him a gobful before Scrubber puts his hand on her shoulder. "Hey mate, is that a prepaid phone?"

The young man says, "Yeah, why?"

Scrubber asks, "What did you pay for something like that?"

"A hundred and twenty," the lad replies. Wanting to get on his way as it was not cool to be seen talking to old relics, he starts to walk away.

Scrubber raises his voice loud enough for the young man to hear. "I'll give you $500 for it."

The young bloke stops in his tracks. "What did you just say?" He turns back towards the old fogies, who now have his full attention. "It's only got $15 credit left on it," he stammers.

"Sold," says Scrubber, counting out the bills. The young bloke couldn't believe his luck, receiving the ten $50 notes in the hand. Scrubber adds, "On one condition – text all your mates and tell them this is no longer your number. I don't want them bothering me."

"Yeah sure," the lad says gleefully as he starts working out how much free credit and what brand of new phone he could get for the bucks.

Max looks at Scrubber. 'What the?' is written all over her face. He gives a wily smirk and says, "We now have an untraceable phone cleanskin. Let's find a car."

Back at Hatchet River Station, they are now into day five and, other than to expand the search area, they are starting to run out of options. The tip off cost them two fruitless days. The Captain had to report their lack of success to head office every afternoon, then word came through that a black tracker was on his way from the Northern Territory to try and pick up where Ray is.

Arriving by police troopy, Jimbo is taken straight to where the shots were fired and spends hours covering the area around the crime scene. Walking back into the police camp, he goes straight to the command tent and shakes his head. "No good no good."

"What's wrong, Jimbo?" one of the constables who is there getting new orders asks.

"A lot of cattle been through there and the chopper has come down to low and blown all the signs away boss. Nothing left to follow, boss," Jimbo replies.

Frustrated, the Captain swears and slams down the topographical map he is holding onto the table. He runs his hand through his thinning hair that was becoming more apparent by the day.

Right at that moment, the two-way crackles. "Cap, I think I've found something" comes across the airwaves.

Quickly grabbing the two-way off his hip, the Captain says hastily, "Who is it and what sector are you in?"

The reply is, "Constable Reeves, sector one with the metal detector. Sir, I think I've found splatters of blood."

"Stay exactly where you are, son. Well done, we will be there shortly." The Captain's spirits lift at finally having something found. He starts bellowing orders. "Get that team of forensics out of the house now. I want them in that troopy with their gear in five minutes. Jimbo, you can come with us." Turning towards his two most experienced homicide detectives, who are still standing close by, he asks, "What are you pair doing? You two come as well and refresh my memory. Have you thoroughly questioned the brother?"

"Yes, Captain," one replied. "Haven't been able to get anything relevant out of him at all."

The other added, "He's as dumb as dog shit."

The first detective replied, "He seems harmless and you can bet he hasn't been the one reading the scores of law books in that house."

Neither of them were aware of the fact that Price, on his way back from his early morning muster after letting all the cattle in that had spoiled any remaining evidence, stashed the 357 Magnum and his belt full of shells, as well as Ray's keys, under a large boulder on the river bank.

Both vehicles pull up on site 20 minutes after the original call. Nobody was to be seen. Constable Reeves comes across the two-way again. "Not down there, sir, up on the side of the ridge to your left, sir."

"Roger" is the reply. "Get us around to that ridge but not too close. We will walk the last 100 metres, don't want to disturb any remaining evidence."

Pulling the troopies up on the opposite side of the ridge, they send in Forensics and Jimbo the tracker first. When they get to where the officer is standing with Tim's detector, "Here," he says, pointing towards the ground where blood splatters, dried and nearly black, could be seen on some rocks.

"Yep," replies Forensics, "that's blood all right," and he pulls out his camera to photograph the splatters after they had been marked and numbered.

Jimbo starts scouring the area like a blood hound. "If it's his blood, he went this way" and follows the trail for a brief period of time until he can't pick up on it any more.

Reeves goes over to brief his boss on the finds. "Well done, son," states the Captain as the young cop walked towards the troopy.

"I most probably wouldn't have found it if I was not using the detector, because you move so slow, watching where the coil of the machine is going in relation to the ground and rocks, Captain," proudly, getting a pat on the back from his superior.

"You have given us a start point along with the best
evidence so far. There's cold water and juice in the esky, help yourself."

Forensics return with a couple of samples of rock with blood on them in evidence bags. "Well, before we go getting carried away, best we go back to camp and check if it's even human blood."

"How long will that take?" asks the Captain.

"Well, first we have to run a swab test to confirm if it is blood, then we have to run a second test to see whether it is human or animal; about half an hour give or take."

"OK," replies the Captain. "Have all of those firearms you found in the homestead been sent for analysis yet?"

"Yes, Cap, they all went out yesterday."

"Good," he says, nodding, starting to feel like they were getting somewhere.

The radio crackles again on his hip. "We have dragged all the dams down this way, Cap, where would you like us to look now?"

Taking two steps to the troopy, he picks up the search map off the dashboard. By now knowing the search grids as well as he knew his own kids, he replies, "Move to sector four and help that crew. They're going over the sand and rock tailings."

Leaving Jimbo to get back to camp under his own steam, the troopies headed back to camp with purpose and pull up in a plume of bulldust, with Cap saying to Forensics, "I want to know the results ASAP. He desperately wanted to call head office and finally give them an update that was beneficial to the investigation. To keep himself occupied while the tests are being done, he pace the tent, calling all his search teams, including the two remaining choppers that were now working well away from the station homestead. The forensics crew enter into the main command tent and confirm that the blood is human. "Right," says the Captain as he grabs the phone to fill head office in on the news.

"We need access to the missing prospector's medical files to find out what blood type he was, and we can now upgrade this from a person missing under suspicious circumstances to suspected murder. Yes, Chief, and we will also need some ultra violet lights to cover where the blood was found as the area has been wind swept," but he does not elaborate on that, cursing that one of the choppers had flown so close to the ground. "Bloody cowboys," he says to himself. On cue, he can hear the choppers landing a short distance away in an area that would not blow bulldust through the makeshift headquarters.

Both chopper pilots and the four police spotters walk into the camp at the same time as Jimbo does and they all head into the main tent. The jet ranger holds three spotters whereas the mustering chopper only holds one spotter. The jet ranger pilot Ron is the first into the tent with his highlighted map of the area he has covered today, followed by the mustering pilot, who passes the maps to the search co-ordinator for him to add to the areas already covered. The Captain cuts in on their chopper chatter. "Who's being flying low?"

Both turn to look at the Captain with blank looks on their faces. "What do you mean?"

"Well, someone's been flying low and blown any sign of tracks to the shithouse with the down draught."

Both chopper operators look at each other. Steve the musterer answers. "With all respect, Captain, but we are not going to see jack shit travelling too high, and for a down draught, the chopper would have to be hovering not far off the ground."

Ron the jet ranger pilot adds, "The lower the better but you can ask your spotters, the only time we have been that low is on landing or take off. Have you asked that other cowboy you got flying around?"

The Captain sternly states, "He finished up this morning after kindly offering his services free for the past two days. We have now established a crime scene and it's been blown to Burke and back! Other than some blood on the rocks."

"Yeah we heard that earlier on the two-way," replies Steve. "So if a crime scene has been established, will I keep going on the search patterns or am I done?"

The Captain ponders on this. "Well, you're not that far away. Have a day off, I will get someone to ring you if you're needed again. Hand in your flight hours and you will be paid for your services."

Turning to Ron, he says, "You can do a run to Cairns, pick up some supplies, and also some bigwigs from Brisbane have arrived that want to come out for a look. The pressure is on to get this pair behind bars before the peak tourism season kicks off, which traditionally starts in three weeks' time. This could get uglier than what it already is. We got feedback this morning that a total of thirteen people have been listed as missing in or around this area over the past fifteen years."

Back at the Oasis, the trucks are packed. Jack says to Sue, "I will give Tonga a quick ring to ask if he can check in on the place every now and again."

Tim is ready to go. "Well, best we head off one at a time so we're not up each other's arse."

Rob yells from the seat of his truck, "Channel 20, Dad."

Tim waves and slowly heads out as well, after giving Rob time to get a head start, not wanting his truck's air cleaner to be sucking in bulldust. Tim turns on the two- way, flicks it onto channel 20 and picks up the mic as he changes through gears. He says to Rob, "Get that bucket of bolts moving, bro, because I'm right up your clacka."

Rob laughs. "Righto, bud, I'm on it." Still chuckling to himself, he pushes down harder on the accelerator. Sue, sitting in the passenger's side of their 4x4, listens in and smiles at the light humour between the men on the two-way, even at such a bad chapter in their lives, knowing that what they are about to do is life changing but necessary nonetheless. They were totally unaware of what trajectory their life would now take.

C, wanting to keep abreast of happenings, dials his cop mate Marko, twirling the ring on his finger subconsciously as the phone starts ringing. When the cop picks up the receiver to answer, C cuts him off. "I want updates from you on what's happening, not have to watch the TV or listen on the radio to find out what the fuck is going on second hand. That's what I pay you for. And I want you to report back before the day's end where Scrubber and that bitch are."

C hangs up then rings Ox. "Get your gear together. You might have to clean up some things quickly for me."

Ox, knowing what C means, replies, "Righto. The chopper got the crew out no problems but it was over loaded, so bugger all meth come out. I've fixed him up for it and I'm ready to go on your word." Getting off the phone, Ox packs two hand guns with silencers, a high- powered rifle with a variety of day and night scopes and plenty of shells into the canvas bag along with some binoculars, an assortment of clothes, and knives.

About half an hour later, C's phone rings; knowing the number, he picks up the receiver. Marko has already sourced the intel on Scrubber. "Right, they have a tail on them. They've rented a car in Bankston and are now booked into a motel in Midtown." He gives C the details and the number of the motel. "Bankston police also took photos of the three witnesses so I will fax them through with their names. I'm running a search on the addresses now, I'll text them to you when it's done."

"Now we're getting somewhere," C says to himself, ringing Ox back. "Righto, here's the number of the motel. Ring the clerk, tell them it's urgent and it needs to be passed on to them personally. Give them your mobile number and pass on the message to ring Ox now!"

Doing as he is directed, the hit man phones the motel and what sounds like a pimply teenager answers. Ox lays it on thick and heavy the importance of the message that needs to be hand delivered ASAP. The young bloke writes down the details and at the end, Ox sweetens the deal by offering to pay the young man $50 for his services. The bored young man had been Googling the internet for porn sites; 50 bucks would get him into at least five sites. He quickly walks up to room eight and knocks on the door.

Scrubber is lying comfortably on the bed in the air con, flicking through channels. The news comes on with all the hype on the missing prospector. He smirks and speaks back to the TV, "You guys ain't got a clue."

Max answers the door. "Message for you." The pimply young bloke passes the note to Max; reading it, she turns to Scrubber. "Need 50 bucks."

Scrubber says, "What the fuck for?" He is cranky about being disturbed while watching the news about their handiwork.

Max replies to the outburst with frustration. Gritting her teeth, she says, "Just get your fucking wallet. It's from Ox and C."

Just hearing the name makes his whole body language change. Fumbling for his wallet out of his back pocket, he throws the whole thing at Max. She catches it easily and opens it to reveal a huge amount of cash. She pulls out a $50 dollar note and pays the adolescent, shutting the door abruptly before the kid could even say thanks. By the time Max turns after shutting the door, Scrubber is at her side, grabbing the note from her hand, anxious to read it.

Max can tell by the twitching of his right eyelid that he is under stress. Reading the brief note, he groans. "Right, best I ring him then." Knowing that they had fucked up big time and had to bear the brunt of the backlash, Scrubber felt like he had been caught with his pants down. He was used to dishing out the fear, not receiving it. He rings the number.

Ox picks up. Not knowing the number, he still answers in the normal manner. "Speak" is the only word said.

Scrubber, picking up that this isn't C, says, "Who's this? Ox?"

"Yep."

Scrubber starts to spill it all. "Ox, we thought it was just one lousy stinking prospector. We didn't see anybody else around, they must have been hiding and saw what happened. I've got their names for you though and they will never find the lab."

Ox replies, "I already have their names and photos, the lab has already been shut down, C is extremely pissed off that all this attention has stopped production."

Scrubber, now trying to right the wrong, says to Ox, "I know where one of them lives. If C wants me to get rid of him, I will."

Ox replies, "You hopeless fuck, your lucky to still be breathing" and hangs up.

Tim, Jack, Sue, Rob and John are all pleased to be arriving at their homes. Jack is the first to act. "Sue, first thing in the morning, I want you to ring the bank and tell them we want $30,000 in cash to pick up that afternoon. I also want your mother to go into the communications shop and buy a prepaid phone. All credit cards are to be burnt and I will ring a mate for a loaner car for a while. Pack some clothes and whatever else you need because we aren't hanging around here like sitting ducks. Rob can look after Bumpy; we want to be out of here tomorrow night at the latest."

Tim arrives home to a loving welcome from Danni. "I have been so worried."

Tim replies, "I need to get you to safety, and quickly."

Danni breaks the embrace and looks into Tim's eyes affectionately but with a worried look on her face. "What do you mean? What's going on?"

Tim grabs Danni by the waist gently. "Babe, this is going to get worse before it gets better by the looks. Don't worry your pretty head over it, just stay at your girl- friend's place when I'm not around."

John also arrives home and starts to unload, turning off and unpacking the freezer. His wife Meg walks up to the shed at the back of the house to greet her husband. "So how did you go?"

"Up the shit," John replies. "They wouldn't let us into the search area as it's now classed as a crime scene." Meg was saddened to see her husband so disappointed and frustrated over the trip.

Jack and Tim are taking this as a more serious threat than Sam, who is a bit of a loner and lives by himself on 30 acres near a small Tablelands town in a tidy, two-bedroom house with a lean-to beside it for his four-wheel drive. It is surrounded by grazing cattle in paddocks for agistment. Having no neighbours close by suited him down to the ground.

Jumping into his 4x4, Sam preheats the diesel motor and lets it idle until the oil pressure picks up. Looking out of his side mirror before reversing, Sam is releasing his grip from the hand brake when he feels a sharp sting on the top of his hand just above the knuckles. Before he can react, another painful sting hits his wrist then another. Pulling his hand away, he sees there are eight puncture holes in his hand with small droplets of blood on the surface of the skin. 'Snake bite.' He looks down near the hand brake and spots a very large angry death adder. These snakes are renowned for having the fastest strike rate of all Australian venomous snakes. Sam knows he is in big trouble. Grabbing the car door, he levers it open with his fingers, turning off the 4wd to retrieve the house keys.

Knowing that time is of the essence, Sam opens the front door and quickly goes to the phone. Picking up the receiver, he dials 000; no ring tone comes through. Now starting to panic, Sam frantically presses the dial tone button repeatedly, willing the phone to give any sound, but the line is dead. Having spent the best part of his adult life as a loner, he had never felt the need for a mobile phone; he wished he had one now. Trying to think clearly, he looks down at his hand. It is turning red with a mix of deep purple swelling like a balloon around the bites. "Fuck," he says to himself. Realising the nearest neighbours are a good 10km away, he decides to try and make it to town.

Walking back outside the house with keys in hand, he spots a timber rake leaning up beside a post in the car shed. Grabbing it, Sam swings it hard against the steel shed pole beside the car, snapping it in half. Probing the timber shaft down near the hand brake, he can feel the adder hitting the rake handle. 'Why is this happening to me?' he thinks. Finally flicking the snake onto the driver's side floor mat, Sam can see it is a fat adult death adder. Having run across them many times in the bush over the years, he knows the venom from one bite can kill ten full grown cattle. Being on the car floor made it easier for Sam to kill it. Striking it with the rake handle with all his force, he flicks it out of the Hilux with the timber handle that is now showing multiple strikes marks from the adder on its end.

Sam jumps back into the 4x4. Waves of nausea come over him and he is having difficulty with hand eye co- ordination. He anxiously fumbles the keys into the ignition. Forgetting about the preheat, it took several times for the cold diesel to fire. Quickly reversing out, he selects second gear and guns his Hilux towards the front gate of the property, which is a good 400 metres from the house. As he skids to a halt in front of the gate, the engine starts to splutter and miss. "What the hell," he says, managing to open to gate as the engine died.

Climbing back into the truck, Sam winds over the motor again and again, but it shows no sign of kicking over. He does not know what to do. His vision blurs. Aware that the venom is starting to take its full effect, Sam's survival instincts kick in and he suddenly remembers the first aid kit back at the house. He kicks himself for not thinking about it earlier. Turning, Sam starts to stagger back towards the house; looking through blurred vision, he can just make it out in the distance. He gets a bit over half way. With blood and venom pumping through his veins, he falls flat on his face. He tries valiantly to get to his feet but to no avail. With his last breath, he mutters, "Scrubber." The penny finally drops on who has orchestrated his demise.

Sam's body goes into convulsions. Less than 300 metres away, Ox is concealed behind a hedge of trees watching the drama play out through his binoculars. He is relieved that it is finally over; not for Sam but himself as he has had a very uncomfortable wait since cutting the phone line and releasing the death adder into Sam's vehicle the night before. After enjoying the show, Ox puts the binoculars into his duffle bag, slings it over his shoulder and walks towards the Hilux whilst putting his gloves on. Popping the bonnet of the car, he produces a screwdriver from his back pocket and reconnects the fuel line hose. Whistling to himself as he closes the bonnet and leaving everything as it was, he walks towards his own 4wd that is parked at least half a kilometre away, well hidden off the road, thinking to himself the best hits are the ones where the victim doesn't even realise it's happening.

Tim and Danni have been busy back at their house. Danni has her car packed with all the stuff she needs for an extended stay with friends. Tim's truck is also loaded to the hilt with everything he can fit for a prolonged bush trip; he is not exactly sure himself how long he will be out there for. Tim told Danni the bush is the safest place for him; it is his backyard and he feels in his element there while still earning an income. Saying an emotional good- bye, Tim says, "See if Johnno can feed the bird and keep an eye on the place for us, sell some of that gold and put $500 bucks on my satellite phone account so I can ring you. I have also organised John to run supplies out to me if need be." With a final kiss, Tim drives off. Danni, with tears in her eyes, walks over to finalise the last few matters with Johnno, their friend and neighbour, before leaving herself.

Tim eventually arrives at a spot he had found many years ago; it was well off the beaten track and extremely hard to access from any direction. It has taken him six hours to get there from Claytown as, being very cautious, he swept his tracks thoroughly. With only one way in, he knew this is as safe as it is going to get.

The area is well shaded by the large mango trees planted by the Chinese miners back in the Hatchet River heyday. There is a fresh water spring close by that was still trickling when he had first found the area in the driest time of the year. This camp is not going to be a quick shift camp with the barest of essentials that Tim is used to working with, but more of a permanent stay. He had brought a large green tarp for shade and rain and his solar panels to run his freezer. BBQ plate, gas cook rings and frozen water bottles to exchange from the freezer to the esky daily to keep his vegies, bread, butter, drinks cool. It takes the rest of the day to set up properly and he finishes just on dark. He sits down to enjoy his first sip of rum and cola.

Jack and Sue, also having packed up, are on the move after organising a mate's car as a loaner. They have the car pointed south, heading off at 4am in the morning, leaving everything but the essentials behind.

Back at the station, the results had come back positive that it was a match to the missing prospector's blood and a warrant had been issued for the arrest of Scrubber and Max for murder. The big boys from Brisbane had arrived at the crime scene command site; not being accustomed to the north Queensland heat they are sweating profusely. Crammed into a police troopy with the aircon on high, the bigwigs are driven to the area where the dried blood was originally found. With sweat still running off their faces like a tap dripping. They were waiting in anticipation to use the high-powered ultra violet lights to be turned on and sweep over the local vicinity.

Within half an hour, there is enough darkness to start. The blood trail stands out in a weaving line and they follow it over to the other side of the ridge to a slightly larger pool of blood in one spot, after which it stops for no apparent reason.

With the nearest old mining road a good 50 metres away, the men from Brisbane ask the captain in charge of the investigation, "You find any vehicle tracks on that old road?"

"Not that we could find, sir," he replied. "There have been a lot of cattle through here lately." Not wanting to bring up the discussion on the area being wind swept by a chopper for fear of the city boys labelling him incompetent, he changes the conversation by saying, "Well least now they are going to be behind bars for the tourist season."

The two large-framed city cops agree. "We want a written report on today's, including tonight's, findings and organise that jet ranger to take us out of here first thing in the morning." Both are looking forward to getting back to their air conditioned offices.

A swarm of police turn up at the motel that Scrubber and Max are staying. A loud thud on the door has Scrubber on his feet instantly. Grabbing the note that been delivered by the young man from reception and the mobile phone, he runs into the toilet, pulls the top off the cistern and drops them both in, quickly replacing the lid. He rips his pants down and his arse cheeks just hit the toilet seat as the door is shouldered in by two burly officers with guns drawn. Both the officers are citing him his rights for the arrest, with one officer still levelling his service pistol at him while the other spins Scrubber around and cuffs him, with his pants still down around both ankles. Moving him back out towards the most spacious part of the room, one officer begrudgingly pulls up the prisoner's strides while Scrubber looks across at his wife sitting on the bed, also handcuffed. The unit is searched and all their personal items are placed into evidence bags for further investigation back at police headquarters.

The Hatchet River Station owners find themselves behind bars, waiting for a court hearing. The detectives who had interviewed the three witnesses try to contact them on their personal numbers to inform them that the accused have been locked up. With not one of them answering the calls, serious concern sets in with the experienced detectives, each of them having decided that the three men were on the up and up after their interviews, as each of statements concurred with the other, without one difference. In haste they organise to visit the witnesses' place of residence, knowing that without them, they did not have a solid case. All three detectives leave in separate cars, accompanied by a uniformed officer.

The first to arrive at one of the house addresses is the detective who conducted Tim's interview. After knocking on the door repeatedly without response, they check the property over thoroughly. The residence is locked tight with not a car in sight and no apparent evidence of foul play. They go over to the neighbours to question them on the last time they noticed any movement next door.

After the first knock on the door, Johnno answers; the detective introduces herself and asks a couple of questions about Tim's whereabouts. Johnno replies, "They left yesterday morning. Don't know where they were going but it looked like they weren't coming back for some time. That's all I know, have never gotten on with them that well. We are not what you call close neighbours," not knowing whether he could trust them at all.

The detective that had interviewed Jack finds the same thing; the house is locked up, but he is puzzled by the two vehicles still parked in the shed, both registered to Jack and Sue. After interviewing the neighbours, he also comes up empty handed. As they live on a small acreage block, the neighbours didn't even know that they had left, claiming that they come and go all the time. "Sometimes nobody is there for months."

The detective for the last witness Sam found the total opposite. Turning onto the dirt track to Sam's property, they can see a vehicle in the middle of the driveway with the door open, and the gate swung wide as well. Pulling up at the gate, both officers jump out of the squad car and scan the area for the owner. Looking back down the driveway, they can see a black mass moving about 250 metres away. With Sam's 4x4 blocking entry through the gate, the officers walk towards what seems to be birds feeding on something lying in the grass to one side of the driveway. When they are only 30 metres away, six crows become startled and fly towards the tree line, revealing Sam's contorted body.

The detective turns to the young officer. "Get back to the car and call it in." The young cop runs back towards their squad car quick as his black shiny boots will allow. Fumbling with the hand piece of the radio, he calls through to the station. "We have found a body at…" Caught up in the fact that this is his first dead body, his nerves are making his thoughts race and he can't remember the address. Finally he gets himself together to accurately give the address, adding it was one of the murder witnesses.

Within an hour the place is overrun with police and ambulance, with Forensics on their way from Cairns. One of the homicide detectives examines Sam's body intently without touching anything then straightens up off his haunches. "Looks like a snake bite to me." Pointing to Sam's left arm, he says, "Look at the puncture wounds on the hand." Eventually Forensics finish with the body; zipping it into a large black bag, they request that the coroner makes Sam's body a priority. The Forensics along with detectives go through the house and car for prints or any sign of foul play but come up with nothing.

Once they are done, the young officer first on the scene is instructed to move Sam's 4x4 that is still blocking the driveway so they can get the body to the morgue for autopsy ASAP. Though he winds the motor over continuously, it refuses to start. One detective walks over to see what the holdup is. "Did you pre-heat it? Has it got fuel in it?"

He looks at the gauge. "Yep, on both counts."

"Well, it's either electrical or fuel," the detective comments, knowing a bit of a backyard mechanics himself.

"Hook it up with a tow rope and get the bloody thing out of the way," the detective in charge of the crime scene orders, annoyed that proceedings were getting held up over something so trivial.

Within a week, an article on page five of the local newspaper read "Man dies on Tableland from snake bite, no suspicious circumstances." A detective quoted by the newspaper reporter said, "It looks like the man was bitten multiple times and had tried to drive himself to get help when his car unfortunately encountered mechanical problems. He had then proceeded to walk back to his house but regrettably did not make it that far."

The young news reporter had done his homework thoroughly and returned a question to the detective while doing the interview, "Is it correct to say that the deceased was a witness in the suspected murder case at Hatchet River Station?" The detective winced. "That is correct but there are no suspicious circumstances here. He died from a snake bite."

The weeks went past without any further incidences. With Scrubber and Max in prison waiting for their bail hearing, Danni was relaying the events surrounding the investigation in the media to Tim via sate phone. John does one run out to a designated drop off point with a gas bottle and various other supplies that Tim was running short on. He pulls up near a barely visible side track and unloads the supplies, carries them into the bush and stashes them out of sight from the road on the off chance that he has been followed at a distance. Tim knows exactly where the drop off spot is as they had both found some nice nuggets in the spot and had the area plotted in on their hand-held GPSs.

Tim arrives a good hour after John had run up the road for 5kms before turning around to head back towards town. He parks about 100 metres out from the supply drop, not wanting to leave tyre tracks, walks in and starts ferrying the supplies over to the tray of his truck then backtracks towards his hide out.

With the bail hearing being set, Max is transported from the Brownsville Women's Prison to the Cairns Watch House the day before while Scrubber, based at Lotus Glen Prison only an hour away, is transported to Cairns on the day of the hearing. Inside the courtroom the judge goes through the case, saying, "There is a strong case against you on the charges of murder and interfering with a corpse. As a part of your bail conditions, neither you nor your legal team can make contact with the three witnesses that are critically important to the case." Then, flicking through the pages of information in front of him, he raises his head and says, "Sorry, now two witnesses, after an unfortunate turn of events."

The judge continues, "Seeing the lack of criminal history and also having such strong ties to the station with the need to tend to your stock, I consider you a low flight risk. With the investigation now finished at the station, you can return on the condition that you ring police three times a week. Bail is set at $40,000 each, with the case coming before the court again in three months from this date." Hitting the hammer down on the desk, he says, "The court is now adjourned."

Out at the station, the investigating officers are packing up after running an extensive and expensive search effort over 25500 hectares of wild terrain over many weeks, with no sign of a body. Even a dive team had been brought in to search every dam on the property with still nothing; the best evidence they had was the blood trail that mysteriously stopped and the witnesses' accounts of events, which was now down to two. Exhausted from the gruel- ling weeks of extreme temperatures and inhospitable terrain that continuously hampered the investigation, the Captain issues a few remaining orders in relation to packing up camp then, loud enough for everyone to hear, says, "Listen up. They have been released from custody and we need to be on the road out of here before night fall." He continues to load boxes full of reports for the crime scene investigators to sift through at the command centre that had been relocated to Cairns.

Jack and Sue, heading back closer to home through the western route, pull into a service station. Jack fuels up while Sue goes in to pay. She also picks up a few snacks and drinks and walks out with a newspaper under her arm. Getting back into the car, Sue says, "Best you pull up over there," pointing to some empty car parks and waving the paper. "I am sure you are going to want to look at this."

After reading it twice, Jack puts down the paper, shaking his head in disbelief. "Fair dinkum, how high does this go?" he says. "What, because they don't have a recorded criminal history, they get set free. Where is the justice in that? What a joke. On 40 grand bail each that just makes me sick."

Sue adds, "There's more. Sam's dead! By snake bite apparently."

Jack's jaw drops. "What? When?"

Sue replies, "A few weeks ago. We haven't been following the news at all; there's a small article on the opposite page linking him to the court case."

"You're kidding," retorts Jack, reading the smaller article. "Right, let's go," says Jack.

"Where to?" asks Sue.

"Back up north, closer to home, in case anything else happens." They take turns driving through the night.

Tim, now well into week three, had seven ounces to show for his efforts. Getting sick of listening to the same CDs, he leans into the open window of the driver's side door and turns off the stereo. He starts the truck to charge up the batteries even though installed in the vehicle is a dual battery system that automatically cuts out, always leaving enough power to start the truck. It was more just out of habit. "Too far to walk if the old girl won't start," he thinks to himself. The only contact Tim has with the outside world is with Danni, every second night at 7pm on the sate phone.

Tim also feels a bit down after Danni relayed the news about Sam's death. Tonight is phone call night and Tim has the sate phone antenna extended to pick up the necessary satellites for reception. He is ready and waiting, sitting at the plastic table in his fold-up chair at five minutes to 7pm. After 20 days in the bush alone, he eagerly awaits its ring. Right on 7pm, the phone comes to life. "Hello, bub," Tim says, only to be met with sobbing at the other end of the line. "What's wrong?" he asks.

Danni, taking a deep breath, says, "They're out on bail. They are both out and will be back at the station tomorrow."

Tim couldn't believe it. "For fuck's sake," he let out, "How? Why?"

Danni, now more composed, reads out the article. When she is finished, Tim is very concerned. He says to Danni, "Stay at Sandy's and don't worry about me. I'm nowhere near Hatchet River. I am fine, you just keep safe. Have you heard from Jack or Sue?"

"No," says Danni, "not since they rang me to give me their new mobile number before they left. I haven't rung them but Sam and Hatchet River Station have been all over the papers and radio so I'm sure they would know.

"John rings me regularly to see how you're going. You know, all the macho men's shit aside, I think he really does miss you, you know." A small smile crosses her face.

"Yeah, I know." After a minute or two of personal conversation, he presses the red button to end the call. Sitting the phone down on top of table, he gets up to pour himself stiff rum and cola. Sitting back down, the phone beeps and continues to do so. Tim had heard the phone do the same thing during Danni's call. He picks it up, trying to work out what is going on. It couldn't be a flat battery, he had charged it the night before. Scrolling down the menu settings, he sees that there was a missed call earlier from the chopper pilot. Tim was thankful he had remembered to programme the number in before he lost it.

Relieved to have something else to occupy his thoughts, which were starting to run wild, Tim rings back the number. Chris is halfway through washing up from an early meal. He grabs a tea towel, wipes one hand dry and reaches for the phone. He is puzzled that the screen reads an overseas number. On answering it, he recognizes Tim's distinct way of speaking. "Hey Chris, it's Tim, how you going?"

"Not bad," he replies. "Listen, mate, I've got a few days up my sleeve if you want to go for a run in the chopper to look for those Chinese stacking's I told you about. How's a fifty-fifty spilt on the gold you find sound?"

Tim is barely able to hold his excitement. "Done deal."

"Righto, bud. Where are you?"

Tim laughs. "Mate, you would never find me. Hang on, I'll grab my GPS." He reads out the co-ordinates.

Chris asks, "Anywhere close to land the chopper?"

"Yeah, mate, a bit of a clearing not far from my camp."

"No worries then. I will see you bright and early in the morning."

On the tail end of the phone call, Tim adds as an afterthought, "Hey, it's not near Hatchet River Station, is it?" "No. Why?" asks Chris.

"My missus rings every second night and told me that they fucking let them go."

"True?" replies Chris. "No mate, I hadn't heard that, but believe you me it's a long way from Hatchet River."

Tim hangs up and starts to buzz around the camp, getting what gear he needs for tomorrow, putting the detector battery on charge while he throws a couple of pork chops in the frypan on top of the gas ring. Adding a few tins of fish along with other assortments into his backpack for the morning, he finishes off dinner and washes up. "I'll have a rum for a nightcap and then it's bed for me," he said to himself.

Tim is up before dawn. While the water is boiling for coffee, he decides to stash the seven ounces of nuggets he has found to date, not wanting Chris to think that he had found them out of the chopper. Finishing off the coffee, he replaces the detector battery pack into his harness. He hears a faint noise that sounds like a chopper heading his way.

As the sound becomes distinctly louder, Tim finishes sliding the snake protectors down over the top of his boots, grabs his hat, backpack, detector and also the pick then starts walking towards the small clearing. The chopper comes into sight, a small black blob which is moving fast. By the time Tim gets to the clearing, the chopper is doing circles above him. After about the third circle, Chris drops the chopper into a confined spot and powers down. Tim runs over in a crouch and starts to position his gear on the skid rack. Chris comes around to help him, shaking hands first then pulling out an elastic type cargo net to go over the gear, fixing it all securely in place.

Chris giving the thumbs up, returns to his side of the chopper, and harnesses himself in. Tim follows suit then reaches for the headphones and places them over his ears. Chris says, "This is very well camouflaged camp from the air. You've obviously done this before?"

Tim modestly replies, "Once or twice," with a grin on his face.

Powering the chopper to maximum, Chris explains to Tim, "She's a bit of a tight spot. Hang on, let's see if we can get out of here." Revved to the limit, the chopper lifts off, hovering then slowly gaining altitude. Chris turns his head to look behind him for protruding tree branches then skilfully manoeuvres the chopper backwards as far as the trees allow. He moves the joy stick forward and they manage to get just enough forward momentum to clear the trees in front of them.

Chris and Tim chat while the chopper heads towards the most remote and unexplored locations on the Hatchet River Goldfield. Tim points at old timers' workings as they fly over; he removes the GPS from his top pocket, pushing the mark button on anything that took his fancy. Winding their way in and out of sandstone gorges as they go on further, Chris spots the old Chinese stacking's and points them out. Tim nods, giving the thumbs up and saying into the mic, "I can smell the gold from here, bud."

Chris laughs. "I hope you're right, mate. These choppers don't run on fresh air."

"I bet they bloody don't."

"I can land over there no worries," said Chris. "What do you reckon?"

Tim looks around to see some old timers' surfacings. While they hover, he points towards them, saying, "There's a good place to start." Landing the chopper and winding the engine down to idle, Chris turns off his machine and reaches for his hat before going around to help Tim get the rest of the gear sorted. When he is all suited up, with the pick over his shoulder, Chris says, "Lead the way, wonder boy."

About 15 minutes later, Tim is working a high terrace well out of the creek with the odd Chinese pot hole, swinging across a nice sweet-sounding target and, not wanting to look too confident, he casually swings his pick into action. Chris says, "True? Already?" and moves closer to get a good look.

"Yeah, bud," says Tim, throwing the pick slightly to one side behind him and kneeling down to dig out the broken dirt by hand. "Don't reckon any one has been here with a detector before," he adds, waving handfuls of dirt over the coil of his detector and eliminating the dirt that the detector does not respond to. When he feels the extra weight in the next handful, hears the squeal of the coil and senses the gold, Tim's face lights up.

Standing behind him, Chris reaches for the pick on the ground and, swinging it high above his head, sinks it deep into Tim's muscly shoulder blades. A huge gush of air comes out of Tim's mouth as does a trickle of blood. Trying to stand up with the pick buried deep in his back, Tim staggers and looks at Chris in disbelief before falling over the side of the terrace. The prospector tumbles down through the razor sharp slate rocks and lies face first near the small stream below. Chris looks over the bank at Tim's lifeless body and, satisfied the job is done, pulls off his gloves, which have blood splatters on them. Lifting a large piece of slate, he gets rid of the evidence by throwing them under it and letting the rock slam back down. With his right hand clearly visible, he begins to twist the thick gold band ring encrusted with sapphires on his finger.

Walking back towards the chopper, he says to himself, "Yep, if want something done properly, you do it your- self." Throwing Tim's backpack on the passenger's seat beside the GPS, he swings the door shut. "I'll ditch the pack on the way home." He starts the chopper and heads off towards his property.

Landing at home, C phones Ox. "Well, that's two down." They discuss other details in a low tone, with Ox doing a lot of nodding on the other end. Hanging up, C is happy with his achievements for the day.

The following night Danni places a call to Tim's sate phone at the usual time. Two things puzzle her: there is no ring tone and he doesn't answer, so she rings on the hour every hour until 2am. Unbeknown to her Tim's sate phone is turned off and sitting on the plastic table in the deserted camp. Although worried, she figures she will try again early in the morning and goes to bed with the phone by her side. She wakes at 5am after a couple of restless hours sleep. Picking up the phone, she tries again with no success. Breaking into a despairing sob, Danni holds her face in the palms of her hands. After having a good cry, she thinks to herself, 'Pull yourself together. Crying isn't going to help my husband.'

Thinking what to do, she decides to ring John's mobile at about 6am. It goes to message bank. After trying a couple of times, Danni then tries John and Meg's landline number. Three rings later, Meg picks up the phone. "Hello, Meg speaking."

Urgently Danni says, "Meg, it's Danni. Is around John around?"

"No, he had to go interstate on business, told me that he would be out of mobile service for about ten days so his mobile is diverted to mine to take care of local business. Why? What's wrong, Danni?"

Danni, who by now is getting more frustrated, started, "I can't get a hold of Tim. I tried all last night and also this morning."

"Shit," says Meg. "I don't even have a clue where to try and get a hold of John, his return flight is a week from today. Can I help at all?"

"No, not really, thanks," says Danni, hanging up before she breaks down again.

She dials another number as tears start to swell again. Jack answers the phone. "Hello, Jack," Danni says in a shaky voice. "I think Tim is in some sort of trouble."

"Bloody hell," he says. "What's happened?" She fills Jack in. "Shit. So we don't even know where his camp is set up then? This will be like looking for a needle in a hay stack."

Danni says, "I know John dropped up some supplies for him about a week ago."

"Well, where's John?" Jack asks, slightly confused. Danni fills him in on that situation as well.

Jack, being a quick thinker, says, "Well, if it's work related, he would not have taken the GPS with him. The top-of-the-range GPS that Tim and John have leaves a trail if it is turned on. We need to get to John's GPS to have a look."

"Righto," says Danni, with a glimmer of hope. "I will give Meg a call back and pick it up on my way through town. Where are you?"

Jack replies, "I can be in town in four hours. Just take it to work and I will get Sue to come in and grab it, OK?" Danni feels better now that something is in the pipeline.

Around lunchtime, Sue walks into Danni's workplace and is given a brown paper package with her name hand written in large black Nikko pen, with a co-worker saying, "Sorry, Danni has gone home sick for the day."

"Thank you," says Sue as she grabs the package and walks outside.

Jack rips it open and starts the GPS, holding it outside the car window to log onto the satellites. After about two minutes, Jack scrolls down the map and pushes the button with waypoints plotted in everywhere. On further inspection, Jack notices a way point with a green track line to it. "That will be it," he states. While driving home, he rings Danni on the mobile and talks through the hands free. "Danni, it's Jack. I found the drop off spot. Sure as shit I will just have to walk around the bush a bit to find his car tracks, I know how Tim operates. Danni, don't get too upset yet. His bike could have broken down and he might have had to walk back towards camp, sleeping the night in the bush. It wouldn't be the first time."

Danni quietly replies, "I know but the sate phone pouch is on his detecting harness, why wouldn't he have it with him?"

"Hmmm," says Jack. "Well, by the time I load up, I won't be getting away until the morning."

"What, you're going alone?" Danni gasps.

"Yeah, I will be carrying my rifle as a precaution but going off the GPS, it's well away from Hatchet River and any obvious danger. He's probably sprained his ankle or something, I've got my sate phone on me so I will call or get Tim to call from out there." Saying goodbye, he ends the conversation.

Sue looks at her husband. "Are you really going alone?"

"Well, babe, John's out of the state. If something is wrong up there, I really don't want to put either of our boys in harm's way so I will go alone. And don't tell them where I am going because I know they will want to come guaranteed."

Sue, thinking ahead, says, "Well, I want those GPS positions for where the drop-off point is."

Jack sighs. "Here you go." He reads them out as Sue jots them down on a notepad. "Don't worry, babe, I've got my sate phone as well."

When they get home, Jack walks straight from the car to the shed and starts loading on his bike, swag and other gear needed for the trip. A few hours later, he gets the call. "Tucker's up," Sue yells towards the shed. A couple of minutes later, he enters the kitchen while Sue is taking cutlery out from a drawer. "I have cooked your favourite corn beef fritters and I've made extra to cover lunch for you and hopefully Tim."

Sitting down at the table, Jack says, "It's good to be home but when I leave in the morning, I want you out of here, your mum's, a friend's place, it doesn't matter. I just don't want you here by yourself. What's your new mobile number? I will programme it into the sate phone."

Leaving in the grey of dawn, Jack is on the road back to the Hatchet River, a road he travelled countless times but not one he thought he would be driving back along so soon. Hitting the start of the dirt road, Jack glances at the digital clock in the dash; 7.45am, making good time, he thinks. About three quarters of an hour down the track, Jack slows the 4x4 to a stop and gets out to open the only station boundary gate along the road. Once through, he swings it shut. Pausing for a leak on the side of the dirt road before getting back into the truck is the last thing Jack does as a single gunshot echoes out. More than half of Jack's skull is blown apart by the velocity of the high- powered 308 rifle. The momentum of the bullet lifts him off his feet and propels his large frame backwards, snap- ping his vertebrae like a twig.

Ox lifts himself up from his well-concealed vantage spot overlooking the gate. The bolt action had glided effortlessly, locking the projectile into place and spitting out the spent shell once discharged. Replacing it with another shell, he sounded off another two rounds into the air in quick succession, alerting his offsiders the job was done, then bent over to pick up the three spent shells off the ground in a well-practiced discipline. He looks around for any traces of his being there while he had waited patiently in ambush for his target. A 4x4 station wagon drives up the road at pace. It had also been well hidden off the road, waiting for the tell-tale rifle shots from Ox. They'd taken turns sleeping, for two of them it was going to be a long couple of days on the road. Three bikies, heavily tattooed, emerged from the wagon with a large blanket and tarp. "Ya got him, hey?" one bikie says as they wrap Jack's body in the blanket to soak up any blood then roll him into the tarp and secure it with rope. The three struggle to lift Jack's large frame into the back of his own truck.

"C was right about him coming to look for his mate and to think we only had to camp out for one night to get it done." Ox instructs the two bikies, "Righto, you two keep driving until you get to WA and dump the truck. Any good spots along the way, ditch the body. We don't want it found ever!" Loading on a 60-litre drum of spare diesel, they both jump into Jack's truck and roar off down the road, trying to get as much distance between them and the Hatchet River Goldfield.

Ox takes off the binoculars from around his neck, throws them in the wagon and pulls out the fax of Jack's mugshot from his top pocket. He had studied it carefully before squeezing the trigger. Ox jumps into the driver's side of the wagon, with the bikie settling into the passenger's seat. He looks across at the leather-clad heavily- tattooed accomplice. "Well, you got to open the bloody gate so we can get out of here, ya dickhead," he says to the bikie. Once through the gate, Ox says, "It's got me stumped how you dumb pricks stay out of jail, honestly!" The bikie, though seething over the comment, knows better than to reply as this killer was the real deal.

Ox pulls out a GPS from his bag to find the waypoint where he had exited the dirt road with his own vehicle. The crows and hawks have already started to circle, swooping to pick up small fragments of what is left of Jack's brain matter. There was a battle of nature happening as there are also swarms of meat ants joining in the fray, quickly congregating to carry off their share of brain splatter to their nest. About 40 minutes' drive up the road, Ox pulls up and the bikie jumps back into the driver's seat. With the duffle bag over his shoulder, he walks into the bush to retrieve the car that was hidden 50 metres in. The bikie, who is glad to see the back of the hit man, continues back towards Brownsville.

Getting back onto the bitumen, Ox thinks aloud, "Well, that's another job finished." Setting his cruise control and turning up the music, he makes himself comfortable for the long drive back to Brownsville. As soon as Ox is in mobile reception, he rings C. "Job done," he says.

"Good," replies C. "Get that chopper organised to get them men back out there and tell them to back load what product they have in the cave. Pack it in garbage bags if they have to, we are running on fumes in town and I want you to do the runs from the factory until things settle down. When you see Scrubber, I want them pulled into line. Tell them this is their last chance, no more epic fuck ups. I am over it!"

Ox replies, "OK, C, but I will have to check out the station first. They have brought a lot of heat on themselves of late, just in case they are being watched." C agrees.

With Forensics finished with their vehicle, Scrubber and Max pick it up in Cairns and leave straight back to the station. Pulling into the Huego servo for fuel, Max grabs some cash out of the ashtray to go pay. Scrubber says, "I got this." Pulling out the wallet, he walks inside. After having a good yack to the attendant, he gets back in the truck.

"What was all that about with my dead shit cousin?" Max asks, knowing her husband was not one for small talk.

"Do you need to bloody know everything!' he snaps back. The rest of the trip is mainly in silence, until they start passing some of the huge ant hills on the side of the road that seem to run for miles. Max tries to strike up a conversation with Scrubber. "It's amazing, Mother Nature, isn't it?"

Scrubber grunts back, "What do you mean?"

"Well, our little friends here, for example," pointing to the anthills, "how quickly they repair their nest in just over 24 hours."

"Yeah," returns Scrubber, "I can't even remember which ones they're in anymore," adding, "The coppers didn't have a hope from the start."

Max replies, "Yes, that was one of the more useful things Dad taught me."

Max was reflecting back to the innocent age of six when her father caught a cattle duffer red-handed. He flicked the stock whip with accuracy, wrapping it around the man's neck and pulling him abruptly off his horse. Landing heavily, the man tried to rise quickly and reach for his pistol as Max's father's boot connected with the man's chin, shattering his jaw and breaking his neck. Max was watching from behind a large gum tree, close enough to hear the sickening crack of the splintering bones. Her father then threw the man over his shoulder and walked a short distance to a nearby anthill. He turned to Max, gruffly saying, "Collect some wood, child, don't just stand there," as he walked back towards his horse tethered in some close bushes to retrieve a small pick. While Max did as she was instructed, her father dug out the middle of the anthill to form a cavity and carved out a large hole at the bottom. The dead man's body was rolled into the cavity then the fire was stoked in the hole at the base, acting like a furnace. Within days the ants had rebuilt their home and entombed the ashes of cattle duffer, along with any evidence of Max's father having anything to do with his death.

When they pull up at home, the dogs don't bark or even show interest, being used to that many different vehicles lately, but they are met by Price, blurting out, "They only left this morning and they have been through everything."

Scrubber shrugs. "Good luck to them. Did you stay strong like I told you to?"

Price nods "Yep," says proudly. "They left me alone in the end, thought I was simple or something."

Scrubber pats him on the shoulder. "Thought they would," he says, smirking. "Good lad, we got you a box of chicken." Max grabs out the cold chook from the truck for Price and they all walk inside. Scrubber and Max hit the sack early, leaving Price to devour the nine-piece pack of chicken.

There is no early start around the homestead in the morning though Price has been up for hours. With all his chores done, he is waiting around to get orders from Scrubber which are not forthcoming this morning. Remembering his 357, he decides to walk up along the river bank to retrieve it. Arriving back at the station with it now firmly strapped to his hip, he finds Scrubber and Max sitting on the veranda rail with their coffee. Scrubber says to both of them, "I want you to go through this place thoroughly for bugs room by room." The phone rings as they go inside, Scrubber picks it up. "Yeah?"

"It's Gus."

Turning and pointing to the phone at Price, Scrubber says, "It's for you."

"For me?" Price frowns as he grabs the phone. "Yes," he answers timidly, having never received a phone call in his life.

"Hey mate, it's your cousin Gus from the servo. I know your birthday is coming up soon so I'm sending you out two surprise presents. I'm sure you will like them when you open the wrapping." Gus chuckles as he hangs up the phone. Price, doing the same with the hand piece, is still puzzled as to what the call was all about. After a very hard childhood, he can't remember ever receiving a birthday present.

At the servo, two gorgeous English backpackers come in to pay for their fuel. In a heavy pommie accent, the girls ask, "So where is the station that is looking for workers that you mentioned?"

"No worries," smiles Gus. "He is a good friend of mine and will look after you well."

He hands the girls a map with directions on it. "Thank you" they say as they walk back out to their relic camper-van.

Sue tries Jack on the sate phone all that night with no response. She rings police headquarters only to be told by the young lieutenant, in a tone that made him sound like he was full of his own importance, they have to be missing for over 48 hours before police can list them as a missing person. Slamming the phone down, Sue does what Jack had asked her not to, she rings her sons to let them know what had happened. Both raw with rage, they vow revenge if anything has happened to their father.

Two days later, John finally gets back into service, takes his phone off divert then rings Meg. She tells him that Tim has been missing for six days and Jack, who had gone up to look for him with the co-ordinates from his GPS, seems to have gone missing as well. John is now visibly shaking in anger. "Get me on the soonest flight home" is all the speech he can muster, his look one of stone cold death. Meg adds, "They have just had a brief comment on the radio that Jack's truck has been found abandoned in WA on a bush track by some pig hunters; there's no sign of Jack."

John feels like he has just been gut shot himself. With a seething voice, he says, "Come hell or high water, those fucks have just signed their own death warrant." Meg, with a mixture of fear and adrenalin, knows exactly what her husband is capable of. Only seeing him completely lose his temper a couple of times in their 24 years of marriage was more than enough; she knows that all hell is going to break loose at the Hatchet River soon. Very soon! John plots in the airport on the Navman in the hire car as he makes his way through the congested city traffic.

An old prospector hermit living on the outer-most accessible areas of the Hatchet River Goldfield hears his dog furiously barking at something over the bank. "What's up, girl?" he asks, walking over to the edge, then jumping back startled as a bloodied hand covered in cuts and scratches grasps a handful of slate jutting out of the bank. "My god, son, looks like you have been to hell and back!"

END OF PART 1

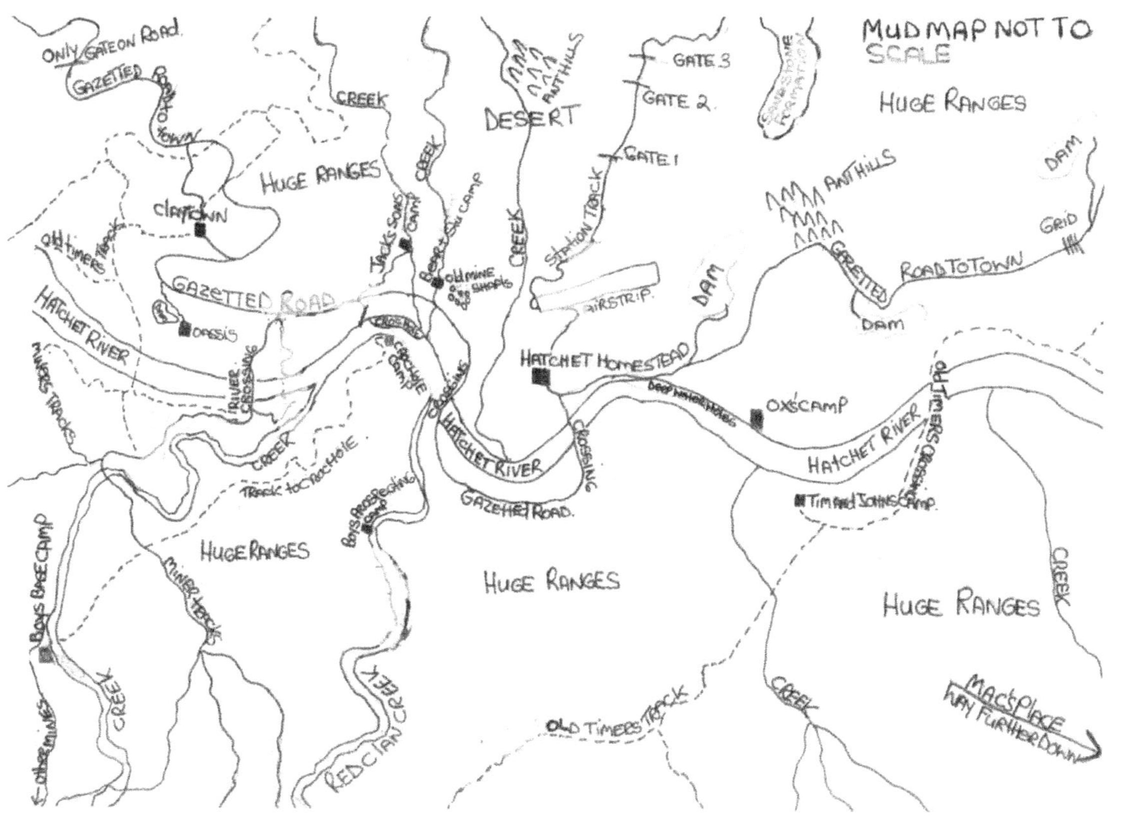

MUD MAP NOT TO SCALE
ONLY GATE ON ROAD
GAZETTED ROAD TO TOWN
CREEK
DESERT
ANT HILLS
GATE 3
GATE 2
GATE 1
SANDSTONE FORMATION
HUGE RANGES
DAM
ANT HILLS
GRID
GAZETTED
ROAD TO TOWN
HUGE RANGES
CLAYTOWN
CREEK
Jacks Sons Camp
Ford + Stu Camp
Old mine old shafts
Station Track
DAM
DAM
Old Timers Track
GAZETTED ROAD
Oasis
AIRSTRIP
HATCHET HOMESTEAD
OLD TIMERS CROSSING
HATCHET RIVER
River Crossing
Crochole Camp
Crossing
Deep water holes
OX'S CAMP
HATCHET RIVER
MINERS TRACKS
CREEK
Track to Crochole
HATCHET RIVER
Crossing
GAZETTED ROAD
Mt Tim and Johns Camp
Boys Prospecting Camp
HUGE RANGES
HUGE RANGES
HUGE RANGES
Boys Base Camp
MINER TRACKS
other mines
CREEK
RED CLAN CREEK
OLD TIMERS TRACK
CREEK
CREEK
MACKS PLACE WAY FURTHER DOWN

Blood Gold
Revenge in the Local Manner

They say you are lucky to find one true mate in your journey through life; to have a mate that unreservedly will put his life on the line to save your own hide without question increases the odds even higher again.

Five hours have elapsed since C had taken off in his chopper from the area, believing Tim dead. The prospector slowly regains consciousness and rolls onto his side, a sharp pain burning deep within his back, originating from the middle of his shoulder blades. Grunting with the amount of effort required to move, reluctantly he slides his calloused palm across the week-old stubble on his face to feel dry blood under the fingertips, congealed from many hours of being baked in the outback sun. Tim's hand continues upwards towards his throbbing temple and tenderly touches a lump the size of an emu egg and the nasty gash that had rendered him unconscious. He was lucky that the blunt steel pick had struck the strap of his solid detecting harness, taking some force away from what would have been a deadly blow and deflecting the pick so that it missed his vertebrae by millimetres. Otherwise he would have been a paraplegic fending off predators in the bush, if not dead already.

With a dry mouth and parched throat, the hardened prospector tries to regain his feet. Stumbling to the water's edge, he drags the newly released GPX 5000 behind him by the power cord, which bounces and skids over the smooth, water-worn rocks. The creek is not a large one, only about 6 foot wide and 2 foot deep, but crystal clear and quite cool for this time of the day, indicating that he was high up and not far from its origin seeping out of the hills.

Kneeling, he drinks small amounts at a time; cupping both palms together, he brings the water towards his face and washes off the dried blood while rinsing out his blood-matted hair. The pain has not subsided from between the shoulder blades, being unable to inspect the wound visually does not help matters. He cringes at the thought of Chris the chopper pilot sinking the pick deep into his back. "Shit, that was only a 10 gram nugget, would hate to see what the prick would have done to me if it was a 5 ouncer." The attempt at self-humour does not come off well and he winces in pain.

As his mind starts to clear, he thinks seriously about his situation. Making the observation of how far he is away from any help, also knowing full well that the back wound needs due attention or the chances of getting out of here alive would become further remote, he knows it will not be an easy task. Unscrewing the power cord from the detector before rising from the water's edge, Tim searches for the only weapon left to him, his prospecting pick. He locates it close to the base of the embankment he had come crashing down earlier that day.

Briefly glancing towards the crest, he flinches when he spots a fully grown male dingo is standing motionless, peering down at him intently. "Great, just fucking great," Tim says, talking to himself, as many men that spend a lot of time in bush alone tend to do. He retrieves the pick; looking up, they stare at each other for a full minute, sizing each other up before the dingo turns and trots out of sight. Picking up the tempo as best he can, Tim shrugs off the detecting harness and slowly starts to collect firewood, limply dropping it all in a heap near the single tree standing beside an open area near the creek bank.

Grabbing the detecting harness, he examines the pick hole that saved his life. Crouching down the injured prospector systematically goes through all pockets that are stitched onto the belt and empties out all contents, examining what is of value to get himself out of this shit fight.

First is a large crepe bandage in case of snake bite, a multi-purpose knife that had now been returned back into his belt immediately after the day of setting John's foot on fire because it had been left in one of the motorbike pockets.

The sate phone pouch is empty; he curses himself for leaving it back on his table at camp when hearing the chopper's approach that morning; and the two-way is busted. It must have got smashed on the way down the bank. The rest is mainly spare detecting components in case of breakdown out in the field, other than a thermal blanket that John had brought each of them the year before; the only reason it was included in the detecting belt was because it was light, slim and compact, measuring the size of your hand; a topographical map of the area he was originally working off at his own camp, which was totally useless for the area he now found himself in, and a head lamp that included three spare triple-a size batteries, which had come in handy over the years not only for getting himself out of problems in the dark but also for night detecting.

The GPS that normally sits in his top pocket had been left on the chopper seat, he'd use it that morning plotting in spots of interest on the way in, Tim assumed that they were only stopping in areas briefly so it did not get returned to his top pocket. The backpack that carried spare food, a first aid kit, a small roll of 20-pound fishing line about 40 foot in length and spare hooks; it had all been left on the carry rack above the chopper skid. The only other items in his possession are a drinking water bladder with one tin of mackerel in brine stashed in beside it, the GPX5000, a lighter and a pouch of tobacco and papers.

Tim stands up from filling the water bag and makes a circle of timber around the lone juvenile gum tree that was about the thickness of his thigh. Picking up dry leaf and small twig matter, he proceeds to scatter it under the dry timber. After setting out his thermal blanket in a sandy patch before placing a rock the size of a man's fist on each corner to hold it in place, he ignites the fire, moving around the circle and lighting it in numerous spots. Examining one particular heavy piece of wood, he places one end into the fire. "That will do the job," he says aloud then sits down to eat the tin of mackerel, washing it down with a couple of healthy swigs from his water bladder to give the food time to digest.

Rolling a smoke, Tim takes a few deep drags, pondering how this is all going to go. Inspecting the log, he nods to himself. It is time. Taking off his belt, he reaches for the log that is now glowing in coals at one end. As darkness falls, he straps it tightly around the gum tree trunk at shoulder height. Tim sheds his shirt and throws it onto the thermal blanket in front of the tree then backs up to the glowing coals of the log to try to seal the wound. Letting out a deep- throated yell as the smell of searing flesh enters his nostrils, he passes out from the pain and collapses onto the thermal blanket, with the ring of fire giving him protection from predators while in such a vulnerable state.

Hours later, with the moon rise, three sets of glowing yellow eyes intently watch the circle of fire from a high creek bank. Cool air has started to descend over the high gorge country, with a mist sitting slightly above the creek as the night grows older. Stirring in the early hours, Tim finds himself shivering from the moisture of the heavy dew falling on the upper end of his naked body. Stiff and sore, he reaches for his shirt and struggles to put it on. The purpose of inflicting such agony on himself by sealing the wound at that time of day was to keep the flies from laying larvae, which would evolve into maggots, in the wound while he was passed out. Also it was cooler and easier to protect himself.

Glancing up at the moon, he guesses it is close to 3am. Falling back onto his knees, he leans over to scoop some sand under the end of his thermal blanket, building a makeshift pillow. Settling in, he flicks half the thermal blanket over himself, keeping the rest under his torso to prevent a chill as the river sand grew colder, then falls to sleep near on instantly.

Waking as the sunlight drills directly onto his face, he slowly starts stretching the stiff muscles. Lifting up his head, he rubs both gritty eyes to try to get the tear ducts flowing. Eventually able to get both knees under him, he stands and steps over the now dying coals towards the creek. Placing one knee on the ground, he scoops a couple of handfuls of what is now cold water over his face, waking up immediately. An array of birds hit the water, their bills open to drink as they go about their daily business. Walking around the fire circle on the way back to retrieve his belongings, he notices numerous dog prints in the sand surrounding the outside perimeter. Concluding they had originated after the heavy dew had fallen, he studies the tracks in more detail and guesses there were 3 or 4 dogs, going by the different size prints in the sand. Shaking his head, "For fuck's sake, give a man a break," he knows they will be back, having picked up that he was wounded and weak.

Organising the meagre amount of equipment he has left to work with, he cuts a length of the snake bandage with the small blade of the pocket knife and wraps it around his head to cover the gash on the temple and knots it at the back. Tim pulls off the shirt and tries his best to cover the large pick wound in his back with the bandage.

He also decides to leave the metal detector in a tree branch above flood level with the hope of returning one day to retrieve the machine, not wanting to carry anything more than what is needed to survive. He starts off downstream, following the rule of thumb for all bushies – a small creek falls into a larger creek that eventually falls into a river, enhancing the chances of finding help.

He opts for not lighting a green fire as a signal to any search parties. He is still unsure who is friend and who is foe as he is trying to fathom the extent of his enemy. Chris is on top of the ladder, which leaves a deep burning anger in his gut. Filled with thoughts of revenge, the prospector picks up his stride as best he can in his current condition, thinking about how well he had been played from the first time he met Chris in the chopper after Ray had been shot.

Ducking and weaving around the semi-rainforest growth along the creek bank, he makes slower progress than he had hoped. The creek has started to widen, with its depth now close to 5 foot. A series of miniature waterfalls appear as well as a few fish lazily swimming in the current, trying to pick up meal of unsuspecting smaller fish coming over the rapids from upstream. Knowing that following the flowing creek down is his best chance of a constant food supply, he does not realise that the dingoes following his scent at a good distance behind are working off the same principle.

It is getting on into the afternoon but he finds it hard to judge the time exactly as the huge sandstone escarpments that tower above him block the sun's position. Only the full sunlight at midday beams into the gorge, which is abundant with many varieties of ferns and moss. The injured prospector starts searching for a safe place to camp, not wanting to leave it till the last moment and limit his choices. The back of Tim's shirt has been covered in flies for the best part of the day, with some even working their way inside from the pick hole in the shirt and slipping under the loose-fitting bandage.

Miles further on downstream, he selects a nice-sized gum tree with smooth bark that is easy to scale and thick branches fifteen foot off the ground. Climbing the tree takes a lot of physical effort after the gruelling trek down the sometimes near vertical water course, which, in places, tested his body to its limits. He shrugs off the harness that held his small amount of equipment and places it over a branch. The temperature starts to cool rapidly in the gorge as the prospector tries to organise sleeping arrangements well above the ground. His back wound feels like it is weeping fluid, and he surmises the quick fix with the burning log had not gone as well as expected.

Reaching for the pouch that held his thermal blanket while also retrieving the pocket knife from inside his trouser pocket, he punches two holes with the small 4-inch blade at the top of the silver blanket then bends down to unlace one of his shoes. Threading the lace through both holes, he ties the blanket loosely around his neck to try to contain body warmth. Unbuckling the leather belt from around his waist once again, he measures the girth of the branch and, adding extra length for his wrists, makes a new notch in the belt with a very blunt blade of his knife. Tim wraps the blanket snuggly around himself. As his mind starts to wander, he reaches for the belt and tightens it around both wrists and the branch to prevent himself from falling to the ground.

The night is full of delirious dreaming from the infection that had now taken hold of the wound; the rhythmic sound of the small creek that normally puts him to sleep when camping beside water is not needed tonight. He slept deeply for what Tim worked out to total three hours before waking at dawn to find he had slipped down the branch overnight.

Twisting his bound wrists to undo the belt buckle, he sits upright on the branch and massages his wrist to circulate the blood back into his hands. Untying the shoelace from around his neck, he lets the silver blanket drop to the ground.

From his higher vantage point, Tim turns his eyes to what could possibly be a busted old boundary fence on a small ridge above the creek bank further downstream where the right hand side of the gorge rapidly dissipated. Sliding down the smooth tree trunk, he walks over to pick up the blanket. A sharp pain shoots through the top end of his back, making Tim gasp in pain. Turning to retrieve his pick from the base of the tree, he notices claw marks on the bark, close to 3 meters up the tree trunk. He mutters to himself, "These dogs aren't going to fucking let me be." Folding the blanket and placing it back in the belt pouch, he snatches up the well-worn pick then starts walking down towards what he hopes are old timber fence posts. Hunger pains are starting to set in.

The old barbed wire fence appears in front of him after he has scrambled up a short, steep bank. Not believing his luck, thankful that his mind had not been playing tricks on him, he produces the - purpose tool and cuts a good five meters off the very old wire fence, laughing to himself as he does so. Looping it over his shoulder, Tim ambles back towards the creek and continues following the game track downstream, looking for the right-sized hollow log while he travels. Feeling the strain of the poison in his blood- stream and exhausted from bugger-all sleep with fever on top of it, his progress is very slow.

About three kilometres downstream, Tim finds what he is looking for – a log that had been hollowed out by white ants, about 1.5 meters long. There are also paperbark trees, abundant in certain areas along the creek. He starts to strip the bark off one large tree and places it on the end of the log while cutting the barbed wire to the right size. Criss- crossing the wire over one of the open ends, he wraps it around the end of the log, plaiting it so it holds tight. He finds a smooth rock large enough to use as a makeshift hammer and hits the wire, burying the barbs into the timber, ensuring there is no chance of escape from the rear entrance. Tying what remains of the wire to the front of the log, satisfied that it can be safely retrieved, he feverishly mutters to himself, "Bait needs bait."

Looking high and low and eventually finding a newly made green ant nest covered in workers on the exterior sealing the nest, he snaps off a thin branch and walks quickly towards the ready-made fish trap. Picking up a rock half the size of his fist, he tears open the tightly woven nest and places the rock inside to act as an anchor and provide bait. Both forearms are now covered in angry ants, biting into the flesh of their new found enemy. Tim quickly drops the nest inside and throws the trap into the creek as ants swarm their way up his sleeve and into his shirt. Trying to brush off the majority of ants with his palms is fruitless. Having no other option than to take off his shirt, he shakes it wildly to rid himself of the annoying freeloaders. He is unaware that a couple of juenile maggots fell onto the sand. His pick wound had become fly blown and maggots were writhing under the makeshift bandage.

With the temperature rising as the sun peaks at its highest point, Tim puts his shirt back on and lies down physically drained under the shade of a broad leaf tree away from the creek, not wanting to scare off the fish in such shallow, crystal-clear water. Thirty minutes later, he pulls in the log rapidly, cutting both hands with the barbed wire in the process, not wanting to let anything trapped escape. He heaves it out of the water and when it lands beside his feet, he can hear success immediately. There is a fish flapping inside. Smiling, he upends the trap to produce a nice size catfish. It starts to flip and flap around on the hot sand. With three poisonous barbs fully extended, it tries to ward off the enemy as its slimy smooth silver and grey skin gets covered in sand and a distinct grunt can be heard coming from its open mouth.

Tim is very happy with his catch. Immediately producing the pocket knife to brain spike the fish from underneath, he yells, "Food," nearly as loud as his belly rumblings. Collecting wood for a fire, his energy level at an all-time low, he realises the importance of nourishment if he is to survive this ordeal. He checks over the fish flesh at its thickest part with his knife to make sure it is cooked thoroughly as it lay sizzling on the hot coals then tears off a slab of paperbark for a makeshift plate from one of the many trees that line the creek bank. He rolls the fish off the fire with a stick and peels back the skin then sits down to devour the lot, busily waving the flies away as he does so. Willing his body to get moving, Tim forges on, knowing if he does not find help soon, he is not going to have a pretty end. The landscape starts to flatten out. As the creek gets deeper, with a multitude of gullies starting to feed into the main stream. Tim decides to cross the creek to throw off the dingoes that are persistently tracking him, not about to give up on their hunt anytime soon. He wades into the clear water. The depth was deceiving and he soon finds himself up to his neck but as he gets closer to the other side, the water shallows out. In a little washed-out gully that cuts through the silt bank to enter the main stream, his trained eye picks up on a glimpse of gold between the tree roots exposed under the bank. "That's gold, I'm sure of it."

Grunting, he bends over to dig into the soft wet clay from the moisture of the creek with his fingers, not able to remember where he left the pick. His judgement is clouded by the blood poisoning that is now rampant throughout his system, leaving large lumps inside the groin and both sides of his neck. As Tim works to dig out the nugget, it grows larger. Finally prying it out of its resting spot, he holds a weighty chunk in his hand that nearly covers his palm. He gives a slight weak smile as he slips the 9-ounce nugget into his wet trouser pocket then turns all his attention towards negotiating the steep slippery bank out of the water. He is positive that he also spotted at least a couple of smaller gram nuggets exposed on top of the soil exiting from a small boulder-strewn gully flushed out from the previous wet season. "The old timers missed this one," he slurs but does not have the strength to inspect the new find further.

With survival the name of the game, Tim tries to put his wandering mind back on task and continues downstream. As the afternoon passes, instinct kicks in and he starts the search for a safe place to camp. The terrain had flattened out on the opposite side of the creek though the mountains still loom to his left as he pushes on, following a cattle pad/ game trail weaving parallel to the creek for another hour and a half. Pausing, Tim thinks he can see a wisp of smoke coming from the top of an escarpment to his left. "There's no one this far out," he says, not sure if his mind is playing tricks on him. Having worked it out roughly earlier in the day while waiting for a fish to enter the trap, he guessed there was at least another three days' hard walk back to his camp, but this was not possible in his condition. Mumbling, "Can't be a bush fire, the grass is too green," the prospector, following his gut instincts, starts to climb the long steep bank on unsteady feet, legs cramping and muscles screaming, burning up the last of his energy and will power, knowing, if he is mistaken, it would be his last roll of the dice.

Back on the bank where Tim had eaten his feed of fish, the three dingoes try to pick up on his scent, with the male dog following his footprints to the waters' edge and standing with ears pricked, its eyes scanning for any hint of their prey on the other side. Looking back at his pair of bitches that are still scouting around aimlessly, the rangy male balked twice at the water's edge, willing himself to take the plunge. Finally, driven forward by hunger, it dives into the creek, making way to the opposite bank, with the bitches following suit. Digging his claws deep into the muddy bank to gain traction, the lead dog shakes his coat dry waiting while the other dogs do the same. Working the area, noses to the ground, they regain the prospector's scent and, picking up pace, follow the cattle pad downstream.

Getting the best part up the escarpment, Tim finds himself tripping over numerous sharp, jagged rocks that become more prevalent the higher he climbs. Falling over frequently as his vision also starts to diminish rapidly, his entire body starts to shut down and he has no strength left in reserve to physically lift his own body weight off the ground. He is positive he can hear a dog barking above the loud ringing in his ears and he continues crawling on his stomach towards it. Finally succumbing to the poison that has riddled his body, he reaches out in desperation to grab a handful of jutting slate feebly trying to pull his body forward with no success, though he is sure he hears a voice way back in his subconscious before blacking out.

The old prospector had just settled down on his outside chair in front of the aged corrugated iron hut to enjoy the oncoming sunset from the high vantage position of his camp. Swearing under his breath, he rises to see what Jonah, his wolfhound ridgeback cross, is barking so vigorously about. "What's up, girl?" he asks, walking towards his best mate standing on the bank's edge watching Tim's last ditched effort to climb onto the plateau. "My god, son, looks like you have been to hell and back," the old timer exclaims, as he grasps Tim's hand. Jonah starts to growl, her ears are laid down and the hair is standing up full length of her back. Mac turns his wrinkled neck to see what has the dog's attention now. After spending many years together, he knew to trust his best mate's perception of trouble. Mac follows the dog's stare and picks up on three dingoes working as a team, scampering up the rise at a faster pace with the scent growing stronger.

"Dammit," he says, knowing there is no time to get this young man safely to the hut before the dingoes arrive. Old Mac makes his way back towards the camp as fast as his spindly old legs will take him and reaches for the loaded double-barrel shotgun resting just inside the corrugated iron door of his hut with shaking hands. He can hear Jonah confront the dingoes below; before he can return armed to the scene, he hears the yelp of his dog as the three dingoes rip into him after putting up a valiant fight to keep them away from Tim. Both bitches latch onto his throat and Jonah goes down hard under the sheer force of the hungry dingoes. The male dog's attention then moves back towards its original prey. Teeth bared, he sinks them deeply into the young prospector's leg, shaking it wildly.

Squinting into the sunset, Mac lets one shot go at both dingoes on Jonah; instantly spinning, he lets the other barrel loose on the single dog attacking the young man. It misses its mark for a kill but is still close enough for the lead male dingo to release its hold of Tim's leg and snarl at Mac, the new intrusion disturbing his meal, before vanishing into the fading light. The dog fight has continued further down the bank from where it started. Both dingoes yelp at the spraying of lead but the shot was too far away to draw blood. The pair of bitches, now without direction, scamper down the steep bank, following their leader into the darkness. Mac drops the shotgun and moves to retrieve Tim. Puffing from the sheer exertion to his emphysema- filled lungs from 45 years of smoking, he is finally able to drag the young prospector inside.

Lighting the kerosene lamp after laying Tim on his mattress, Mac solemnly goes back to retrieve his only mate, that had been by his side for the last six years. Lifting the lamp as high as possible to shed more light on the steep terrain, he makes his way down. Kneeling, he talks softly to his dog as it lets out a soft sigh of content that his master got back in time to say goodbye. Looking Mac in the eyes in the flickering light of the lamp, Jonah lets out a large groan and closes her eyes for the last time. Picking up her limp frame in his arms, Mac struggles to the top of the bank in the dark with the extra weight. Placing the dog's limp frame onto her hessian bed, the tough old prospector's chin quivers and a tear rolls down over the wrinkles on his face. The last time Mac had shed a tear was at the tender age of five when his dog died saving him from a king brown snake in mating season. Composing himself, tough man he is, Mac turns and says aloud to Tim's slumped body on the bed, "You better be bloody worth saving, mate." Mac cuts open his shirt and bandage to reveal a sour-smelling, infested back wound, rife with maggots. "Holy bloody hell," he exclaims, "a low- life back stabbing." The old timer opens his extensive medical kit and works through the night using his bush techniques to save the prospector's life.

Back at the Hatchet River Station access road, the two English backpackers are driving the old beat-up campervan that they had brought in Cairns for $1800, thinking it was an absolute bargain at the time. Maybe it was for bitumen roads but they now find themselves struggling with the steering wheel against the deep bulldust that kept trying to spear them off the dirt track. The bargain vehicle rattles increase dramatically the more corrugations they travel over. "Can't be that much further," says Terri, her long blond hair falling to one side of her face as she plays with the radio, trying to pick up a channel.

"No," replies Suzie, adding, "How exciting to be working on a real life cattle station in Oz. Hope they teach us how to ride a horse." The girls, both in their early 20s, start to giggle.

All the dogs around the station start to bark simultaneously as the girls' vehicle approaches. Scrubber appears from the homestead door and lays his rifle up against one of the veranda rail posts. The girls' van rounds its last corner, coming into Scrubber's line of sight. He immediately dismisses the threat. Price, who also heard the dogs, walks up beside Scrubber. "Who is it?" he asks, puzzled that Scrubber doesn't have a rifle in his hands.

The girls emerge from the van, a wide smile breaks across Price's face. Scrubber quietens down the dogs, his gaze still on the girls walking to the gate. He says to Price, "That's your prize for keeping your mouth shut when the pigs were nosing around, and a birthday present from your cousin."

"Cool," is all Price can get out, barely able to hide his excitement as they both walk towards the gate.

"Hi," the girls say excitedly, "are you the owner?"

"Yes," replies Scrubber with a slim smile, "and this is my foreman, Price. Got a call you were heading out, may as well bring your car in and park it behind that building down there till we get you settled." He points towards the shed.

"Great stuff," reply the girls in their heavy accent. Price opens the gate and the van drives through.

As Price closes it again, Scrubber says, "Right, we need them to clean up that shed proper. Everything on the bench side needs to be well out of reach, give them a hand so it's done before dark."

Price nods and shuffles off quickly behind the settling dust of the van.

Driving slowly, Suzie comments, "Did you see the way that foreman was looking at us? Gave me the creeps."

Terri laughs. "He most probably hasn't been in town for a couple of weeks. Of course he's going to check out these hot bodies." She smiles, motioning her open palms down both sides of her body and grabbing both firm breasts on the way back up, pushing them out to reveal more soft, silky-white skin. "Live a little on the wild side. Can't wait to meet the rest of the cowboys, they want to be a lot better looking than him to even be in with a chance."

"Hmm," answers Suzie, "maybe I should chill some," being the more reserved of the pair. She still feels somewhat uneasy but is not able to put her finger on why.

Price walks around one side of the shed as both back-packers open their car doors. Having never been in charge of giving anyone orders before, he feels out of place. "Girls, we have to clean out the shed."

"What, now?" the girls say in unison. "Where do we put our bags? Where are our rooms? Isn't that a man's job?"

All these questions overwhelm Price. He bows his head and replies, "Be back in a minute." He shuffles off to get Scrubber.

"Some foreman," says Suzie when Price is out of earshot, more doubt forming in her mind.

Both men return and Scrubber says in an authoritative tone, "Righto, girls, this is how it stands. The rest of the station hands are out mustering cattle and will be bringing back two head of cattle to cut up for meat before dark. We need that shed cleaned up and wire rope hung from the rafters to hang the beasts overnight to cure. This is station life," Scrubber continues, "if you can't toe the line, best you leave now." He turns to Price and, with his back to the girls, gives him a wink. He looks back to the backpackers and says, "You in or out?"

Suzie touches her friend's arm. "Come on, let's go" Scrubber, seeing that some doubt had entered their minds, quickly adds, "Tomorrow we will teach you how to ride so you can both help the crew muster."

Terri smiles on hearing this and, throwing her arm over Suzie's shoulders, replies for the both of them. "Let's get to work."

Scrubber walks away towards the homestead pleased with his performance and is met by Max pulling up in the oldest cruiser. "What's going on?" she inquires, curious after seeing the conventional tread pattern left in the dust.

"Not much. Price's girls turned up," Scrubber replies. "You get something for dinner?" Max nods towards the back of the dusty old truck; Scrubber peers in to see ten squatter pigeons all plucked, with every bird a clean head shot.

The girls and Price get stuck into it, cleaning the shed and placing the steel wire cable through the roof beams of the shed. Price measures two lengths of chain that reach to the floor. Cutting them with the oxy, he threads the top chain link through the cable so that it is like a running chain the length of the shed before bolting both ends of cable down. "What are these for?" asks Suzie.

Price, happy that the shed is all but finished, reaches for two D-shackles off the bench, walks up behind Suzie, says, "You ask way too many questions," and grabs a handful of Suzie's firm bum cheeks. Letting out a scream, Suzie spins around and slaps Price's face with all the strength she can muster.

He smiles. Without even blinking an eye, he backhands Suzie and leaves her sprawled out on the ground, unconscious. Moving quickly to one side, blocking Terri's run for freedom, Price picks her up by the waist. She fights valiantly for her size but with Price's brute strength it is no contest. Ripping her top off with his free hand to reveal Terri's breasts, Price remarks, "The hardest part was trying to work out who was going to be first. Looks like it's you're lucky day." He forces her down onto the bare earth of the shed and tears off her short skirt.

A long scream is heard from the open shed. Inside the homestead, Scrubber and Max look at each other and smile. "Looks like the games have started."

Max added, "You can have your turn with them both when I am in the right mood. Could you go grab a couple of extra spuds seeing as we have a few more mouths to feed for a while."

Scrubber grunted, responding, "Well, it better not affect the chores he has to do around here or I will get rid of the pair of them in my own way. When he is finished down there, get him to bury the van."

An hour later, Price emerges from the shed, smiling, then returns with two buckets; one full of water, the other empty with a roll of toilet paper inside. Both girls are huddled in semi-darkness, sobbing, their wrists heavily bound by the chain while also D-shackled. Placing one bucket at either end of the shed, Price is about to walk out when, "Shit, nearly forgot." Moving over to the welder, he starts dragging it behind him towards the backpackers. "I wouldn't look at the flash, it could blind you," he says as he tack welds the thread of all the D-shackles so they cannot be undone. Closing the squeaking old door behind him, the inside of the shed falls into complete darkness.

From a boulder-strewn hill on the downstream side of the homestead, a set of powerful binoculars are focused on Price as he buries the backpackers' van in some deep soft river silt with the backhoe. "In-bred fucking hicks," Ox says to himself, lowering the field glasses. "No wonder we got fucking problems out here."

John's plane lands at the Cairns airport and, wasting no time, exiting the terminal and turning on his phone. He is talking to Meg while he preheats the work truck. "I will need fresh food for a week," rattling of a list as he drives straight through the long-term-parking automated boom gate. He enters the highway, his luggage left abandoned and travelling continuously around the airport carousel. Going through the phone contacts, he rings Jack's home number, anxious to get up to speed on what exactly had happened while he was away.

Sue picks up the phone, answering in a monotone voice then, realising it is John, more emotion comes into her voice; both of her sons had called in to see how their mother was coping after she'd strongly refused the offer stay at either of their places. Both young men agreed that their mum seemed to have aged considerably in the last week. They walk closer to the phone with the noticeable change to her tone. "It's John," she mouths silently. "No new leads from the cops on Jack or how his truck ended up in WA, no prints, no witnesses, no suspects." Sue continues. "Jack left here with your GPS to find Tim's camp; how the bloody hell his truck ended up in WA has got us buggered!" Sue's voice starts to crack so Rob takes the receiver off her, while Rick puts an arm around his mother's deflated shoulders and leads her out of ear shot of the phone and towards the lounge room.

"John, it's Rob. Look, bud, me and my bro want in on anything you are organising to sort out these fucks. Dad did not raise us to take a backward step from anybody and we want blood!"

John replies, "Rob, it's not just one man, it's a very organised syndicate. The station owners are just the front. Don't worry, bud, you will get your chance, but it will be a bloodbath if we go racing in there unprepared. Here is my mobile; text me your number."

Rob hangs up the phone. Walking into the lounge, he nods at his brother's questioning gaze and sits on the other side of his mother. Sue grabs her sons' hands. "Boys, we have lost a friend, a nephew, and now by the looks your father to these animals. I do not want to lose you as well but I am no fool and I know I am not going to be able to stop you. Your father was a proud man and taught the pair of you well to be good bushmen and handle yourself. If you can, bring home some answers, or better still your dad. Here is the number for Ray's two brothers, they are still seething with anger as well." She reaches for a note book full of names and numbers, with half a page of questions for the police, all ending in question marks.

John dials Tim's home number; Danni picks up. "Hi Danni, it's John, any news on Tim?"

Her voice quivers. "No, they run a chopper out there for a couple of days, couldn't find any trace of Tim, not even his camp."

"Yeah," replies John, "it's a big country out there and once that camo net goes over the vehicle, you don't realise it's there till you nearly walk on it. I'm going out for a week to see what I can find. If anyone can pick up where he is, it's me," he says, knowing his prospecting partner's mindset from years of working with him. Danni agrees and the conversation ends as John drives into his yard to be met by Meg. "You get everything?" he asks, walking into the house towards the gun safe.

"Yep," Meg replies, finding it hard to keep up with her husband's pace. "It's all in the truck. You just need to turn the freezer on, it was unplugged." John nods and throws the rifle and packets of 44 shells on the passenger's seat. Warming the truck, he winds down the window and kisses Meg. "Please be careful," she says, more to herself as the 4x4 is already roaring out of the yard and heading west.

The hours roll on as does the truck's odometer. John opens and shuts the gate where Jack was shot; there is no sign or clue left at all of what had occurred. Finally John arrives at where he had dropped off the supplies for Tim, close to two weeks previous. Moving off the track, he weaves the truck through the trees as the sun starts to spray its golden display before setting. Backtracking, John sweeps his exit from the disused old miner's road with a sapling covered in leaves, returns to the truck and unties his swag off the back. "No good looking for tracks in the dark," he says. Crawling into the swag, he is asleep within minutes, which is not surprising considering that he was on the cold, busy, smog-ridden streets of Sydney 12 hours previous, fighting traffic to reach the airport on time.

Back at a local pub in Midtown, Ray's two brothers enter and sit on stools in the main bar. There is a scattering of patrons mingling as Bear (got this nickname from being the size of a mountain and being the slightly larger of the two men) pulls a $100 note from his top pocket. With a deep, powerful voice that seems to originate from within his thick barrel chest, he says, "Stubby of any mid-strength beer." Turning to his brother, he says, "Stu?"

The younger of the brothers, slightly smaller in height but made of the same build replies, "Yeah, rum." The men get into a discussion while the young barmaid serves their drinks.

Bear states, "How the fuck can there be not even one eyewitness left for the goddam trial?"

Stu shrugs his broad shoulders. "One's dead, the other two are missing or dead with no suspects so they have thrown it out of court from the lack of evidence, and still no sign of Ray's body." Lifting the glass of rum to his lips and taking a large mouthful that leaves it half empty, he says to his brother, "We have to take care of this ourselves, like we should have in the first place."

Bear moves the bar stool closer towards his brother's to discuss matters in more detail. "Another round," he directs to the barmaid, placing his empty drink on the bar, as does Stu.

The barmaid returns with fresh drinks just as five footballers come through a door from the gaming lounge, pushing each other, swearing and carrying on. Both brothers turn and give them a quick eye over. On seeing the men's reaction, the alert young barmaid says, "It's Mad Monday pub crawl. All the senior league players take the day off and they hit the grog, going from pub to pub. Looks like we are one of the last stops this year," and rolls her eyes at the brothers. They shrug their shoulders and get back to the conversation at hand.

As Bear lifts the stubby towards his mouth, a large young front rower bumps his shoulder, making the beer spill down the front of his shirt. "Hey, sorry, bud," says the young man in his early twenties, as he breaks into laughter, along with his four team mates.

Bear puts down what is left of his stubby and turns to look into the young footballer's eyes. Half cut from grog, the young bloke does not read the danger in Bear's stare. "Just replace the drink and fuck off to where you just come from and we will leave it at that."

The young bloke, not used to being told what to do, laughs. He looks towards his mates for support and backup if things go wrong; all are egging him on to proceed with the encounter, wanting some entertainment. "How about you buy me a drink and get the fuck out of this pub while you still can?"

Bear, hidden from the footballers' view, looks at his brother with a wide grin from ear to ear. Stu just rolls his eyes as he knows exactly what comes after that grin: pain quickly followed by destruction.

The footballer aims a widow maker at the temple of his adversary. Bear, still seated, had been in more pub brawls than hot dinners in his time. He pre-empted the swing, engulfing the fist with his huge hand and applying a vice- like pressure. Everyone in the pub could hear bones snapping. Standing quickly for a large man, Bear twisted his fist viciously, snapping all the footballer's wrist bones. The footballer screams in pain; the last thing he sees is a large fist smashing his nose to a pulp. He slumps to the floor, out cold.

The other four footballers sober up quickly. "We have no beef with you, mate," one says.

Bear, not even warmed up, wants to vent some more pent-up anger. "Well, one of you want to replace my drink? Your mate can fix you up when he gets out of hospital," he says, hoping like hell they refused.

All in the bar had witnessed the devastating, cold, calculating efficiency of this stranger. One of the young men fumbles in his tight jean pockets for some crunched-up notes. Producing a fistful, he places them on the bar. "Get this man what he wants." The young barmaid already had one in hand, not wanting the job of explaining to the boss how the pub got wrecked on her shift.

Still standing while finishing the drink in two huge gulps, Bear says, "Let's go before we get locked up. Ring me when you're ready to go bush, and keep it to yourself." They leave the pub in separate cars. The barmaid picks up the phone as soon as both brothers are outside and calls for an ambulance.

Dawn's grey light signals the introduction to a new day. John already has his swag rolled and back on the cruiser. Taking a healthy swig out of an orange juice container from the esky, he waits patiently for more sunlight before even attempting to pick up his prospecting partner's tyre tracks. With boots on and a camel pack over his shoulder, he slips the car keys into his pocket. With enough light to work with, first he walks south, his eyes alert for any sign of a vehicle passing. An hour lapsed. Nothing. Deciding to swing out wider and change direction to the north, after twenty minutes of studying the ground, he notices a rock that had been moved out of place, leaving an indentation in the ground where it had originally sat. Taking a slow look around, John says aloud, "Got to think like Tim."

He follows a slate ridge bearing little to no grass and finds a bit of slate that had been loosened by the weight of a fully loaded vehicle and had sliced a small amount of tread from the tyre. Picking it up between his fingers, he sights the path Tim probably took. "You didn't want anyone finding this camp, bud," he says to himself. His stride increases on his way back towards the truck. Now having his prospecting pard's measure, he travels slowly west, pulling up numerous times to get out and relocate the faint tracks.

Three hours later, John pulls into the well-camouflaged, abandoned camp. The crows have gotten into everything that was not in sealed containers, and there is bird shit covering the table. Beside a chair leg is Tim's sate phone, probably knocked off the table by crows squabbling over the one-kilo pack of sugar that had been left on the table. It is now demolished. John picks up the sate phone and tries to turn it on. "Dead flat, that would be right." He moves to the glove box of his truck, retrieves the charging cord and inserts it into the cigarette lighter.

He walks slowly through the camp, trying to pick up on anything out of the usual. Tim's bike, with its camouflaged seat and tank cover, is on its stand under a tree, not far from the covered 4x4. Pulling the cover off the truck, he checks where Tim always stashed his car keys, under a rock that he had placed in front of the passenger's side front tyre. Picking them up, he juggles them in his hand. "Well, mate, you knew you were leaving camp or the truck would not be locked. Your bike is here, the pick and detecting gear is gone so you must have been working within walking distance of the camp."

Leaving the sate phone in the camp was a bit odd, he thinks. It usually sat on Tim's detecting belt. John starts checking through the truck; everything seems to be in place. Slinging the 44 rifle over his shoulder, he spends the rest of the day searching in probable gold areas that Tim could have followed, finding numerous areas where he had been with soil being moved then replaced. After a fruitless afternoon of walking up gullies and across ridges, he arrives back in camp exhausted. He starts a fire from the wood pile beside the old fire place then tears the pull-top lid off a tin of baked beans. Placing it beside a log near the edge of the fire to heat up, he went in search of a green forky stick to lay his bread on for toast, picking up Tim's sate phone, now fully charged, on the way back after reaching for his own so he could ring Meg. Before sitting near the flickering light of the fire, he reaches for an ice-cold middie out of the esky.

The phone call to Meg is brief, just letting her know he is OK and had found the camp. Placing his phone back in its pouch, he reaches for Tim's phone, and turning the power on, goes through his recent call list, scrolling down the many unanswered calls from Danni. One number stands out after the last time he talked to his wife, lasting one minute, 25 seconds. Also a missed and returned call to that same number. He resists the temptation to call to find out who it was, not wanting to alert anyone outside the close circle of friends he can trust.

John dials Tim's home number. Danni can see from caller ID it is an overseas number that sate phones display. Her heart racing, she picks up the receiver excitedly, hoping it is her husband. "Hello, is that you, Tim?"

"No, mate, it's John. I found the camp but no bloody sign of him."

Danni's wishful thinking crashes to reality. "OK, well, that's some good news." Now she sounds a bit deflated.

John continues, "Hey, his sate phone was left at the camp. Do you know anyone on this number?" He reads it out.

"No, not off the top of my head but I will check our refidex. Why?" she asks.

Explaining the call list, he continues, "Are you still good with that chick cop?"

"Yes," replies Danni. "She calls in quite regular to see how I'm going and gives me new updates if there are any."

"Good. If it's no one you know, give the number to her and hopefully she can check out a name along with an address. It's worth a shot; the worst she can say is no." Both agree and the phone call ends.

Over the next four days, John thoroughly scours the surrounding bush with no success. What he does find is Tim's seven-ounce gold stash under the wood pile, which he only picks up on after using most of the timber on his fire. Packing up, disappointed with the result, he says as he gets into the cruiser, "I'll have to get one of Jack's boys to come out with me to pack up and bring all Tim's gear home."

Stu, waiting on the outskirts of Bankston in his 4x4 loaded for the bush, sits tapping the steering wheel to one of his favourite songs being played on the radio. Big brother Bear pulls in behind him, bouncing out of his truck that was similarly loaded, and walks up to the window. "You all good to go, bro?" he asks.

"Yeah," answers Stu. "I told the girlfriend I was going on a fishing trip to the Cape for two weeks. And you?"

"Yeah, I said pretty much the same sort of thing. Follow me out, bro, and put your two-way on channel 12."

Both trucks leave town in the direction of Hatchet River Station. Bear had done some homework on Google Earth in the days before leaving, selecting a small creek about 4km upstream from the homestead to get the trucks well off the road but still within walking distance of the station. He just hopes now that the country is drying up. There would still be some isolated water holes remaining along the creek's winding course where they could set up camp. Water is not essential, with the men carrying enough on their trucks, but more for having a bath or cooling down in the heat of the day. Neither has planned to be there long anyway. They estimated two, maybe three, days for scoping out the station from a distance, one day for the kill, with a further day to dispose of all the bodies and cover their tracks. Then head to the Cape for a couple of days to make their alibi concrete, making sure to get fuel dockets along the way and to be seen at popular tourist points during the trip.

After many hours on the bitumen, along with the same again on the winding dust road, the brothers are getting close to their destination, only talking on channel 12 briefly along the way. "Watch for me on the left after the creek," is all that Bear says as he slows down the truck to find a good spot to exit the road. Wheeling his vehicle into the bush for a good 50 meters or so in low gear to try to avoid staking a tyre, confident the truck is not visible from the road, he walks back to wait for Stu. As the dust from his passing starts to settle on the nearby tree leaves and grass, the other truck comes into sight slowly. Bear points where he had turned off. Stu stops beside him, the bull dust keeps rolling on past the vehicle. "Follow right on top of my tracks, park up behind mine, and we will cover up."

Both men spend a good twenty minutes standing the grass that the trucks had flattened back up. Satisfied, they walked back towards the 4x4s, talking as they went. "I reckon we check out if there is any water holes for a bogie in the arvos, then set up about three to four hundred meters away. Camps beside water are too easy to pick up on by air or by foot."

Stu nods in agreement, saying, "Yeah, best we play it safe. We don't want anything coming back on us down the track."

Moving off once again, they drive slowly in the long grass up the creek till they find a spot to their liking. They set up a very basic camp, wanting to be able to pack up quickly and get out of the area once the job is done. They'd opted not to use an open fire but cook on a portable gas stove so there was no trace that anybody had even camped there. Sitting down in their outdoor chairs, they start going over the plan for tomorrow while feeding shells into the magazines of their rifles.

Neither of brothers has a clue that Ox is only seven kilometres away from them, the veteran hit man being camped three kilometres on the downstream side of the homestead below a large water hole. Having just finished cleaning his rifle, Ox leans it against the car door for tomorrow's sweep, muttering, "Another week and a half of babysitting these halfwits, just need to get this run done and get the hell out of here. There're no cops watching this joint." He is satisfied with his perimeter sweeps around the station but as always, does what C asks him to do down to the letter. Throwing a steak on the compact BBQ plate, he lowers into the chair beside the fire with tongs in hand and waits to turn his steak as it sizzles away.

Ox is up early, finishing a hearty breakfast of bacon as well as a tin of spaghetti for a change. After washing off the plastic plate, he fills his water bladder from a container, adds some tinned fruit into a backpack the finally slips the 308 rifle over his shoulder. He leaves on what is now a regular perimeter search of the Hatchet River homestead. The hit man follows his now well-worn track along a cattle pad that had been cut deep into the edge of the bank beside the river by passing stock, with a steep bank falling down to the edge of a large, deep water hole. Walking upstream, he spots a few large barramundi swimming around lazily near the surface amongst some tree branches protruding from the river's edge. He is not aware at all that his daily routine has also attracted the attention of a five-meter saltwater crocodile that has followed him nearly the full kilometre of the hole every morning with just a slight ripple giving away its position.

The brothers wake late, with dawn left way behind and the sun starting its steep climb. "Shit a brick," says Stu, rolling out of his swag. Neither men had a great deal of sleep, with mossies swarming over them from midnight onwards.

Bear rolled out with gritty eyes from the lack of deep sleep. "Did you bring any repellent with ya, bro?"

"Yeah, it's in my glove box, mate. These little pricks must be thick in this long, green grass," replies Stu, who is lighting the gas stove for a quick coffee as they get their gear organised for a day of surveillance. Bear grunts in response, ties a knot on his boots then walks over to his truck, picking up the cheap GPS he had bought a week before off the passenger's seat. Not having had much to do with a GPS previously, he had spent a few hours with the manual before heading bush learning the basics. Switching it on, Bear waits for the satellites to lock on before plotting in the camp's position then he places a set of high-powered binoculars over his thick neck and reaches for the 223 rifle along with the backpack. "You ready? It's about a 4km walk from here."

Stu, finishing his coffee, nods and picks up his old but very accurate 303 rifle as they walk out of camp on their first mission.

After over an hour's stiff walk, they come to the crest of a ridge and find themselves looking down on the station. It is anything but a hive of activity. Bear hands his brother the binoculars as the scope on his 223 is well up to the job. Not realising that Ox had passed them half an hour before in his circuit of the station, they both watch as Price enters the shed with a bucket in each hand. They are not quite sure if they heard a female scream or not given the distance they are away from the homestead. The brothers gave each other a questioning look. "What was that, you reckon?" Stu asks.

"Sounded like a girl screaming to me, coming from the shed that bloke walked into," Bear replies, lifting his scope back up to train it on the old building. Price swings shut the shed door and makes his way back towards the pair of vehicles parked out the front of the homestead, not having the faintest clue that he is squarely in the cross hairs of the 223. "I could take him out right now," Bear mutters, moving the rifle barrel slowly and evenly, keeping his target in the kill zone.

"Do you know how many we are up against?" Stu asks.

"Going off what I have read and heard in the media, there are three of them, not sure if they have any station hands though," says Bear, setting down his firearm while adjusting his hat. A bead of sweat forms on the big man's forehead as the heat of the day increases.

Rising off the ground, they make their way back towards the tree line, seeking out a shady spot to have some food after scrambling out of camp late and missing out on breakfast. In between mouthfuls, Stu comments, "It wasn't that Scrubber fella, he looked too young."

His brother agrees, adding, "Yeah, we will have to spend the rest of the arvo working out how many there are," as he finishes off tucking into a cold tin of baked beans. Discarding the empty can, they move back into position.

On the opposite side of the homestead, higher up again than the brothers, Ox sits down in the same spot as he has done now for weeks, sweat running out of the pores in his skin freely. He turns into the breeze that has now picked up, cooling down his body temperature almost immediately. He sucks on the camel pack tube to quench his thirst. With the first mouthfuls being hot water, Ox swills it around with his tongue to break down the built-up saliva and spits it onto the ground then takes a few large swigs of cool water.

Down at the station, Price climbs into the old truck and heads off to collect a load of firewood for the donkey. This consists of a 44-gallon drum lying on its side and copper piping leading into the top of the drum for cool water to enter whilst the hot water exited from the bottom tubing when the shower tap was turned on, all being heated by a fire underneath. Having not showered since the arrival of his two female guests, Price says to himself, "The girls will be happy to see me tonight, freshly showered and all," smiling while he drives out of the station gates.

Ox, noticing some activity below, lifts his field glasses to take a better look at what is going on. Sweeping the glasses along to focus on the truck's movements, a reflection from a ridge on the opposite side of the homestead catches his eye. Moving his high-powered army-issue binoculars straight back to the spot he had seen the flash, Ox adjusts the glasses to focus clearly on the two brothers lying in between some dying clumps of grass. "Well, I'll be fucked," he says aloud then spends the next half an hour scanning for any more intruders, but only coming up with the two men. He notices they are both armed. "Well, they're not here for a friendly visit." Moving backwards in a commando crawl as a precaution, he lifts himself off the ground only after getting a safe distance from the edge. Not taking anything for granted, he decides to return the 3 km back to his vehicle to retrieve what he aptly calls the peace-maker backpack. It is filled with different rifle scopes, silencers, hand guns and various knives, all tools of his grizzly trade. Moving quickly back through the bush towards his camp, he is happy to finally have an adversary to contend with.

An hour had lapsed before Ox arrives back overlooking the homestead, now fully equipped for any situation. Lifting the glasses quickly, he sweeps over to where the men had been earlier, disappointed to come up empty-handed. Swearing under his breath, he unzips the backpack and places a large bladed combat knife onto the belt that rests snugly around both hips, and slips a smaller sticker knife into a blade pouch stitched onto the middle of the belt that was positioned in the centre of his back, out of sight from any opponent. Zipping up the bag, the hit man stealthy makes his way towards where he last saw the men, arriving 45 minutes later at the spot where the brothers had laid. Working backwards from that point, slowly observing every detail including their empty lunch tins, Ox picks up on their tracks slowly, following them until the footprints entered onto a game trail that led towards the east, making it easier to pursue the men. The hit man increases the pace.

Bear and Stu return to camp both hot and sweaty, and move the table into a shady spot to get out of the glaring afternoon sun. Before sitting down, Stu reaches into the esky and pulls out two icy cold tins of beer and slings the rifle off his shoulder and places it in the front seat of his truck. He passes Bear a cold can. "Thanks bro. Hey, while you're up, just throw mine in too," he says, passing Stu his firearm. "Thanks, bud." The first two beers don't touch the sides. They sit hardly speaking, enjoying the cold amber fluid. Taking off his boots and slipping into his well-worn rubber thongs, Bear stands up. "What do you want for dinner?" He starts to run through all the different selections and cuts of meat.

"Snags with spuds will do me," Stu replies.

His brother sorts through the bush freezer to locate the snags and places them on the truck tray to thaw in the afternoon sun. "I'm going down for a bogie in the creek," says Bear. "If you got nothing better to do, some spuds need peeling." He walks out of camp with a towel over his shoulder and a fresh change of clothes under his arm. Stu just grunts his reply.

Five minutes later he sits back down with two pots, one full of water, the other full of spuds. Pulling his razor sharp pig hunting knife from the sheath on his hip, he starts the chore, pulling up every now and again for a swig of beer.

Ox notices the brothers' white 4x4 bonnet through the tree line and stealthy moves closer. He sits on his haunches just below chest height of the guinea grass to study the area in detail. Only finding one of the men in camp, he changes plans quickly. Taking off the backpack, he slowly unzips it. Producing a large silencer, he screws it onto the end of the 308 barrel, not wanting to alert the other man of his pres-ence, wherever he is. Ox raises his rifle, the large man directly in his sights. Stu, not scared of any animal or man he has ever come across, is absolutely petrified of spiders. While sitting peeling the potatoes, a large huntsman spider runs up the inside of his trouser leg. Stu stands abruptly just as Ox squeezes the trigger. He knows instantly it is not the head shot he had planned for.

Stu staggers back from the impact of the shot and looks down to see his intestines pushing out of the large hole in his stomach. Instinctively upending the table for cover, he dives towards the ground to retrieve his knife. He knows he would not make it to the rifles in the car without being an open target.

"Fuck it," Ox curses, losing sight of his mark behind the camp table. Dropping the 308, he swiftly covers the short distance with knife in hand and rounds the table where Stu is lying, motionless. "Might have got a heart shot," he mused, walking closer.

Stu lashes out with his legs, with surprising speed for such a large man. The move catches Ox off guard, he falls heavily as his legs are taken out from underneath him by what felt like tree trunks. Rolling in nearly the same movement, Stu, with knife in hand, slashes it down his opponent's side, making a deep gash in between the rib cage. Ox rolls too, realising this man is no slouch in the art of combat. The blade just misses him the second time around, and buries into the earth up to its hilt. Regaining his feet swiftly, Ox stomps on the huge hand holding the knife handle repeatedly until it finally releases its grip, followed up by a precision kick aimed viciously square onto Stu's jaw with his steel-capped boots as he tries to rise off the ground. Having inflicted that exact move on many opponents before, Ox cannot remember one that had not been knocked out or sometimes even killed. Stu just shakes his head and rises to his feet minus a few front teeth, which he spits onto the ground, with blood and intestines oozing from the gunshot wound.

Realising his strength is dwindling, Stu charges like a wounded bull, one punch splitting the hit man's cheek bone, spraying blood over his face. The nimble-footed Ox stands to one side with perfect timing and in a fluid motion reaches for his sticking blade in its back pouch and thrusts it full force into Stu's neck, severing the jugular artery. With an astonished look on his face, Stu tries to contain the swift flow of blood with his hands, eventually collapsing to his knees.

Bear walks into camp shocked at the first thing he sees, his brother kneeling on the ground with a knife sticking out of his neck. "What the fuck," he booms, dropping his clothes and sprinting towards the car for the rifles. Spinning around, Ox does the same, diving headlong into the long grass as Bear's 223 booms, nicking his shoulder. Locating his rifle, he raises the 308. Not having enough time to look through scope but having had many years in which to hone his skills, he lets a cluster of lead go. Bear is hit in the chest, including two piercing his heart, and slumps over the bonnet, slowly sliding down unceremoniously to land on the ground with the top end of his torso nearly torn in half.

Tim groans and tries to get up. Feeling instantly weak and light headed, he opts to lie back down until his vision clears. He looks around, and has absolutely no idea where he is or how long he has been here but he feels the bandage wrapped tightly around his chest restricting movement. Old Mac walks in with a couple of skinned rabbits and places them on an old timber slab table. "So you made it back, young fella. Didn't think you would a couple of times there." He fills a large camp oven with some water over an old sink that is fed from a natural soak, giving the old timer a year-round water supply. "Rabbit stew sound good, young fella? You got to be hungry, haven't eaten in over a week."

Tim replies, "Yeah, I am. The name's Tim." He tries to sit up again, successfully this time, and swings his legs over the edge of the old mattress to place his feet on the uneven slate floor. He looks down to see his calf is bandaged as well. With memories starting to come back to him, he says, "So you saved my sorry arse?"

Mac's voice lowers. "Yep, that I did, and I lost a bloody good dog over it too." Placing the rabbits and spuds that grow wild out behind the hut, and adding a liberal dose of mixed herbs from a jar into the camp oven, he says, "So, who are you, son? Where do you come from? What is your business out in this remote country?" Things Mac had wanted to ask for over a week now, wanting to know if he had wasted his time saving a deadbeat or someone worth- while. Mac knew one thing for sure, he had neared on emptied the medical kit.

"Hey, whoa up, old timer, I will fill you in. What's your name?" Tim asks.

"The name's Mac. Hang on, got to get this stew on the heat," Mac says, placing the lid of the camp oven back on before walking outside to position it beside the coals. He comes back quickly to sit at the table. "Righto, let's hear it."

Tim begins and from that moment on, they quickly form a solid friendship, only stopping conversation to grab the camp oven off the fire and eat the stew with yesterday's damper. They talk well into the night.

The next morning, having slept soundly overnight, the battle-worn prospector wakes and walks steadily outside the walls of Mac's corrugated iron hut for the first time. He takes in the awesome view, looking over the countless winding gullies and creeks with the Hatchet River barely visible on the horizon.

Mac is sitting on a chair beside a makeshift cross with recently turned soil, talking to himself. Tim, feeling way stronger after last night's dinner, turns back to the hut and gets a chair. Carrying it, he sits beside Mac. The old timer nods, "Been thinking of what you told me last night. I reckon you're better off letting them think that you are dead." Tim agrees. "Oh, and by the way, this was in your pocket when I had to strip you down to try and slow the fever." He passes over a near-on solid nugget with a touch of buck quartz stuck to one end.

Tim laughs. "Mac, I thought nothing was real at that point."

Spending quality time with Mac, their friendship grows as does Tim's strength. As the days pass by, they find they both have a lot in common as prospectors despite the huge age difference. Having a clear head, with the wounds well on the way to healing, Tim has time on his hands to think things through properly for the first time. He thinks back to the police captain going off his head because a chopper flew too low and blew away all the evidence of tracks. "Hey Mac, I reckon he had it in for me ever since I got in his chopper at the search, and I bet my bottom dollar that's the reason he nominated us to do that sandstone run past them gates in his chopper. It wasn't to keep clear of the other search choppers; it was so he could mark that area off the search grid as being completed. The cunning prick was protecting his asset. Least now I know the general area he seemed most interested in, he hovered around one particular area. The cops didn't stand a chance from the start; he has been in this up to the hilt from dot one."

Realising he had been well played, Tim starts forming a plan. The more he thinks about it, the more detailed and clearer it becomes. The old timer picks up that he is getting itchy feet. "Come over here, son," he says, standing beside the door of the hut, "see that calendar marked off on the wall?" pointing at it with a gnarly old finger.

"Yeah."

Mac continues. "Well, that is when the chopper is due in with my next load of supplies, comes in every three months." The chopper drop was organised by his daughter, who ran around gathering everything on a list, from tinned food to soap, and placed it all on a pallet. When his list was complete, the pallet was covered with shrink wrap, which is a heavy plastic that holds it all in place tightly, and driven to a hanger in the general aviation section of the airport. It was then strapped up by the ground crew ready to swing under a heavy cargo lift chopper from Cairns, all paid for by Mac's gold finds.

Mac continues. "Well, he would have room to take you out of here, but like I said before, reckon you will achieve a lot more with people thinking you are dead."

In agreement with the old prospector, Tim asks, "You got a pen and paper? Where exactly are we?"

Mac smiles, takes a few steps and slides open an old drawer to produce a crinkled old map. He places it on the table. "We are here," he says, pointing on the map. "There are no roads, no tracks, nothing leading to here. It's a three- day walk if you're fit and know where you are going, otherwise it's by chopper."

Tim replies, "Yeah, I'm used to no tracks," and studies the map intently before putting pen to paper in earnest.

Two days go by and it is the morning the chopper is due in, both men are up early. Over coffee Tim passes Mac an envelope. "Could you get your daughter to forward this on for me?"

"Sure," is the reply. "Guess I won't need any dog biscuits on the next order," Mac says, drawing a line through his list. He had started the list months ago, jotting down stuff he needs when it came to mind. Finishing off with a short note to his daughter, he places it in the envelope balancing on his lap.

Tim says, "Look, Mac, I am very sorry about your dog, mate. She saved my life, no doubt."

The old prospector's eyes glaze over, the memory still raw. "Yes, that she did." Getting up, Mac walks into the hut to change the subject and places both letters on the table. "I've got something to show you." Tim walks in behind him over to a corner covered in cobwebs from the harmless Daddy-long-legs spiders. Raising the lid of an old steel chest, he grunts as he lifts a huge specimen covered in thick veins of pure gold.

"You're kidding me," Tim exclaims, taking the rock out of Mac's hands and feeling the weight. "There's got to be 20 ounces in this at least."

"Yeah." The old timer smiles. "Found myself a good reef over the hill, probably pulled out about half a million's worth so far, but I get knocked up quick these days because the reef is dipping deeper into the hill. Don't know what I am going to do with it all, having everything a man wants here, I am content with my life exactly how it is. Probably give it to my daughter, she runs round for me without question." Placing the specimen back in the large box, which was nearly full to the top with other samples, all varying in size, the old prospector finishes off with, "Tell you what, son. You go finish what you need to do then come back and we will work it together, 50/50 split." Before shutting its lid, Mac reaches into the corner of the box and passes Tim a Glock handgun and two boxes of shells. "Reckon you will need this before I do."

Both men hear the choppers approach well before it comes into sight. Tim ducks out of view as the machine hovers and lowers its load down slowly till the pallet touches the ground. Flicking a quick hitch switch, the cable releases from the chopper, he then does a tight circuit before landing in a cloud of dust. Mac walks over with the cable rolled up, holding both letters in hand, to talk briefly with the young man who had now done a few runs out for him. Not even stopping its engine, he powers up as soon as the old prospector is at a safe distance away from the chopper. Mac knows it would not be long now before someone came to pick up his new found friend.

Back in town, the female detective who had taken Tim's statement arrives out the front of Danni's house. They had become quite close since he had gone missing. Some things in this case did not add up as far as she was concerned after spending considerable time researching the station owners, and she has not totally ruled out help from someone within the department. Having thought long and hard after Danni's call about the phone number, Grace is still fighting her conscience as she knocks on the door. It swings open. Danni smiles weakly. "Hi Grace, I saw you pull up. Want to come in for a cuppa?"

The detective declines and reaches into her top pocket to produce a folded piece of paper. "Not today thanks, Danni. I have a fair bit happening back at the station. Here is that name and address you asked for but it didn't come from me."

"No, of course not," Danni replies.

The detective turns, saying, "I will call in if we can find any new leads on what happened to Tim." They walk a short distance to the unmarked police car. "Whatever you do with that," she says, nodding to the bit of paper, "think about it carefully. You have lost far too many loved ones already."

Coming into mobile service areas intermittently on the way home, John receives a text message from Danni with a name and address. "Shit," he says, "I was over that way fishing years ago. I'm over half way there." Slowing down he turns the 4x4 around and pushes the sub tank button on the dash, confident there is enough fuel to get him to there and back. He opts to pull off the road for a camp, not wanting to arrive there in darkness. Waking up in the driver's seat in the morning, he continues on, crossing the last grid and entering into a 20-acre property overlooking the ocean at 7am. John notices the house is well kept, the lawn green with huge shade trees that had been planted strategically long ago. Exiting his truck out the front, he starts to move towards the steps.

"Oi" sounds out from beside the house. Looking around, John changes direction and makes his way to the chopper parked a good 30 meters to the side of the building. There are a few drums of avgas close to the machine, one with a pump that is being used by a fit looking man in his mid-thirties, at a guess.

"How's it going, mate? What can I do for you?"

John replies, "You Chris?"

The man stops pumping fuel into the chopper. "Yeah, that's me. Who are you?"

"I'm Tim's prospecting partner."

Chris looks over at John as he starts to twist the gold and sapphire ring on his finger. "Yeah, right. How's he doing?"

John stares intently at Chris, who has gone back to winding the pump. "Not real good. He has been missing for over two weeks."

Chris tries to show some concern. "Shit, that's no good. He might be digging out a gold reef and keeping it quiet." With his chopper now full, Chris replaces the fuel cap hanging up the fuel hose. John says, "Well, he talked to you last. What was that all about?"

Though taken by surprise that this bloke would actually know that, Chris comes up with a reply almost instantly. "Yeah, he gave me his number when we were looking for that missing prospector, had a few days with not much on so I gave him a call. No answer. So he rung me back, must have seen the missed call. We were organising a prospecting run in the chopper but he never got back to me." John thought to himself that don't sound like Tim, he would jump through hoops to prospect out of a chopper. Chris adds "Hey I haven't got much on today, we could go for a run in the chopper to have a look around for Tim. Do you know roughly an area you would like to check out?"

"Sounds good," replies John. "Yeah, I have a few areas in mind. I haven't got much cash on me though, what's it going to cost for the hire?"

Chris replies, "Let's not worry about that now. How about we just try and find him first it will only be the cost of avgas anyway, just got to duck in and grab the chopper keys" as he walked towards the house.

While waiting, John opens the passenger's door of the chopper and notices Tim's GPS lying on the floor, wedged between the seat and the door. Glancing over to the pilot's dashboard, he sees the keys sticking out of the ignition. His mind races. So what the hell has he gone inside to get? With the penny dropping, John looks at the distance between himself and the safety of his truck with the 44 rifle inside. Not waiting to see what Chris has in store for him and being unarmed out in the middle of the bush, he decides to make a sprint for the vehicle.

Inside the house, C is swearing. "Why they cannot just leave fucking things alone beats me." He walks into his bedroom and takes from a drawer a 357 Magnum, jams it into the back of his jeans and conceals the butt with his tee shirt. "Could have taken out the prime minister of the country with fewer bloody problems than this."

Walking back through the house, he hears John's truck roar off. "What the-?" is all C says as he runs out the front and pulls up beside his chopper. He'd figured everything was going well up until this point. What the hell that was all about? He notices that the passenger's door on his chopper is ajar. Walking around to close it, he sees Tim's GPS as he swings the door out further to shut it firmly. "Fuck me dead," C voices loudly as he picks up the GPS. Holding it in his grasp, he looks up the road as the dust of the 4x4 starts to settle, quickly calculating what damage could be done with the prospector's findings.

John is doing the same, pushing his accelerator flat to the floor, changing through all gears, drifting sideways around corners and narrowly missing a couple of roos that decided at the last minute to dice with death. "So that's why I couldn't find you, bud. You had left in the bloody chopper." It all starts to fall into place. "So that's why the bike was left at camp and that's why the truck was locked." Thinking aloud, he puts good distance between him and the enemy. "Right, now I know the head of the snake. Best I catch up with Jack's boys as promised." He is dirty with himself for not taking Tim's GPS in the heat of the moment.

John arrives home. Unlocking the front gate, he drives towards the back of their acre block and pulls up beside the shed to be met by Meg half way from the house. "I've been worried about you being out bush by yourself." She gives him a meaningful hug.

"Yeah, babe, well worth the trip. Had a breakthrough finally." Walking towards the office in search of his business credit cards, he shuffles though the mountains of paperwork on his desk, with the majority of them bills.

Meg is not far behind him. She pokes her head through the door, saying, "This has consumed you fully. There is one letter that arrived in the mail today that was not a bill." Meg is concerned that what was a successful business four weeks ago had now fallen to the wayside.

Nodding to Meg in acknowledgement, he continues the search for the cards, muttering, "I know I put them here somewhere." He slumps into his office chair.

Meg walks into the office to stand beside him, placing her arm over his shoulder. "Just slow down, babe. You're rushing things." Seeing the letter lying on the carpet beside a chair leg, she says, "That's the letter I told you about," bending to pick up the envelope and placing it in front of him.

"Yeah, maybe later. I have shit happening. Got to get a hold of Jack's boys," John says, reaching for the mobile phone clipped on his hip.

Meg replies, "OK, will go sort out something for dinner," kissing him on the cheek.

"For fuck's sake." As the number he had dialled goes to message bank, he slams his mobile phone on the desk top in frustration beside the envelope Meg had placed in front of him. Tearing it open, he reads the first sentence then stands bolt upright with the chair flipping over from the quick movement. John's hands start to tremble as he reads on. Looking up, he walks over to the door and locks it. A grin from ear to ear forms across John's face as he reads on. Placing Tim's letter on the desk along with a mud map on where he was located, John studies the many maps covering his office wall. Finding a particular one, he tears it from the wall. His eyes scan the river bends then follow a creek that joins the Hatchet River, moving up with his pointer finger, he finds some unusual creek bends on the mud map. "Game on," says John to himself as he reads and re-reads the letter then stashes it in his top pocket.

Unlocking the door silently, he makes his way to the safe in their bedroom. Punching in a 5-number combination, John pulls out a layer of $50 notes all banded in thousand dollar lots that Meg had been putting aside the last 18 months for a cruise. "Sorry, babe," he says, stashing it all into his short pockets. Composing himself before lying to his wife, he walks through the house into the kitchen. "Got to go for a couple of days," complying with Tim's letter not to tell anyone he is alive, "then I will be home for good, I promise," he says, giving her a quick goodbye hug.

Meg turns and looks her husband directly in the eye. "You come back to me safe," she says, knowing that look in his eye after 25 years of marriage.

He assures her, "Yeah babe, it's all good. See you in a couple of days."

John walks with purpose up towards the shed. Parked alongside the wall is a 4X4 trailer; he drags it over to the tow ball of the truck with ease. Placing down some loading ramps, he starts the 300cc quad bike, reverses it out of the shed, lines up both ramps and rides it onto the trailer then straps it down tight. Leaving the house, he buzzes around town, splashing cash as he goes through the extensive supply list Tim had obviously spent considerable time working it out in detail.

Wheeling into the servo last, he fills up the truck and 3x10 litre plastic fuel containers with petrol, the last thing on the list. With a tip truck hogging the only diesel bowser, he reaches for the topographical map he had taken off the office wall. Working out both latitude and longitude, he enters the coordinates into the GPS he had just purchased then zooms the screen in to find the nearest dirt track to his destination. With the bowser now free, John finishes off the last task, reflecting on the way out of town, and also agreeing with Tim's letter, that it is best for our loved ones to know nothing of what is about to happen. Revenge in the local manner!

Getting as close as possible, according to his GPS, he follows a sketchy old gold-drilling exploration track from the early 80s. He approaches some badly washed-out gullies that cannot be negotiated towing the trailer. Deciding to unload, he burns a small area, putting it out swiftly with a wet hessian sack, then drives his truck and trailer onto the burnt area and unloads the quad. Placing a few goods into a sack and tying off the neck of it with rope, he piles it onto the back rack of his quad and secures it with bungie cords, adding one of the 10 litre fuel containers at the same time. He throws his swag on the front rack and ties it down the same way. With the GPS in hand, he fires the quad into life and is on his way.

John slips the GPS into his shirt pocket; once having the general direction sorted out, he starts to read the country on the best ridges and saddles to follow, climbing and bashing through the rough country until near on dark. Throwing his swag off the quad and unrolling it, John does not even bother with lighting a fire or eating anything. While trying to fall asleep, he starts to second guess what his prospecting partner has in mind with the list. He sleeps restlessly all night, anxious for the next day to begin.

Having a crap night's sleep, John wakes on the first chorus of birds and, with gritty eyes, rolls up the swag, ties it to the front of the quad and gets back on his way.

In mid-afternoon, Mac picks up on the faint sound of a motor while sitting in his chair overlooking the whole basin. He nods to himself as Tim walks to his side. "I'm guessing it's your mate coming to collect you, son. By the sounds of it, he will be here within the hour."

Tim smiles. "Yep, that will be him for sure," as he looks into the distance, trying to pick up on John's current whereabouts. Striping off some branches from a nearby sapling, he throws them onto the coals in the fireplace. They start to smoulder, sending a trail of smoke into the air so John can spot the exact location of Mac's camp.

With the quad motor labouring and tyres spinning trying to gain traction up the last steep incline, he finally appears over the rise with both front wheels off the ground. His boot on the rear brake lever brings them down to earth instantly. Turning the quad off, John places one foot on the ground and is swinging his other leg over the seat when Tim starts, "What took ya so long? Some bush tracker you turned out to be, got to send you a letter along with a bloody map to get your attention!"

John, smirking, replies quickly, "Go away for two weeks and as soon as my back's turned, you get god dammed lost. Can't hold your hand all the time." Both men break into laughter and give each other a slap on the shoulder and a strong handshake. John says, "Well, can't be that shabby. Here's your gold stash," reaching into his pocket to place a plastic zip seal bag containing seven ounces of gold in Tim's hand.

The old timer, smiling at the bond of mateship between the young men, walks forward with his hand out. "Call me Mac," he says and shakes John's hand.

"Hi Mac, thanks for taking his sorry arse in."

Picking up on the humour, Mac replies, "I did not really have much choice in the matter. He made quite an entrance," smiling at Tim.

"It's time to celebrate," says John, producing a 40-ounce bottle of rum from the middle of his swag that prevented it from getting smashed on the rough ride in. "And hang on, there's more." He unties the neck of the sack to retrieve 2x 2liter plastic bottles of hot cola.

Tim laughs. "Thanks, bro. I've forgotten what that tastes like." Mac shrugs his shoulders, thinking haven't had a drop in at least 10 years as they all walk the short distance to the hut.

The three men sit inside around the old timber table. With only two chairs in the camp, Tim swings an end of his bed across as Mac opens the rum bottle, squishing its lid with his old but still powerful fingers from many years of holding a pick handle. Throwing it over his shoulder, he says, "Well, it's got to be drunk now" and the rum is poured freely. The conversation comes round quickly onto what had occurred with Chris the chopper pilot. Tim stands, lifting his shirt to reveal the back wound that had started to heal, the infection now gone leaving a gaping hole that you could fit your thumb in without touching the sides. John recounts his trip to question Chris and finding the GPS inside the chopper.

"It's him, bro. He's boss hog, I'm sure of it now," says Tim.

"Yeah, I agree, mate," replies John. "Both Jack's boys are ready to roll on a phone call," John says.

"Yeah, and Jack will be keen as mustard too, I would reckon" added Tim.

His prospecting mate's head bends down towards the ground at the last comment. "I'm sure he would be in boots and all, but Jack hasn't been seen since he went to look for you, mate." Raising his gaze, he sees Tim has confusion written over his face.

"What do you mean? Is he dead?" Anger rises in his voice, sobering him up immediately. John fills them both in on what he knows, ending the story with his truck being found in the outback of Western Australia, with not a sign of Jack. "They're going down, the fucking lot of them," Tim spits out with venom. Standing while finishing his rum in one gulp, he walks outside towards the fire to have a minute or two alone, shaking in anger.

Mac lifts off his seat to follow the young man outside to console him, John lays a hand on the old timer's shoulder. "Just let him be for a bit." Mac nods and sits back down. The conversation changes to gold prospecting as the pair talk idly, swapping experiences while waiting for Tim to return.

Entering the hut 15 minutes later with a determined look on his face, Tim explains, "Well, this is the plan I had in mind." The night flies by. With extensive input from all three men, they finish off in the early hours of the morning. Tim lifts his bed back into place. "Got to get some shut eye, the pace is going to pick up from tomorrow on."

John flicks his lighter randomly in the dark, stumbling over rocks towards the quad to retrieve his swag and drag it over to some even ground closer to the hut that was not littered with protruding slate. Slipping into the swag, he hears the snoring that has started emerging from the hut. It is nothing short of a jet plane taking off. "Great," he says aloud. "Forgot the goddam gum." Rolling onto his side and placing half the pillow over his head, he falls into a deep sleep himself soon enough.

Old Mac is up before dawn as usual, even though he has only three hours of sleep under his belt, fumbling in the dark around a huge firewood pile that Tim had stacked to find some smaller timber to nourish the dying coals. The old timer waves his hat over the newly placed twigs, trying to reignite the fire for a hot coffee. Hearing the movement not far from his swag, John ducks his head out from the canvas cover that resembles a cocoon. Feeling the cool on his cheeks, he decides to wait in his warm bed until the water is hot. Tim emerges from the hut, rubbing his hands together in the early morning cool. "Hey, Mac."

The old timer puts his finger to his lips, "Shhh," and points to John's swag.

Looking at the green canvas laid out on the dirt, Tim raises his voice, "He's been in the bloody big smoke two weeks doing bugger-all, best he gets back into bush time instead of playing doggo."

A voice comes from the swag. "Don't want to hear your voice till at least I finish my first coffee." Over morning coffee, the mood is sombre as all three men come to the reality of what is in front of them after discussing last night's plans. Finishing the last mouthful of hot liquid in the tin pannikin, John stands. "Best I roll my swag and fuel up the quad," leaving the other men to talk in private.

Mac starts. "Son, my offer still stands on the gold. If I was 20 years younger, I would be coming with you pair."

Tim looks at his old mate and places a hand on his shoulder. "You're a good man, Mac. Don't worry, you haven't seen the last of me yet," then rises to find his boots, the handgun, and the boxes of shells.

The quad fires into life. While it is warming up, they say their good byes to the old prospector. He watches themdrop over the steep bank, following the tracks back the way John had come yesterday.

With two of them on the quad, their outbound journey is more difficult and Tim has to bail off on numerous steep pinches and walk up. Just before dark, the men reach the vehicle, and stretch out, their muscles stiff from riding all day. Tim says, "We will have to leave the quad and trailer stashed in the bush here and come back for them later. The trailer will just slow us down, there's no way it will get where we are going."

John replies, "No worries," as he rides the quad onto the trailer then steps off to pull both tie downs taut holding it in position. "Give us a hand, will ya?" he says, as the extra 265kg now sitting on the trailer makes it awkward for one person to lift from the tow bar. After unstrapping their gear off the quad's carry racks and loading it into the back of the truck, the prospectors leave the area, with the beam from the spotlights cutting through the darkness.

Ox finally makes it back to his camp after dark had fallen, having left the brothers' bloody corpses four hours earlier. He has been bruised, beaten, stabbed and shot; overall, he is not in a good way with one eye now fully closed, blood continued to seep through his shirt from the knife wound in his ribcage and a deep gash on his cheek bone that is also oozing blood. There is no way in hell he would have found his way back in the dark without the aid of a head lamp he'd found at the brothers' camp.

Laying down the 308 and backpack, Ox reaches for his car keys stashed on the spare tyre and unlocks the doors. He scours around for his especially made-up first aid kit, locates it and a bottle of whiskey. Leaning up against the truck body for support, he takes a few large swigs out of the bottle, wincing as the raw alcohol slides down his throat. The injured hit man takes another couple of mouthfuls of spirits before placing the bottle down. Ox gingerly moves a couple of steps to the driver's side door and swings it open to switch on the lights of the truck. He strips off his shirt under the headlights to reveal his two torso wounds. Inspecting the bullet graze, he dismisses it with not much concern, other than a chance of infection.

Going through the medical kit in front of the car lights and finding what is needed, Ox pours some whiskey on the deep, nasty rib wound. Not having any body fat on his lean muscular build, he has to pinch the skin together, which adds to the blood flow from the wound inflicted by the thick-bladed pig hunting knife. Forcing the suture needle through his flesh, Ox starts stitching himself up proficiently, placing an adhesive wound dressing over the stitches when he has finished.

Making his way back to the truck cab, again needle in hand, he turns on the interior light and adjusts the rear vision mirror to examine his cheek. Grunting, "That's gonna make a nice scar," he winces as he stitches it up in the poor light with one eye. Completing the job, he reaches for a fresh shirt out of clothes bag, slips it over his head then turns off the headlights and interior light. Picking up the sate phone lying on the passenger's seat, he flips up the aerial to turn it on, and then finally, takes the weight off his feet and sits down in the camp chair. "You were lucky to get out of that one alive," he says to himself as he pushes the only number in the phone. He had organised to ring the boss every Tuesday at 7pm since arriving out bush to check in, unless something went wrong. He is now faced with ringing his boss two days early.

C looks at the overseas number and picks it up on the second ring. "What's up?"

Ox informs him, "Ran across two human mountains, both armed, and they had the station staked out."

C asks, "What? Cops, army, Special Forces – what are we dealing with here?" Turning the phone onto loud speaker, he starts to pace, twirling the ring on his finger continuously.

"No, boss, not sure. They were not carrying any government issue weapons, more like hunting rifles. Anyway, I have taken care of it," Ox says then adds, "A bit banged up though, closest I've come to meeting my maker in hand-to- hand combat."

C sighs with relief that the problem is gone, telling Ox, "Yeah, well, I had the prospecting partner of that Tim bloke turn up at my property asking questions." Knowing his hit man must be injured significantly for him to even comment on his own condition, he asks, "You OK to stay out for another week till that run needs to be done?"

"Yeah, no worries. I can stick it out. You want me to pay a visit to this other prospector when I get back in?" asks Ox.

"No, we have enough on our plates even though he did spot the GPS in the chopper. I can claim it's been there since the search. I've deleted all the way points on it since. He might have some suspicions but I'm sure there wasn't enough time to check out the GPS. He's only one man, what can he do?" replies C confidently.

"Righto," says Ox as he presses off the power button, feeling tired, probably from a mild concussion and loss of blood. He decides to seek out his swag and take a couple of days off to mend.

Three kilometres upstream at the Hatchet River Station, Scrubber, Price and Max are sitting around the table, finishing off their dinner of stew. Max says, "There has not been much traffic or radio chatter around lately," in between mouthfuls of food.

"Yeah, word must have got round to stay away from the place," says Scrubber.

Price speaks up. "Couldn't be sure but I could have heard some gun shots today."

The other two look at him. Max asks, "How many shots?"

Price looks thoughtful. "Hmm, maybe 4 or 5, but it was windy." He shrugs his shoulders. Not wanting to get in trouble for being wrong, he adds, "Na, must have been something else." He gets up from the table and takes his empty plate to the sink. "Can I go feed the girls?"

Scrubber grunts. "Not till you finish washing up," and slides his plate across the table in Price's direction.

Max does the same, saying, "Good. I'm off for a shower then," and walks out of the room. Scrubber walks outside to lean on a veranda railing, rolling a smoke in the dark. Price empties what is left of the stew from the dinner pot to a bucket.

The backpackers had exhausted every effort to escape over the weeks. Bound and chained, they tried desperately to reach anything that had stacked so neatly and effectively out of their own grasp. Their eyes have become so accustomed to the darkness, seeing is not an issue. The monster had thrown a thin mattress in the middle of the shed; they are sure it was more for his comfort while having his way with them than for theirs. Both girls had given up screaming for some time now, their spirit to fight him off has been broken and are becoming more submissive by the day to avoid a beating when he enters the shed for what he calls some fun. Terri says through cracked, swollen lips, "I don't know how much longer I can take this for and I can't even kill myself."

Suzie mumbles, "Someone will come for us. We have to believe that."

Terri raises her voice. "Who? Nobody knows where we are other than that prick at the servo who sent us out here in the first place. We should be in Darwin by now."

Terri starts sobbing and Suzie moves closer to put an arm around the shoulders of her friend. "We have to stay positive."

They hear the latch lift on the shed door and its squeal, protesting from being swung open. "Hello, girls, you miss me today?" Price says, groping for the light cord in the dark. He pulls it down, flooding the shed with light. Both girls squint in what they think is a bright light but in actual fact is quite a dull 60 watt bulb. Placing the bucket containing the cold stew down one end of the shed, he flings the empty one outside. "If one of you is real nice to me tonight, you both will get a bath tomorrow," he says, touching Terri on the leg with his foot. "You?"

Terri starts to shake uncontrollably as if she is having a seizure. Suzie, looking at the condition of her friend, speaks up as he reaches for her arm, and says begrudgingly, "Leave her. I want you tonight. I will be the best you have had."

Price smiles with his broken, tobacco-stained teeth. Suzie has captured his full attention. "That's what I want to hear." Finding a chair down one end of the shed, he places it in front of brunette. "Show me your best then," he says, spreading his legs. Suzie crawls closer, trying to stifle her sobs, having some problems unzipping his fly with both hands still bound.

The prospecting duo finally hit the bitumen after many hours on the dirt. They have been catching up on all the events since they had last met. Turning on his mobile phone,

John says, "As soon as we hit a service area, my messages will start to sound out."

Tim replies, "It makes the plan a lot easier to work, knowing Rob and Rick are prepared to help out. I am proud of them boys, just like their old man, tough and staunch, standing up to the plate to fight for their own. They're not boys anymore, they are men, real men."

An hour and a half down the road, John's phone starts to go crazy, vibrating all over the seat. Skidding to a stop off the road, John starts sifting through the work calls to find two messages from Jack's sons. "I've got two bars of service." Pressing return call, he passes the phone to Tim, saying, "This will blow them away."

Rob picks up immediately, thinking he is talking to John. "Missed your call the other day, bud. Where you up to? What's going on?"

Tim cuts him short on the hundred questions, not being able to get a word in since the phone was handed to him. "Hey mate, shit you ask a lot of questions."

There is silence on the other end of the line then, "Fuck me drunk, is that you, Tim?" Rob stammers.

"Yeah bro, it's me. Sorry to hear about, Jack, mate. Listen, this is what I need you to get and what I want you to do. Grab a pen." They spend nearly a full hour on the roadside going through the entire plan before finishing off with, "Wait to hear from you on the two-way, channel 15, in three days. That should be enough time for you to set up."

John starts the truck and they head towards the first part of their plan, a goat track that the gold miners utilised well over a hundred years ago when travelling by horse, bullock drays or on foot between camps in the goldfield. Tim had accidentally run across this track years before. He doubted Scrubber even knew of it. It led into Hatchet River Station from a totally different direction than the modern era of roads and tracks. Even though it's the dark, Tim points to the side of the road. "Pull off here. You got a head lamp?"

John points to the glove box. "Yeah, in there."

Fitting the lamp over his head and opening the door before the truck stops, Tim walks along the fence line, locating the old gate 300 meters up from the truck's position. Getting back to the 4x4, he says, "It's up here." He stands on the side step of the truck as it moves forward. With the help of the headlights from the cruiser, he slides along the 8-gauge wire loop on the top strand that is holding the fence picket parallel with the fence line; dropping it on the ground, the truck goes through. John flicks a switch on the dash and a rear spotlight mounted under the tray illuminates the fence line so Tim can erect and close the gate. Getting back into the truck, he comments, "We may as well make camp not too far in here. It will be impossible to follow this track in the dark."

Parking up, both men are hungry but not being bothered to go and collect wood to light a fire, they rummage through the tucker box selecting tins of baked beans and potato chips. "Looks like a dingo's dinner tonight." Tim smiles.

"It will do. Hey, you forgot to add one thing on the list, a swag. Anyway, I have a spare sleeping bag behind my seat." John gets up and flicks the seat forward to remove a sleeping bag. Glancing at the clock on the dash, he adds, "Shit. No wonder a bloke feels knackered, it's 12.30am," throwing the bedding towards his mate, who catches it in one hand.

"Ta bud, a bag is all good. We won't be out here long and, yeah, it has been a long day." Scoffing down dinner with little to no talk, the weary prospectors each select a spot in which to crash for what is left of the night.

Morning arrives too soon for John. He groans and tries to get his brain in gear. Flipping the canvas cover off his head, he squints over at the empty sleeping bag 15 meters from him. Rising, he walks over to his truck, connects the gas burner hose to an 8.5kg gas bottle and fills a saucepan with town water out of a 20-litre container. He puts it on to boil for a coffee. He walks around the truck looking for any sign of where his mate has gone. He hears Tim coming back towards the cruiser ten minutes later. "What a bloody mission. Found the track but look at this shit."

His partner looks up from pouring them both a coffee to find him soaking wet from brushing against the tall grass heavily laden with the early morning dew and hundreds of spear grass tips sticking out of his shirt and pants. John laughs. "You look like an echidna that's gone for a swim. Here, bud, I got clothes," he says, throwing over his soft carry bag.

With dry gear on, Tim throws the wet clothes into the back and reaches for his mug. Taking a good mouthful of the hot brew, he says, "Might be a good idea to zip tie your shade cloth in front of the radiator now." John agrees. Both prospectors always carried a section of shade cloth cut specifically to stop spear grass from getting embedded into the fins of the radiator and reducing cooling, causing the trucks to overheat. Finishing off their drinks, they get organised to leave, firstly fixing the shade cloth in place. When done, Tim says, "Better lock in your front hubs, bud.

It's going to be one hell of a drive best part of the day I would reckon. The wind this time of year usually blows from the south-east, so the noise of us approaching from this direction will be blown away from the station."

John replies, "This old girl will get us there and back, no worries." Selecting low four, they move off through the tall grass, slowly towards the first obstacle, a steep lipped sand crossing with a meter of water running through it. Tim looks at his mate and waits for a comment, but it does not eventuate, there is just a smile. Poking the nose of his truck slowly down the sand embankment, John guns the truck, giving it the momentum to climb up the opposite bank. With all four wheels spinning trying to grip on the soft sand with the initial speed now lost, the cruiser slowly crawls onto level ground. John turns to Tim. "Next?" he says with a wide grin, knowing that Tim thought his driving skills would be tested.

Four hours down the track, the grin is well and truly gone. They have one staked tyre, another had the wall sliced out of it by a slate bar, they lost the track several times. They both got out, leaving the truck idling, looking in different directions for a sign.

The heat is picking up rapidly. John reaches for a bottle of orange juice out of the esky while watching his prospecting partner skid down a hill to the right hand side of him. "You find anything?" he says, passing Tim the bottle of cold drink.

Nodding, he upends the bottle, polishing off at least half its contents. Pointing towards the hill he had just come down, he finishes off the mouthful. "It goes up there, bud."

The response from John is better than he had anticipated. "What? Fucking up there! How in hell?"

Tim breaks out laughing. Patting him on the back, he says, "Yeah. Tough old buggers probably used block and tackle."

They climb back into the truck. Turning it to face the very bottom of the steep hill square on, John leans forward over the steering wheel to find the crest a long way up. Looking for the best path to tackle, he says "For fuck sake, you sure."

Tim laughs again. The answer is short. "Don't be soft." On that note the 4x4 leaps at the steep incline. After an hour and a half of the truck's front wheels rearing off the ground, skidding backwards under full brakes and winching themselves up part of the way up, they reach the top, with John just shaking his head.

Negotiating a steep gully 4km after arriving on top, John slips the truck back into low gear to crawl over the large, sharp rocks. Tim announces, "Pull up after you get out of this gully. I want to check something out." His partner just looks at him, not even asking why, just happy enough to pull up and inspect the damage on his truck.

Tim heads off through the bush while John gets out, shaking his head at the condition of his vehicle since starting along this track. Both side mirrors were smashed off by trees, one side board carries a large ding from getting wedged on a large boulder that the truck's clearance didn't quite make it over and there are a multitude of scratches along the paint work on both sides, not to mention the flat tyres.

His partner is following a dry gully along from the high bank, looking intently towards the bottom where the water had flowed swiftly in the wet season. "Just as I thought, fresh detector scrapings." Walking down further, backfilled detector holes become more apparent. Who would be operating this far out has him buggered, though the rock type in the area did suggest the possibility of gold-bearing ground. Walking over fresh bike tracks, he decides to follow them. About to give up and turn around after ten minutes, Tim hears an "Oi." Forty meters up on the flat, away from the gully, Allan is lying under some sparse shade, his detector turned off.

Recognising him instantly with no shirt on, Tim walks over. "What are you guys doing up here? I thought you were in WA."

Shaking his hand, Allan stands up and smiles. "Got sick of playing secret squirrel. We were being followed nearly every time we went for a swing. Ran across a couple of crews that knew their shit, the rest were novices; too lazy or hopeless to find their own spots. And I missed the hills of home, too bloody flat over there to hide from the scabs. We did OK though," he says, not elaborating on the amount of gold he'd found.

The prospectors were adversaries in the field but got on well socially, having a high respect for each other's ability to find gold. Allan says, "I have been following the news from over there; all kinds of shit happening downstream, hey? That Ray was a nice bloke, only met him a few times."

Allan's radio crackled to life. "Hey, did you hear that vehicle? It sounded close to me."

Replying, Allan tells his mate, "Yeah, Tonga, it's all good. It's just Tim and John."

"What the hell? The bush telegraph told me he was missing. What they doing way the hell out here?"

The prospectors smile at each other. Tim trusts Allan to keep quiet and briefly fills him in on what had gone down since they had left for WA. While in conservation, Tim asks, "Many junk targets out here?"

Allan answers, "Na, bugger all."

"So all them holes you dug up the gully were gold targets then?"

Allan smiles at being caught out so easily. "Yeah," he says, producing four ounces of nuggets out of his pocket.

Getting up to leave Tim, ends with, "You have not seen us if anyone asks."

"No worries, bud," is the reply as Tim heads back towards the truck.

John has been waiting impatiently. "Where you been?"

Tim responds, "Let's get going, fill you in on the way."

From there onwards, it is all downhill. They follow ridges and saddles for the next three hours to where Tim wants to set up base. This is close to 3km on the northern side of Hatchet River as the crow flies, actually slightly downstream from Ox's camp hidden in the tree line of the river. Crawling out of the door, John says, "Thank fuck for that."

Tim smirks. "No fires at all from this spot. We will work off the gas on the back. We don't to give us being here away." With a stiff south-east wind blowing onto his face, Tim is happy that the vehicle's approach would have missed detection by anyone looking towards the Hatchet River.

Rob and Rick had both rung their work place, taking a week off on short notice, citing family reasons. Being valuable workers for their respective employers, they had no issues with the request. Emerging out of the army disposal store in Cairns with arms full of purchases and walking back to Rick's truck, Rob looks at his older brother. "Hey bro, can you believe it? Tim is still alive, what a spin out, bud. I didn't even know what hell to say, it was like hearing from a ghost."

Rick smiles. "Yeah, it would have blown me away too. Hopefully Dad is still alive as well." On that comment both young men go quiet, reflecting the time their father had spent teaching them how to shoot, catch a variety of animals with snares and traps, and read game signs while being aware of where you were in the bush at all times. Starting at the age of six and eight, their skills had improved rapidly as they grew older. Special events that had occurred out bush came to mind instantly, such as Rob's trapping of his first full-grown boar in a snare he had made and Rick' catching his first barramundi. Loading the gear into the back, they look at each other; their eyes told the story of anger, hope, and payback.

On the way home, Jack's boys talk about Tim's plan in depth and the stuff they have just spent the last of their money on. Rick says, "The only thing that I can't work out is why only one truck? We both have good bush rigs and we could come in from both directions to block anyone leaving other than us."

Rob nods. "Yep that idea works for me too, bro, but Tim knows his shit better than us, even down to the camo gear we just bought. A lot can go wrong with the plan. We are trying to second guess a mad man. Hopefully there will be no surprises."

Arriving out the front of Rob's place, Rick says, "Pick you up at 4am. Be ready. Just your sleeping gear and fire power and we are gone."

Opening the car door, Rob replies, "No worries, bro. I've got a bit of drilling, binding and sharpening to do before I hit the sack."

His brother just gives him a blank look. "Whatever you need to do, just be ready." Rick drives home to finish off packing the cruiser.

The next morning, the young men, both bleary-eyed, leave town early and travel slowly through a heavy fog with wipers on. Spotlights and high beam are useless in the soup-like atmosphere. Rick turns the demister to full boar, concentrating on following the white centre line of the road. The fog starts to lift 80km further on with Rick picking up speed as daylight breaks.

Driving for hours on the dirt road both had travelled countless times over the years, they arrive at a point where the road peels off to the left. Slowing the truck, Rick looks at his brother. "Well, I haven't been any further than this. Have you?"

Rob confesses, "Yeah, a couple of kilometres. I know Dad's strict rule, he would have kicked my ass for sure, but this boar I was chasing had the biggest set of ivory I have seen out this way." He adds, "Tim said to turn on the GPS from here on in and keep at least 3km away from the station and not to camp near water."

Rick nods. "It's in the glove box. Might be a good idea to pull up and grab the guns out just in case we run into them on the way in. No good to us behind the seat, unloaded." With the truck slowing to a halt, the brothers feed shells into the magazines of the 223 rifles that their father had gifted to them on acquiring their gun licence.

Keeping the revs down to a minimum, Rick moves along the road at 70km per hour, trying to contain the noise emitted from the truck's exhaust. Rob has his eyes on the GPS. "Getting close now. There's a creek coming up soon, I reckon we get off before it and find a place to camp." The truck slows down even further, both of the brothers are on the lookout for an area that did not have an excess of breakaway gullies. "Over here." Rob points out the window on his side towards a small clay pan gully that looks fairly easy to negotiate. Driving off the road onto the hard packed clay, barely leaving a tyre print, the brothers make their way up a gully that twists in behind a ridge, well out of sight from the road. Picking an inside bend off the small dry water course that is level enough to set up camp on, the boys get out with Rick making the observation, "Going to be hot as hell in this hollow. There will be no breeze down here and bugger all shade."

Rob nods and looks around. "Must a dead beast or something over the hill," he says, pointing to the circling hawks not that far away as they unload their gear.

Having taken the last couple of days off, Ox feels a lot better. He notices looking at his face in the side mirror of the truck his swollen eye had started to subside. He even managed to wash his clothes in the sandy shallows downstream, preferring it to the large waterhole above camp. Not sure exactly why, he chose to bathe further down the river; call it a sixth sense Ox got occasionally that could not be ignored. It had helped save his life on numerous occasions.

Cooking himself a large feed of bacon and eggs, the hit man is in no hurry to start disposing of the bodies and clean up the mess he had created at the brothers' camp. Sitting in his chair studying mine maps that showed multiple abandoned hard rock mine shafts in the vicinity, and now having a rough idea of the direction he needed to take, folds the map and places it on the table.

Ox reaches for the army-issue hiking boots that hadn't been needed in the last couple of days; he had actually enjoyed walking though the river and barefoot. Being the first to admit he is not a bushie. Always used to city life and fighting crowds of people either on the streets or in traffic, along with his taste for expensive women, the best motels, and good room service.

The solitude has started to grow on Ox slightly, having been out bush for four weeks straight, now was starting to run low on what he considers basic supplies. The hitman is counting down the days before this drug run could be finalized and he could get the hell away from these unpredictable, incompetent, inner-bred bush hicks. Filling the camel pack with water then reaching for the 308, he sets off on the 7km walk to get rid of what would be bloated bodies, unless the wild life had beat him to it. Walking alongside the large water hole as he did every morning for the last month, he thinks to himself that if a man liked fishing, this would be the spot as another Barra flashes silver, chopping for food at the surface.

Getting close to the brothers' camp after a stiff two and a half hour walk, he errs on the side of caution and moves in stealthily for the last 40 meters towards the vehicles, in case anyone had stumbled onto his handy work. Two crows sitting on an iron bark branch sound out the alarm to the others as they fly to another tree forty-odd meters away; close to twelve crows heed the warning, flying to nearby trees immediately, searching for the enemy. Finding the advancing foe's slight movement in the tall grass, all took flight.

Ox stands, shrugging his shoulders, confident there is no other human presence, otherwise the crows would not be there feeding. Walking into the camp and holding his gun loosely in hand, he moves over to Bear's body. His eyes are missing along with all the soft tissue facial features. The exposed skin left to the relentless sun had blistered easily and had peeled off the flesh as the sharp talons of the crows clawed all over the large man's torso.

Resting the rifle on its butt up against the 4x4, Ox notices Stu's body is in no better condition than his brother's. "You put up one hell of a fight, big boy," he says with admiration in his voice. "You deserve better than to be left for the pigs and dogs." Picking him up by the arms, the hit man starts dragging his adversary's bloated dead weight of over 120kg towards the 4x4. Leaving the bodies to Mother Nature goes against his grain as a professional. Leaving no signs of his work around, no matter how remote the area, was common practice. Trying to lift the stinking, heavy carcass into the tray of the truck is a failure. "Fuck this shit," he says, wiping maggots off his forearms. He drops the body and launches into a search for something to utilise.

Ox finds a snap strap used for towing trucks out of bogs in a side aftermarket aluminium compartment fitted to the truck, "this will do." He rolls out the thirty-meter length of thick strap and loops it around both of Stu's arms. It is now 38 degrees in the shade and sweat is running freely down his face as he completes the task of tying Bear in the same manner, looping the end over the tow ball. "Right. Now for the rest of the shit." He folds the chairs, table and miscellaneous other camping possessions, leaving absolutely nothing behind. The door of the vehicle is unlocked and the keys still in the ignition. "Too easy," says Ox with a smile, as he preheats the truck, kicking into life at first turn of the ignition.

Jack's boys, just over the other side of the ridge, have finished setting up camp and are sitting down to work out where they needed to be to lay the trap by the height of hills on the GPS; for Scrubber and co to take the bait, the area had to be easy to access by vehicle. Realising they had to be decisive for Tim's plan to work, they are finishing off studying the contours on the screen when ten crows fly overhead. "That's unusual," says Rob. "Something must have given them a fright," knowing full well from years of bush time how the food chain out here works. He grabs his rifle from the front of the truck. "I'm going to check it out."

His older brother looks at him. "You are jumping at shadows, bro. Maybe a little anxious about tomorrow. What do you reckon for dinner?"

Sitting down momentarily, Rob can't relax and states, "I'm going for a look anyway." He lifts himself off the chair and starts up the ridge with gun in hand. Rick is shaking his head when they both hear a vehicle start. They look at each other. Rick scrambles to his 4x4 and, finding the binoculars and his 223, catches up with his brother who is already lying down at the top of the ridge.

"Is that what the fuck I think it is?" Rob asks as Rick lies down beside him and brings the glasses to zoom in on the white truck skull dragging bodies over the ground, bouncing over any rocks in its path towards the old mine shafts.

"You're kidding me. It's definitely not Scrubber or the others but…"

He passes the binoculars to Rob; he watches till the truck drives out of sight through the trees laying over the long grass in the wake of the bodies before lowering the glasses. "Well, what do you make of that?"

Rick replies, the colour draining from his face, "Fuck knows but we will give this area a wide berth in the morning and just stick to the plan." Both young men now fully comprehend that this is no game by far; this is for keeps.

Ox crawls along in first gear through the bush, moving in the general direction of the mine shafts. After travelling about 1.5km, he knows from his study of the map at camp they must be in the near vicinity. Getting out of the 4x4, he moves forward on foot to find the exact location. Stepping out of a shallow gully, he observes some rock piles standing over the height of the grass. "There they are." On finding the first, he realises the area is littered with shafts. He selects some on the outer edge as it is easier to pull the truck up beside them. Ox takes the time to drop rocks down some of the old shafts to gauge the depth, selecting the one that the rock took ages to hit bottom, bouncing off the sides on the way down to eventually splash at the end. "Perfect." Whistling to himself, he makes his way back to the truck, and an hour later, the job is just about finished as he rolls Stu's body to the edge. "It's a dammed better burial than you pair would have given me," he says, pushing him the last couple of inches over the side with the worn sole of his boot.

"Right now, what to do with the trucks?" Realising the day is coming close to an end, he decides bugger it, "The other three clowns can bury them." Not really wanting to make an appearance at the station homestead until the morning of the run, going through his options he realises he doesn't have much choice. As the white 4x4 makes it out to the edge of the road, Ox changes the gear selector from low four to high four and drives towards the homestead.

The station dogs sound the alarm. With all three knowing well beforehand that a vehicle is approaching, they are standing outside, armed and waiting to sight the truck as it comes around the last bend of the road before the gate. Scrubber sneers. "Only one in the truck. You pair keep the guns levelled at him," he says as he walks towards the gate and lays the rifle barrel on the top rung, pointed towards the driver's side door.

Ox takes one look at them as he brings the car to a stop. "What a freak show." He climbs out of the truck with his hands in the air and says loudly, "It's Ox." With that they lower their firearms and Scrubber goes through the gate to be met halfway by the hit man. "You need to bury this," he says, throwing the keys to Scrubber, adding, "There will be another truck tomorrow."

Catching them in one hand, Scrubber replies, "What the hell happened to your face? You're not supposed to be here for another three days," not liking the idea at all of authority being taken out of his hands on his own station.

Ox picks up on the negative attitude and replies sarcastically, "I had a run in with a one-eyed pigmy. I will be back tomorrow." Turning his back on the three of them to retrieve the camel pack and 308 out of the back, he slips on the headlamp from a pocket in the backpack and starts making his way back to camp as darkness falls.

Scrubber pegs the car keys at Price as now he is in a filthy mood. "Get this around the back out of sight. I want it buried at first light."

Looking over the Hatchet River delta, Tim sits on the spare camp chair John brought as various shades of darkness start to engulf the bush. Carrying over his own chair along with two beers, passing one to his partner, John says, "I will wack some steaks on shortly, my worms are screaming out for some grub-"

Tim cuts him short. "Did you see that?" he says, pointing into the darkening horizon.

"See what?"

"Over there, it was a light I'm sure of it."

After a minute, John spots what his prospecting partner is talking about. There is a light that looked to be flicking on and off but was actually the light getting blocked by the tree foliage as it moved downstream. "Yeah, I got it now. Who would be walking around this time of night?"

Tim replies, "I don't know but we will be checking it out in the morning. Switch your lamp over to infrared so it can only be seen from short distances away."

The men follow the light till it does not emerge back out of the trees. "We know where to look now," says Tim as they get up to organise dinner and have a bird bath, followed by an early night as a good sleep beckoned after the two previous nights.

They wake at about 4am, keen to get the day started, and have a quick coffee whilst organising what they need to take. With John slinging on the 44, Tim opts for the Glock handgun as it is easier to carry and shoves it in the waistline of his khaki pants. "We will take the two-ways in case the boys get set up earlier than we predicted. Now, let's go check out who our nightwalker is," Tim says. They leave camp in Indian file, with John following a distance behind, on a cattle pad and make their way to the river. After being cautiously on the move for close to an hour, he crouches and waves his hand for John to come closer, whispering, "Can you smell that?"

Nodding, he quietly says, "Smells like bacon cooking." Tim smiles and points towards the source, raising a finger to his lips.

Crossing over the dry river sand as silently as possible in their work boots, the prospectors make it to the heavy brush on the opposite side of the river from Ox's camp and lie flat to observe his movements. The hit man, having no idea that it is him now being stalked, finishes off the last of his bacon and baked beans then starts tending to his wounds, lifting his shirt to change the rib dressing. Once finished, he stashes the keys in the usual spot on his spare tyre under the dual cab, grasps his backpack and 308, and mutters, "Go grab this other truck and take the arvo off, I reckon" as he starts the trek upstream once again.

The men lie in hiding for ten minutes before emerging out of cover and into the camp. There are first aid dressings lying all over the table; they also pick up on that the ash has been dug out from the fire place numerous times. Tim says in a hushed tone, "Whoever he is, he's been here awhile," pointing at the pile of ash, "and he's also injured." Thinking aloud, he says, "Well, he's not a pig hunter, no sign of any dogs' stuff all scratches or dints on the truck, standard highway tyres, only one spare tyre." Continuing on, "And he definitely ain't no prospector or fisherman either."

John, leaning his face on his hands to look through the heavily tinted windows, pipes up. "Hey, super sleuth, looks like a hand gun on the front seat. You want me to get his keys and have a look inside? Otherwise we will be here all day using your powers of deduction."

To walk into someone's camp when they are not around is totally against the bush rules that the prospectors adhere to normally, but at this point in time the prospectors needed to find out whether this man was friend or foe. "Yeah, righto," says, Tim working against one of the golden rules of the bush.

John swings under the back of the truck to retrieve where he had seen Ox stash the keys, feeling for them with the tip of his fingers. "Got them." Unlocking the door, he quickly scours through the gear in the front of the vehicle whilst Tim keeps watch in case the mystery man returns. "Holy fucking hell! Tim, best you come check this out, bud."

Tim glances up the river before moving in closer to what see what has his partner so excited.

He looks through the backpack containing various scopes, including a night scope, along with a silencer for the 308. "Well, shit a brick, we have ourselves a real life hit man on the Hatchet River. Wonder which side is paying him?"

John passes him the sate phone. "Maybe this will tell us a story," he says, powering up the phone.

"There's only the one number and I'm sure I recognise the last three digits," Tim says, passing it to John, who recognises the number instantly.

"It's Chris's number, the fucker."

Tim, with anger flooding into his body, says, "Right, well, let's give this prick a real bush welcome. That's who took Jack out for sure, bet my balls on it." He quickly works out a plan in his head. "Any pliers in that truck?"

John opens the over-flowing glove box and paperwork falls to the floor. John instinctively picks up a handful to shove back in; quickly flicking through some of the pages, he pauses on the mug shot of Sam. Slowing right down and going page by page, John uncovers Tim's and Jack's mug shots as well. Looking across to his mate, he says, "Hey bro, you need to come look and have a look at this, bud."

The prospectors walk upstream, following the well- worn track with steely resolve. Tim picks up on the slight ripple in the river following them at a distance. Pausing to get a better look, he says to himself, "He's a big boy." The ripple ceases as the croc submerges fully. Smiling to himself as it all falls into place perfectly, he follows the track further till it turns sharply to a tight pinch rounding a high rocky outcrop, with the bank falling steeply into the deep water hole as the river narrowed considerably at this point. Pausing to survey that exact spot, Tim says aloud, "He has to walk through here, there is no other easy way around. We need to lay out a snare right here," being fully aware he is dealing with a pro killer not a greenhorn.

John, bringing up the rear, catches up to Tim and asks, "What's the go?"

"We will set up a snare trap here. There's a holding paddock just above the high flood mark above us, I'll go cut some barbed wire." He estimates roughly the length needed to make it across to the opposite bank comfortably. "Change your two-way, bud, to channel 1. If you see him heading back, just say the word 'fish.' We don't want Scrubber scanning the radio and picking up on us."

Nodding, John moves off the track to a higher location to conceal himself, alert for any movement from upstream. Not knowing how much time they have up their sleeve, Tim moves with haste. Returning with a large bundle of wire, he has it all worked out. "Right," he says, passing John one end of the wire as he approaches, "see that gum tree up there?" pointing above the rocky outcrop. "Tie that end to the bottom of the trunk real good." Peering over the steep bank to the water's edge, he adds, "That's got to be a good 10-meter drop so add that by measuring it with your arm span." Looking at the length of John's arms, he says, "With both extended, it would be close at 2 meters, so five spans then lay that on the ground spread out. We don't want it to get knotted up." Completing what he was instructed, John watches as Tim painstakingly cuts off all the barbs along a four-foot section of the wire and places the off cuts in his top pocket.

Bending the wire in half then feeding it back through itself to make a loop the size of his fist, he reaches for the loose end and places it into the loop, pulling through all the excess wire. When done, Tim tests the action of his snare to make sure it will tighten quickly and smoothly where the barbs had been removed then places it in an oblong shape on the track where their victim would have no choice other than to step into it. Concealing it well with a light cover of dirt and leaf litter, he turns to John. "Hey mate, you want to grab a decent rock. We need to throw this end of wire to the other side."

Selecting one that is the appropriate size for the job close at hand, John passes it down to Tim, who wraps the wire around it many times before twitching it off at the end. Getting as much as a run up as possible, he throws the rock with all his strength; as they are a good 15 feet higher than the opposite bank, the rock makes it over, landing in the sand a good eight feet above the water line. Smiling he makes one turn of the wire around the base of a small sapling about three feet high. Watching him, John asks, "What did you do that for?"

Tim smirks. "Watch and learn," he says as they both lightly sweep all the prints they had created, making it as natural as when they first arrived. The men then walk up half a kilometre to cross the river, keeping well away from the track Ox has been using. Making it back to the rock covered in wire on the opposite side, Tim replaces it with a sturdy lump of timber. Holding it in both hands, Tim is satisfied and starts explaining the plan to John. "Now we just have to wait till he is in line with that sapling I looped that wire around then we take off with this like a bat out of hell," he says, holding up the timber handle.

John makes a suggestion. "Do you want me to move upstream and give you a call on the two-way?"

Scanning the other side, Tim confidently replies, "Na, she's right, mate. We will see him close to 80 meters before the snare."

Ox arrives at Bear's vehicle and wastes no time in getting it started and making his way to the station. Jack's boys are not in earshot of the truck starting up today as they left camp on daybreak, taking a wide detour around what they had witnessed yesterday. Following the marker point on the GPS that they added last night, just before climbing the last ridge Rick says, "We got less than a kilometre to go." Pausing under the shade of a gum tree, he unzips his backpack and takes a few mouthfuls of water out of his bottle. Rob pulls up beside him and shrugs off his pack also. Rick looks at what his brother is carrying. "What is that frigging thing sticking out of your pack?"

Rob looks at the dangerous-looking object standing at least two feet out of the top and laughs. "That's what I had to make up the night before we left. Haven't you seen one before?"

His brother shakes his head. "No bro, it looks a weapon though."

Rob feels sad thinking about all of the things their father had taught them over the years. "Don't know where you were. Dad showed me how to make them years ago; you just need the right branch at whatever height the prey is you are targeting." Returning their water bottles to the backpacks, the young men continue on, arriving on top of the last ridge before the country started to flatten out in front of them.

Sitting down, the brothers could now visually work out how to set up the plan other than just working off the GPS. With it still in hand, Rick starts. "Well, the station is 8km in that direction. Tim told you that track with the locked gates runs parallel to the sandstone formation in the distance. Going off the GPS coordinates, they only have to drive across three small creeks to get a vehicle in here," he says, pointing lower down in front of them.

Rob adds his thoughts. "OK, so they pull up down here then we need to get them all well away from the truck and hope like hell Tim is right and we are closer to their lab than the homestead." The young men spend the rest of their day setting up Tim's plan in detail, leaving a huge pile of green branches in a steep gully before they depart for camp.

Parking Bear's truck at the front gate of Hatchet River Station while the dogs go off, hitting the end of the chains with force before Scrubber quietens them down as he walks towards the gate, Ox does not even bother talking to the station owner; he just retrieves his 308 and camel pack from the back and starts making his way back to camp. Scrub-ber's face turns crimson with anger at being ignored;

feeding a round into the chamber of his rifle, he levels the barrel at Ox's back. The hit man is close enough to hear the mechanism lock the shell into the breach. Stopping in his tracks, he turns around slowly, raising the 308 to his hip, to face Scrubber, scowling. "I've had a gutful of you pricks running around our station throwing orders round like you own the place. I own the fucking place," Scrubber spits out.

Reading the situation, with every fibre of his body ready to react, Ox coolly and calmly made his mind up which side to dive towards, calculating the success rate of injecting a shell while putting a bullet in the station owner's forehead in mid-air at the slightest indication he was about to pull the trigger. Through gritted teeth, he replies, "Well, best you take that up with C, not me, old man. Now if I were you, I would lower that gun before I put a bullet in you."

Scrubber's face changes to a look of doubt. He is used to men backing down under gunpoint. Studying the hit man's stance and resolve, he slowly lowers the rifle. "Well, you can tell C from me I run this joint, not him," he adds weakly, knowing well that is not the case.

Ox replies, "Be back in two days for the run," and walks off.

Making the way back to camp, his mind starts to wonder on which call girl would be first when he got home, what would be his first meal and which brand of vintage whiskey he would select. Rounding a sharp point on the track home overlooking the water hole, Ox catches a movement in his peripheral vision, which is Tim at full sprint over the sand, timber handle in his grasp. Raising his rifle and loading a shell with the bolt action at the same time, he takes aim. The snare tightens around his ankles; the shot fires wildly into the air as Tim pulls him over the edge of the river bank. Sliding down the steep bank, Ox loses grip of his rifle. The small sapling beside the track tears completely out of the ground as all twenty feet of the wire John had measured out above the rock ledge quickly follows, snapping taut when it comes to its end and bites deep into the river gum's bark, leaving the hit man trapped by the simple but effective snare in the soft mud at the water's edge.

Trying to work out exactly what has just happened, Ox's natural instinct is to try and climb back up. He grasps the barbed wire with both hands. It cuts profusely into his soft palms and he slips on the steep muddy bank as he tries to gain his footing over and over again. Both men on the opposite side hold the tension on the wire before wrapping it around a large river gum. Not being able to move now in either direction, the hit man quickly works out he is going nowhere and starts to laugh out loud, "Can you believe this? Fucking caught out by bush hicks." Turning his head upwards, he can see the 308 butt caught on a tree root protruding from the steep slope, not that far out of reach. Both men move into sight from the opposite bank, with Tim noticing a ripple slightly breaking the surface and moving towards the hit man's direction. Pegged down, Ox thrashes his boots in the water, trying to break free.

Knowing time is not on Ox's side, Tim bellows out, "What have you done with my uncle, the big bloke that was a witness?"

Realising now who this adversary is that had trapped him so successfully and knowing he is not getting out of this alive, Ox yells, "You should be dead" as he lunges for his rifle, picking up some slight slack in the barbed wire, letting out a grunt in pain as the wire loop cuts deeper into his flesh to the bone at the same time. His fingertips stretch to their limit and grasp the end of his rifle butt. It slides free of the roots and comes within his reach. He smiles in triumph as both men are out in the open and easy targets just as the head of a huge croc emerges out of the water. With amazing speed its powerful jaws latch onto his feet and it goes into a death roll, flinging the gun out of Ox's bleeding hands and encasing the hit man in barbed wire every time it rolls him like a rag doll. Snapping the wire bound to the gum tree like cotton, the large reptile drags its prize into his domain while snapping the barbed wire also bound over the prospectors' side of the river with ease. Ox lets out a maniac laugh till his lungs fill of water.

Within seconds it is all over. Other than a tell-tale sign of muddy water where the croc went into its death roll and the large ripple effect that made its way to the opposite bank rapidly before dispersing, nothing remains. Both men are amazed at the size of the croc. John is the first to speak. "Fuck a duck, did you see the size of that thing?"

Tim replies, "Yeah bro, I knew it was big but not that bloody big! One down, four to go. I've been thinking we will go back and get that sate phone of his too. It could come in handy tomorrow." The prospectors first head to Ox's camp then towards their own, still having over an hour's walk ahead of them.

Pulling up to have a piss half way back, Tim mentions, "Haven't heard from the boys yet."

John replies, "Shit, I'm still on channel 1. What about you?" He reaches into his shirt pocket and changes it to channel 15.

"No bro, I changed mine back to fifteen when I come back with the wire." He gives it a good shake and zips up his fly then looks up at the position of the sun. "It's got to be close to three in the arvo now, way too late in the day to start it all off. We are going to need a full day, I reckon."

John agrees, adding, "Hopefully it will go as well as today." They climb back towards their truck. As the heat starts to drain out of the afternoon sun, they come over the last rise and make their way straight to the esky for a cold beer. Tim, passing one on, says, "Cheers, mate."

Tearing off the ring pull and taking a few healthy swigs, John says, "So tell me, how did you know that croc was large enough to be a man eater?"

Smirking and seizing on the moment, Tim step up on his soap box. "Well, being the super sleuth of deduction that I am-"

At this point John just rolls his eyes and says, "Here we go."

Tim's smile widens. "Did you notice on the sand bank at the shallow end of the hole the width of croc slides entering the water at that point?" Not even giving John time to answer, he continues, "No, I didn't think so. They had to be a good four feet wide, which told me the croc was at least 14 feet long." Striking while the iron is hot, he adds, "With your powers of observation, did you notice the croc followed us from one end of the water hole to the other?" Answering again before his prospecting partner can reply, and enjoying every minute of it, he says, "No, I didn't think so."

John just smiles, thinking to himself now this is my old mate back, just slinging shit at each other.

Tim finishes off by saying, "That's why I knew he was an aggressive croc. He followed us up the river. No doubt he had been doing it to that other prick the whole time, just waiting for a chance to strike. They love a creature of habit."

John claps. "Well done, bud, I am impressed. It worked out well in the end. I'm going to have an early shower." Sifting through his bag of clothes, he realises he has run out of clean shirts. "Damn," he mutters to himself. He is going through the shirts quicker than normal as he is supplying Tim clothing as well. Sorting through his discarded shirts, he picks out the cleanest one, which happens to be the one he left town in. John finishes up in the shower, which is strung from the closest tree, while Tim tends to a dinner consisting of lamb chops and a pre-packed salad. "Bloody beaut, bud," says John, polishing off the large plate of food.

"Yeah, good tucker, hey?" Tim says, as he does the same. "We need to be up near the station early tomorrow to pick up the boys on our two-ways. Hopefully they're organised by now. I'm going to head for a shower and get an early night as well."

Jack's boys wake well before dawn and dress in the full camo gear they had bought in Cairns. Neither is feeling very talkative over coffee, each is in their own mind frame about how the day's events would unfold, conscious that their part was the make or break of the entire plan. Breaking the silence, Rob says, "If we don't move soon, we will miss them having breakfast. They'll have eaten by the time we get there."

Rick agrees. "I will carry the diesel," he says. After going through the check list, the young men move off.

Tim and John wake slightly earlier than the boys. Though not wearing camo, they are both dressed in the khaki coloured clothing that they pretty much wore as their prospectors' work attire anyway as it blended into the bush well. "You ready?" asks Tim.

John replies, "Yeah, just got to fit in this 10 litres of petrol."

His mate, rearing to go, says, "Come on, mine wasn't that hard to get in. You got them windproof matches, hey?" John throws a box of the matches to his partner after finally closing the backpack zip and they move out of camp just on light and head upstream.

The boys arrive at the spot where they had piled the huge amount of green branches and, wasting no time, pouring the 10 litres of diesel onto the pile and set it alight. They give it time to start billowing smoke. "Here we go," Rob says on the two-way before starting to walk away so they were not close enough to get radio feedback from each other. "Hey bro, just picked up a 5 ounce slug. How you going?"

Rick replies, baiting it up, "Yeah, a 4 ouncer but a lot of grass. I'm going to fire it up, got to be more here."

Tim and John look at each other as they pick up on the boys' chatter. "It's on." They pick up their pace, jogging the last half kilometre to watch over the station.

Max is just finishing off washing up the morning breakfast plates and has the radio on scan as usual. The two brothers come through as a strong signal, which means they are relatively close. Both station men are in the middle of an oil change on the town cruiser before the planned drop tomorrow when Max races outside to the veranda, yelling, "We've got prospectors on the radio and they're close." Not used to being so inactive in the main prospecting season, all three are keen to get out on the hunt. They move swiftly inside to try and pick up where the intruders are.

Rob replies subtly, trying to give away their position, "Yeah mate, have a shit load of anthills over my way, driving my detector crazy."

The three standing beside the radio know roughly where they are operating. Scrubber mutters, "There are only two places on this station that are full of anthills." The radio goes quiet.

They make their way outside arguing about which direction they should take until Price points to the billowing smoke in the distance and says, "I reckon that's where they are."

Scrubber, spinning to look at what Price has spotted, yells orders. "Fill that motor with oil, we will get the rifles."

Tim and John had followed Ox's well-worn track to his elevated position overlooking the station; they did not need binoculars to see the three pile into the station truck and take off towards the smoke that stood out like a nun in Kings Cross at night. "Right, our turn," says Tim as both of them skid down the steep bank towards the station, reaching Price's hut first as the dogs go off their heads. Dragging Price's bed closer to the timber posts, they cover the mattress with petrol then trickle a line of petrol on the bare earth towards the door. Reaching for the windproof matches, Tim quickly strikes one and throws it down on the petrol line. The fire moves quickly till it hits the petrol- soaked bedding. Woof. Up it goes in a ball of flame.

Jack's boys can see the truck coming from the long line of bulldust swirling behind the cruiser. "They're coming in quicker than blowflies to a fart." Rob smirks. "Be a good 15 to 20 minutes away yet. Best we get in position."

Rick turns to his younger brother. "Keep safe, bro. Will talk to you on the two-way a bit later. Keep the volume low when they get here," he adds as they part ways.

Scrubber is driving along the dirt track at speed, bouncing over the uneven ground while Price hangs on tight to the head board in the back of the truck. Max is giving directions for the easiest way towards the smoke. "We have to go through the second locked gate then, after the first creek crossing, head east. We need to cross two other creeks that aren't too bad."

All three of them look towards the billowing smoke. Scrubber hits the brakes hard at the first locked gate; Max fumbles for the gate keys in the glove box full of bullets. Scrubber looks over at her impatiently, saying, "Come on, woman, leave the gate open. This won't take long." Max quickly dives out of the truck and swings open the gate. Scrubber launches the truck through, not even fully stopping as his wife scrambles back inside and slams the door. After progressing past the second gate, they cross both shallow sandy creeks with ease, swerving through acres of ant hills then slow the motor revs so the unsuspecting prospectors cannot pick up easily on their approach. "This will do. We will walk from here, don't want to scare them off," Scrubber says with a smirk, pulling in behind a small clump of tea trees to hide the truck from view.

Price is first to jump out and draws his 357 magnum, ready for some action. Max, also keen to stamp some authority on the hunt, starts to give Price orders. "Price, cross the creek and move up the gully; we will take both sides out wider if they run," she says, loading the 30/30 with a flick of her wrist while her husband gives her a questioning look. Max retorts, "About time he took the bull by the horns." Scrubber just shrugs his shoulders. Price moves off first as the others fan out on either side. Working his way up the steep gully with his magnum in hand, he rock hops till he comes across the purposely made fire. Scratching his head, he tries to fathom what was going on. Walking wide past the heat of fire that had now spent most of its fuel of green branches, he clambers out of the gully without seeing a single prospector or detecting hole.

From Rick's concealed position in some thick shrubs on the bank of the dry creek, he spots the three as they fan out and move towards the smoke. Slipping out of the low shrubbery, he moves silently towards the abandoned truck partly hidden in the juvenile tea tree clumps. He knows it will not take that long for them to work out it is a diversion. Unsheathing the knife from his hip belt, he plunges it into the walls of the truck tyres. There is just a slight noise after he retracts the blade; the quickly escaping stale air smells like rubber. After doing all four tyres and the two spares in the back, Rick puts his pack down and retrieves the sheet of A4 paper that he had done up the night before with a large smiley face on the bottom that read 'Have a Nice Day'

"Arseholes" he said out loud.

Smirking to himself, he places it proudly under one wiper blade on the windscreen then bends over into the cab of their truck and rips out the mic from the two-way radio, leaving them with no communication as a precaution. He takes the keys from the ignition and, placing both the keys and the mic in his pack, moves off, weaving through the anthills. He walks to a slight rise a safe distance away to get a better view of the proceedings. Lying down, Rick instantly blends in with the landscape in his full camo gear. Sweating heavily in the heat, he reaches for the binoculars, already able to pick up the heat shimmers appearing out on the flat country. Sweeping his view back past the station vehicle, he can see the three of them making their way back across the creek bed towards their truck, guns still at the ready.

Scrubber leads the way, still scowling at being sucked in. "The pricks still have got to be in the area, can't be more than an hour's walk away at best."

Max agrees. "Yeah, but in what direction? I did see a few footprints but no bike tracks so they are on foot, and I can tell you there is no water close to here."

Price adds his ten-cents' worth. "Could be more than two of them."

Now up out of the creek, they pass the innumerable large ant hills. Forty meters out from the vehicle, Scrubber raises his voice. "What the hell is that?" he says, looking at the white paper on the dust- covered windscreen through a gap in the tea trees, giving the other two hand signals to spread out and move in on the vehicle.

Max is the first to move in and picks up on all the flat tyres straight away. "These are dead men," she grits out as Price comes in from the rear and Scrubber rips the smiley face out from under the wiper blade. Crumpling it up in his calloused hand and livid with anger, he spins around to Price, who nearly jumps at the look of hatred radiating from his boss's wrinkled, weather-burnt face.

"Go get the other truck, then we will find these arse wipes and see how funny they are staked out over a meat ant's nest." He adds, "And don't bloody stuff around either. We will try and pick up on the tracks to their camp while you're gone."

Price goes to protest about the long walk back to the homestead, but, in Scrubber's mood, there is a good possibility he would end up with a bullet himself. Nodding, he walks to the truck and reaches for a two-litre cordial bottle filled with water, warm from the heat escaping off the 4x4 transfer case. Raising his head to dash height, Price notices the broken two-way and yells out to Scrubber, "They've stuffed the two-way as well."

"What the fuck?" scowls Scrubber, stomping to the driver's side door and looking in to see bare wires where the mic used to be. Adding, "And they've taken the keys," he goes off on a rant like a madman. Price had never seen him this bad before. He punches the door of their truck, his eyes wild, and saliva runs out of the corner of his mouth. Just wanting to get out of there, Price starts walking, following the tracks they had come in on.

Max yells, "Where are you going? Follow the creek line over here. There is more shade and you will only have to cut across country the last 2km to home. You will run out of water before you get there going that way." Price spins on his heel and changes direction, going back towards the dry creek.

Rick sighs with relief. Lowering the binoculars and working the hand-held two-way out of the top pocket, he calls his brother. "One coming your way." Rob, who had now been sitting in position for quite some time waiting for the heads up from Rick, has noticed that all the trees had started voluntarily dropping their leaves to reduce their need for moisture intake, as water would become non- existent as the days grow hotter.

At the station the dogs are still hitting the end of their chains with force, flicking them sidewards as they do so, all frothing at the mouth from barking constantly. Tim looks over at them. "John, you want to run the gauntlet past them measly mutts and take out the phone and radio, while I light up the shed? There's got to be fuel and oil in there for sure."

John replies, "Pig's arse." He looks at the dogs and shakes his head. "How about I light the shed up and you get past the mutts?"

Tim smiles. "Geeze you can be a wuss at times. Here, hold this," he says, passing the fuel container to John.

It is now John's turn to smile. "Now this is going to be entertaining," he says, watching the dogs go more berserk as his prospecting partner gets closer. Tim walks just out of strike length past the dogs to the nearby old, beat-up cruiser, jumps in and fires it to life as it spits out a black plume of diesel soot from the exhaust. Slipping the truck into gear,

Tim reverses it all the way till the tray is backed up level to the veranda, passing all but one dog, which tries to leap into the window before hitting the end of his chain, sending a spray of dog salvia over the side of Tim's face. Sliding over to the passenger's side, he scrambles out the window, giving John, who just stands there shaking his head and watching, the thumbs-up and a smile. Tim swings onto the tray of the truck, walks over the veranda and disappears out of sight into the homestead.

John turns back towards the shed, fuel container in hand, and makes his way to the door, saying to himself, "He's not as dumb as he looks." Lifting the latch on the door, he swings it open. With it squealing in protest, he could swear he can hear sobbing in the darkness to one side of the shed. "Screw a roo, what the hell was that?" he says aloud just as Tim pulls up in the old cruiser.

Climbing out with a smile of triumph painted over his face, he asks, "What's up, bud?"

John, intrigued, answers, "Not sure," as he slips the 44 off his shoulder and puts a round into the breach. He picks up on a slight movement in the darkness as his eyes try to adjust. "It goddam stinks in here though."

Tim follows him in. Brushing the light cord with his forearm, he says, "Hang on a tick," and pulls down on it. The light flickers twice before illuminating the shed. Both men stand speechless, looking at the backpackers huddled in the corner, barely clothed, covered in dirt, bruises and abrasions. Both are softly sobbing. Shadows of their former selves, their pristine looks and charisma are gone. They are now physically and mentally damaged women. Tim is the first to snap out it. "Bloody hell. Let's get these poor things out of here!" Glancing around the shed for something to free the girls from their binds, his eyes rest on the oxy set.

"Perfect." Wheeling the gas bottles closer to the girls, he cuts them free then both men help them out of the shed into the bright light of day. They are instantly blinded; the men, realising this, look for some shade.

Sitting down at the base of a large fig tree, Suzie, with tears rolling down her cheeks, croaks out a "Thank you" through cracked lips. John quickly passes her his camel pack of water, which she passes straight on to Terri who is clearly in the worst state. Between them they empty the two-litre water bladder.

John quietly says to Tim, "Well, what do we do now? Can't take them with us and we can't leave them here in case things go to shit."

Tim replies, "Yeah, it has thrown a spanner in the works. Didn't expect this." His mind is racing for a solution when the two-way crackles. It is Rick, letting Rob know he had one heading his way. "Shit, we are now running behind schedule. That shed should be well and truly alight by now. Let's just get the girls further away and get this sucker lit, then we will have some time to work out what to do."

Both men move into action with John slowly walking the backpackers well away from the shed. All the dogs are still going off in the background, protesting at the movement of unfamiliar people on the station.

Tim is busy in the shed, opening a 44-gallon drum of engine oil and toppling it to the ground. The oil makes a glugging sound as it pours freely out of its large bung hole onto the bare earth. Moving around the interior of the shed, he empties all the contents of his plastic petrol container, splashing the accelerant excessively while he walks out backwards and trickles a trail outside. Striking a windproof match, he throws it where the petrol line ends. Woof, up it went while Tim runs towards the truck. Dropping the clutch as its rear wheels spin in the loose topsoil.

He steers the old 4x4 towards John and the girls, who are a good 300 meters away. When the shed ignites into flames, it instantly sends billowing black smoke high into the air as the fire engulfs the spilt oil. The oxy and acetylene bottles explode, sending a mushroom ball of flame like a miniature atom bomb a good 150 feet into the atmosphere. the dogs instantly stop barking and take cover under the veranda, no longer worried about the intruders. Both Terri and Suzie are now fully coming round, realising that their time of torture is over and this pair of knock-around prospectors their saviours.

Skidding to a halt in the old truck not far from the three of them, Tim turns to watch his handiwork. "Righto, girls, this is how it is going to have to play out. For a start, you have never seen us. We will take you down beside the river. If things go wrong for us, a text message with your location will be sent from a sate phone to the cops so you will get picked up. No fires and keep out of sight, other than to any vehicles crossing the river from the opposite direction of the homestead. We will rat through their place for tinned food and other gear."

Suzie nods in comprehension. "Yes I understand. In our eyes you men are saints."

The prospectors look at each other and break into a light-hearted laugh, with John replying, "Saints? Na, you got the wrong blokes."

The men climb into the truck, realising time is of the essence, and, reciprocating what Tim had done earlier, reverse towards the homestead veranda. The dogs are a bit more subdued this time around. Finding a sleeping bag in the spare room, they go through the tinned food in the old timber pantry and throw some into the bag. "Not much here other than beans," John observes.

Tim replies, "Be a damn sight better than the swill they have been eating. The smell in shed nearly made me dry retch." They finish up by stripping a grubby blanket off Scrubber and Max's bed, also snatch some clothing from both the bedside drawers. Returning to the truck, Tim climbs back through the passenger's side window as a precaution, thinking to himself it was very smart on the station owner's behalf to have the dogs staggered on chains of different lengths so nobody could enter the homestead from any angle without being confronted by at least one of these vicious dogs. The prospectors drive back over towards the backpackers and relocate them to a safe concealed spot beside the river.

Price moves briskly along the well-worn cattle pad that meanders parallel to the creek bank, in the rough direction of the station. Walking into a clearing in the tree line when he hears what he thinks is a clap of thunder in the distance. Looking towards the horizon, he can see a large black cloud of smoke rising into the air from the direction of the homestead. "What the hell? My girls," he yells, doing his best to break into a jog towards home. Coming back into another tree line after the clearing and still following along the cattle pad, he does not realise that he has just broken a light brown thread that was tensioned to a sapling half the circumference of a pencil, slightly bending it before the thread snaps.

This gives Rob the signal and he cuts the green nylon rope that held a large springy branch, taut as it had Rob's spiked timber creation bound onto it. With no noise other than the leaves that were left on the branch, it swings swiftly back into its original position across the cattle pad, impaling Price. Five of the timber spikes bury deep into his broad chest, including one into the heart.

Grunting as the spikes slam home, Price stands there in disbelief as his legs give away from under him, snapping off the whole branch from his body weight as he hits the ground with a thud. Knowing there was only one coming his way, Rob scales up the creek bank to inspect his craftsmanship. "Pity it wasn't Scrubber," he says aloud then calls his brother. "He's down. What's going on?"

Rick's voice comes across the radio. "The other two are climbing higher, looking for tracks. By the looks, they've just seen the smoke from the homestead," he says, watching Max pointing towards the billowing smoke through the glasses.

Max screams at Scrubber, "Our fucking house is on fire!"

He makes his way over to his wife as quick as he can. "It's a goddamn trap, we have been set up from the start."

Max starts moving down the slope, screaming, "I'm going to kill them all."

Scrubber yells, with authority in his voice, "Stop. That's what they want us to do, ya bloody idiot. Could be twenty of them at the homestead for all we know. I reckon we head for the lab; it's closer. We'll get more manpower and guns then have a look. Go pull up Price and bring him back before he gets himself shot. He can't be that that far up the track yet."

Max nods. Letting her wicked temper cool, she raises the 30/30 lever action and fires off three shots in succession, signalling Price to return to the truck. They had used this signal many times in the past when separated. Making her way down the incline, she decides to meet him along the track to speed things up. Now is not the time to be stuffing around. The quicker they got to the lab, the better. Travelling along the cattle pad at pace, Max approaches the clearing where Price first spotted the smoke; 30 meters ahead, she recognises her brother's crumpled body. "No," she screams. Sprinting the distance, she kneels at his side and with tears starting to well in her eyes, she rolls him over to see the professionally crafted weapon sticking out of his chest. "Price," she whispers, closing his eyes with her fingers, "I will be back for you. I promise whoever did this are going to pay for it with their lives."

Picking up what water remained in the plastic bottle that lay by Price's side, she turns around. When she gets back within sight of the sabotaged truck, Scrubber notices that Max is alone. "Where is that overgrown dickhead now?"

She looks up to stare at him with anger burning in her eyes. "He's fucking dead."

Scrubber, shocked, says, "What? How?" Max fills Scrubber in on what she knew. "Right," he replies in a terse voice, "let's get some help and go kill the lot of them, including the bitches." They start the long dry walk to the lab with little more than a litre of water between them.

Rob had well left the area, circling wide around the ridges to avoid detection. Getting directions from his brother on the two-way, he eventually found Rick's position. Lying down beside him, he asks casually, "What's going on?"

Rick turns his head. "They've just taken the bait by the looks. Put it this way, they are moving in the opposite direction of the homestead." Both smile as the pair head south-west on foot towards the sandstones that loom in the distance.

"Best we give Tim a call and let him know we have a green light." Rob grabs his two-way. "They're leading us the way you thought they would. There's only two of them now."

The two-way crackles in response with a low signal, being right on the extremity of the range. "Roger, roger, keep us updated."

The young men take time out to eat a tin of fish, rationing their water strictly as they have to follow the other pair, at a distance. In between mouthfuls, Rick says, "We'll give them a bit of a head start, we don't want to be obvious."

His younger brother adds, "Yeah, I reckon one of us each side of them would be the go."

"Yeah. Your trap worked good, hey?"

"Yep, like clockwork," responds Rob, looking towards the heat haze on the flat ground in front of them. "They're nearly out of sight; we wouldn't be popular if we lost them."

Tim and John finished setting up the backpackers as best as possible on a grassy bank beside the Hatchet River. Clear water ran past slowly, about three feet in depth, before falling into the deep water holes a couple of kilometres downstream. The girls strip off the grotty scraps of clothing that remained and bathe for the first time in over a month without help from the monster with his bucket of water and a rag that he mainly concentrated on their genital area. The river revitalizes them after their ordeal and they are no longer worried about their nudity, even in front of the prospectors. Those days are long gone. The men, feeling uncomfortable, say good bye and drum into them again, "You have not seen us, and stay away from the road and any vehicles coming from this side. There is easy enough food for over a week but you will be picked up well before then. Just keep to yourselves about that bloke at the servo; we will pay him a visit. And for Christ's sake, stay away from the deep water holes downstream or you won't be around to be found."

The men walk back up along the river bank for 150 meters to the old 4x4 parked on the river crossing. They drive across and up the road about 2km before turning around in case anyone with bad intentions came looking for the girls. John says as they bounce along the dirt road on very old sad suspension that has seen better days, "Poor chicks. They must have gone through hell in that shed. What about that servo bloke sending them out there?"

"Yeah, bud, lucky to still be alive, I would reckon. These scum need to be wiped out, they don't deserve to breathe air." Getting back to the homestead, both prospectors pick up their backpacks. The fires had subsided, with the majority now ash and smouldering timber beams. "Let's go finish this for good," says Tim as he calls Jack's sons on the two-way. "How we looking, fellas?"

The response was a surprising strong signal, with Rob responding, "Bro, all good. We have about 2km left of this bloody desert before we start getting close to the sandstones. They're tough nuts, I will give them that." Rob wipes the salty sweat out of his stinging eyes.

The young men are fit and had youth and water on their side; Scrubber and Max are now staggering, their water expended many kilometres before. They are now solely focused on the sandstone escarpments in front of them. Through a swollen throat, Max whispers, "There is a soak not far from here that is all year round," pointing the direction.

Scrubber, on rubbery legs and feeling like his brain has been cooked, slurs, "Just get us there." At one point he was nearly ready to throw down the rifle to rid himself of the extra weight burden that it had now become, with survival the main focus.

Knowing the exact location of the soak from over 30 years of cattle mustering on the station, Max reaches the base of numerous caves. There is no visible water, just a muddy patch of soil the size of a kitchen table. Falling to her knees, she starts digging with her fingers. After 8 inches of clawing out mud, there is a small stream of water. Slowly the muddy water clears to reveal a fresh source of water. Not even having the capability of speech, Max lies on her stomach and sinks her lips into the sweetest water she has ever tasted, trying to remind herself of the golden rule; don't drink too much too fast. Scrubber, a good five minutes behind his wife, is physically struggling and collapses onto the ground beside her. Max makes room for him to drink out of the pool that is no larger than her two palms held together.

Rick and Rob have gone to ground in their camo wear, lying in the baking sun, waiting for the other pair to lead them towards the lab. They feel a bit frazzled from the crossing themselves. The radio blares into life. "Where's things up to?"

Rick replies, "We are over the other side of the desert, just biding time, waiting for them to move."

Tim replies, "Righto, we will start making a move towards the locked gates and wait at the last one till we hear from you guys."

"Roger."

Tim looks at John. "Let's get this done," he says as they follow the airstrip, swerving around numerous large trunks of timber scattered over the entire length of it. Not even slowing down for the first gate, which Max had left unlocked, they collect it with the bull bar and it slides under the old truck and is dragged 30 meters past the fence line. There is a slight bump from under the rear as it spits the solid gate out from underneath the back tyres.

Loving the action, Tim and John smile. John says, "Bring it on." Tim laughs, his foot flat to the floor in the old truck, moving along at the top speed of 65km an hour, with a trail of black soot and bull dust steaming out of the back as it moves towards the second gate.

Max and Scrubber have a 20-minute break beside the water puddle, letting it absorb into their bodies before willing themselves to keep moving. Heading south, they track along the base of the sandstone formation. After half an hour of walking in what is now the height of the day's relentless heat, Scrubber stops to lift his sweat-stained hat and peer at the position of the sun. Max, slightly ahead, stops and turns to see what the holdup is, impatient to find out what is left of their beloved homestead and kill all responsible.

"It's got to be between one and two," he announces, trying to save face. He is stuffed and is just looking for an excuse to stop and give his weary legs a break.

Reading his condition by the expression on his face, Max replies, "It's not that far to go now. Another half hour we will be close," she encourages him.

Scrubber grunts. "Yeah, where's that friggin hit man when you need him?" he says as he trudges on.

Jack's sons are in close proximity behind, watching them struggle. Finally they change direction to veer more towards the formation and start to climb. The young men, now side by side, look at each other and nod. "Rob, you just want to walk out to the track and drag a branch across it to let Tim know where to pull up, and give him a call. I will keep following this pair."

"No worries, bro," Rob says as he scampers off.

Rob reaches the dirt track that is just a slight set of old tyre imprints weaving through the bush. Briefly looking at the surrounds, he quickly finds a dead log to drag over the track. Lifting the two-way out of his pocket, he says, "Come in, fellas. Pull up at the log across the track then head west. I will leave boot scuffs on the ground for you guys to follow us in."

The two-way comes to life and Tim replies, "No worries. We won't be too far behind you." The prospector's had been waiting patiently for the call and drive through the third gate to add their presence to the fray.

The pair of cattle cockies eventually reach the mouth of a large cave. Stumbling down the incline to the extended black door, Scrubber moves past Max to raise his fist and pounds at the door. After a couple of minutes, the door slide open to reveal seven heavily armed bikies, all with AK47 semi-automatic rifles pointed at them. The disappointment shows clearly on the heavily tattooed bikie in charge. He lowers his firearm, the rest follow suit as they recognise the pair. "What the fuck do you want? Where's the radio call? And you're a day early, we are not finished the load yet. Lucky we didn't shoot ya, you dumb fucks."

Scrubber, not in the right frame of mind to cop any abuse from anyone, raises his rifle slightly; the thick-set bikies instantly retaliates. The bikie warns Scrubber, "Watch yourself, old man, or that will be the last thing you do in this life."

Max touches her husband's shoulder and takes over the situation. "We got trouble, big trouble. We need both water and guns and any man who has the balls to fight."

The head bikie wavers, liking Max's gumption and grit and her steely, unwavering stare. Reminds me of my own bitch, he muses. The hint of some action coming their way is a bonus too. All of the bikies are sick of being stuck in a confined space in the cave. Many have not ridden their hogs in quite some time and are getting toey, oozing too much testosterone of late and clashing frequently. He thinks it would be good for the boys to get out for a bit of the fun on offer and vent some pent-up steam. Ignoring Scrubber, he looks directly at Max. "Come in and fill us in on the problem." After entering the large black door, with Max in the lead, it slides shut behind them.

Rick, leaning behind some large boulders that weather and gravity had brought to rest over thousands of years, lay not far from the mouth of the cave. He informs Tim, "They're inside."

The lab two-way was only set on channel 25 and not on scan so the bikies had missed all communication from the four men who had now been led directly to the mouth of their lab lair. The old 4x4 skidded to a halt in front of the old log across the track, and Tim and John exit the truck with a sense of rushed purpose. John slips on his backpack with the remaining fuel container then collects his rifle from the rear of the tray while Tim only has on his camel pack and the hand gun Mac had given him, with both his pockets full of spare shells. Nodding at each other that they were organised, they move up towards the cave, with Tim on the two-way, "We're on our way up, fellas."

Following the boot scuff marks left for them makes short work of the climb and they soon arrive in front of the cave. Tim, catching a slight movement to his left, spins with pistol fully cocked. Rob emerges from his position. "Shit, bud, I could have put a bullet in you then." They shake hands with Tim adding, "Shit you're hard to spot in that camo gear."

Rob says with a wily smile, "Yeah, I reckon Rick's got that side covered. They've been inside a good 10 to 15 minutes now."

Tim takes a good look at the door. "Well, if that is being kept shut, they must have a ventilation shaft or hole in the cave for the gases to escape."

John, understanding what Tim is talking about, says, "I am on it," and he starts to climb the rock face to above the cave.

When he is near its summit, his two-way comes to life, with Tim saying, "While you're up there, give the big fish a call, see if we can lure him over."

Turning, John gives Tim a wave in acknowledgement instead of replying as he is sucking in large amounts of air into his lungs to slow down his heart rate, racing from the exertion of the climb. Being the oldest of the four, he lacks the energy of the others. Below they move into the best positions for cover against the heavy fire they expected to come from the cave. Scrambling over the last ledge, John drops the backpack off his shoulders and unzips the pocket containing Ox's sate phone then moves the aerial to receive its satellites. While he is waiting for the phone to beep, signalling it has locked on, John takes a few more deep breaths. Trying his best to remember Ox's tone of voice, he presses in C's number. The phone rings five times before C picks up.

After looking at the screen with the overseas call, he knows whose number it is. "What's up Ox?"

In his deepest huskiest voice, John replies, "We've got big problems at the cave. You need to get here quick" and hangs up.

C goes to reply as the phone disconnects. Swearing, he presses in the number and it ring outs. He rings it repeatedly with the same result. John leaves the phone on a rock, smiling as he can hear the phone ring back several times while he searches for the air vent.

On the other end of the line, C is now furious and throws the phone up against a wall in the house; it smashes into pieces. "What the fuck's up now!" C goes inside the bedroom to grab his hand gun and stomps out to the chopper in a foul mood.

After five minutes of searching, John finds the well-hidden solar panels followed by the exhaust ducting. "Bingo." He moves back to retrieve the petrol from his backpack. Returning with the plastic container, he gives the boys a call first. "The call has been made and I've found the ducting so get ready for a stampede."

"Well done, bud," is Tim's reply. The two brothers move a bullet into the breach of their rifles.

Inside the cave, as the bikers are in heated discussion about who should stay and how many would go, petrol pours freely down the ducting pipe and trickles onto the ground inside the lab. "What the hell?" says one as he walks over. Some lands on his shirt as he puts his hand out to fill his palm.

John ignites his box of windproof matches and throws it down the duct before sprinting to a safe distance. Fuel vapours ignite instantly, catching the inquisitive biker alight just as he is bringing the palm full of fuel to his nose for a sniff. The petrol in his hand turns to flames and burns his entire face. He staggers; screaming in pain, he falls to the ground and rolls, trying to put out the fire. The earth floor, where the fuel had soaked in, erupts into flames. The head bikie yells, "It's a fucking ambush. Get out before it all explodes."

Max and Scrubber are getting on their feet when the large bikie raises the butt of his rifle to smash it into Scrubber's skull. "You brought this trouble here, you prick."

Max lifts the barrel of her 30/30 and lets a shot go that enters under the large man's exposed armpit and exits through the top of his skull. Max grabs Scrubber by the arm and pulls him into a small alcove in the cave then pushes him to the ground. "Get down. This place is going to blow."

The single shot is consumed as the first of the bikers opens the door of the cave to be met with a vicious volley of fire. Three of them go down, writhing in their death throes at the mouth of the cave. The remaining three bikies open up with their semi-auto rifles, spraying hot lead over the boulders out front but none of them find flesh. From their well-concealed vantage spots, Tim and the brothers can hold off an army, providing they had enough ammo.

Luckily it is at the end of a shipment and all the 100-pound gas bottles are empty, but the highly flammable ingredients used to make the amphetamines explode, shaking the cave and sending a fireball of flame, smoke and dust out of the cave entrance and up through the vent in the roof.

C is coming in fast along the sandstone formation and sees the explosion erupt from the cave. "What the hell?" he yells, tilting the chopper to try and get a better look on what is happening below, with little success as the cloud of dust and smoke obscure all vision.

Hearing the chopper blades thrashing the thin air to gain altitude, Tim reaches for his two-way. "He's mine," he says, as he bounds down the slope towards the dirt track below.

Spotting only an old, clapped-out station vehicle stationary on the track, C reasons that it must be some kind of accident as there is no other visible threat. Knowing that Ox is down below gives him some reassurance and he makes the decision to land at the emergency chopper pad and wait at a safe distance for Ox to come over and fill him in on what is going on.

Still on the move while keeping a close eye on the chopper above, Tim wills, "Land, you bastard." As if on command, the chopper spins in a tight circle and lands about a kilometre away, kicking up a cloud of dust until the blades lose their velocity. "You little ball tearer," Tim yells in satisfaction as he starts the old truck after placing his loaded Glock on the passenger's seat. Crunching the old girl into gear, he weaves around typical bush features and makes way towards the chopper.

C is impatiently pacing up and down, twirling the ring on his finger and looking in the general direction of the cave, quickly calculating. If everything in production has been destroyed plus the cost of re-establishment, the damage would easily run into many millions. Hearing the approaching vehicle, he lifts his right hand to cut down the amount of afternoon sun glaring into his eyes. Picking the outline of a single person in the truck, he breathes a sigh of relief. "About time," he mumbles, leaning on the door of his chopper as the truck gets closer.

Now in the cleared landing area, Tim pushes the accelerator to the floor. The old truck lets out a plume of black smoke as it slowly responds to burning the extra diesel and gains momentum. Taken unawares, C exclaims, "What the fuck." Realising the truck is picking up pace not slowing, and he is lined up in the centre of the old bull bar, he spins, opens the chopper door and reaches for the hand gun in plain view on his seat.

Judging the distance before impact, he has no option but to leave the Glock where it is and dive to one side as the cruiser crunches sickeningly into the chopper's cab, smashing the perplex screen and tearing through the light aircraft aluminium like butter. Slamming on the brakes, Tim swings out of the truck before C can get off the ground. He sinks his right boot hard into C's ribs, with three of them snapping like twigs. Letting out a grunt of pain, all the oxygen rushes out of his lungs from the force of a blow that rolls C onto his stomach and leaves him dry heaving as he tries to gulp in fresh air. With cat-like reflexes, Tim lands both knees into the middle of C's back. Drawing his knife at the same time as he twists his torso around, Tim slices straight through the muscle and sinew of C's Achilles tendon, effectively hamstringing the man. C lets out a scream of protest. Stepping off him, Tim rolls him over with his boot so he can get a good look at who is inflicting this pain on him. "Remember me?" he says between clenched teeth.

C's eyes adjust quickly and he recognises the prospector. "This can't be. You're dead!" he yells in disbelief.

Tim replies with a sneer, "You fucked with the wrong people this time around. Now this is how it's going to work. You're going to tell me where my uncle is and who else is in this syndicate and I just might let you live."

Not believing a word, C, trying his best to laugh through the burning pain, grounds out, "Your uncle is maggot food somewhere between here and WA. Even I don't know exactly where."

The blood runs from Tim's face as gun fire echoes through the cliffs. C adds, "And you can go to hell on the rest."

"Fair enough then," says Tim. Taking the couple of steps forward, he bends down and with lighting speed his fist connects flush on C's jaw, knocking him out instantly. Grasping one of the unconscious man's legs, he drags him the short distance to the truck and throws his limp body in the back unceremoniously. Reversing the vehicle, Tim pulls up beside the damaged chopper. Leaving the engine of the truck idling, he gets out, tearing off one of his long shirt sleeves as he goes. Undoing one of the chopper's fuel caps, he dips his sleeve into the avgas, gives it a good soaking then pulls the majority of the sleeve back out. Tim then gives it a flick with his lighter. Sprinting the short distance back to the truck, he slams the old girl into gear with his foot flat to the floor.

Lurching forward, he tries to get as much distance possible between himself and the chopper that is now in flames. It explodes seconds later as the heat has built up enough to erupt in the fuel tank. Tim feels the heat from the blast. As a lump of stainless steel pierces though the rear glass of the cab and out through its windscreen, he instinctively swerves while ducking his head in case more is to follow. The old truck moves through the gears as it makes its way to the centre of the desert. Finally satisfied that there is no water close by in any direction, Tim stops the truck.

Dragging C out from the back as he starts to regain consciousness, Tim releases his grip on his shirt and lets him fall to the ground. "This is more of a chance than you gave me," he says. Drawing out his knife once more, he repeats the hamstring process to the other tendon and C screams in agony. "Now let's see you crawl out of this one, you prick." Wasting no time, he steers the truck back towards the cave, leaving C in a cloud of dust. C tries to stand without success; having no other option, he starts to crawl in the general direction of the homestead.

After the explosion at the cave, the smoke and dust is that thick it blinds Jack's sons and hangs in the air for what seems like an eternity. The remaining three bikies took the full brunt of the chemical blast, its flames leaving them unrecognisable due to the third degree burns covering their smouldering bodies.

As the dust eventually starts to clear, Rick, who is the greater distance from the mouth, tries to pick up any movement in his sights. Drawing a bead on a possible target, he goes to eject a spent shell out of the chamber. Suddenly from behind him, Scrubber appears, his face burnt and blistered, his hair singed. After losing his rifle in the blast, he resorts to swinging a large, solid lump of timber and gets Rick square across the shoulder blades, propelling the young man forward as he squeezes off a shot into the air before dropping the rifle. This gets John's attention, who is still above the cave, and Rob's, who fires a hasty shot at Scrubber, missing the mark considerably.

Max, her face totally burnt on one side, locates the origin of Rob's last shot and sends three shots in that direction, the first grazing Rob's shoulder and the other two ricocheting far too close for comfort, shearing a sharp lump off a granite boulder and drawing blood from his cheek. "Shit," he yells, having to withdraw further behind the boulders, realising he is pinned down and unable to protect his brother.

Rick's face smashes into the boulder directly in front of him. His nose breaks. Raving like a mad man, Scrubber strikes again before the young man can react, sending him to the ground delirious as his vision blurs. Scrubber raises the log high above his shoulder this time and aims at Rick's head to finish him off. John takes a slow breath. With the 44 rifle resting on the side of a small ironbark tree to steady the barrel, he squeezes the trigger, knowing this is the most important shot of his life. The bullet stays true; fine bone fragments of Scrubber's skull are sprayed in every direction.

Seeing her husband's head explode like a ripe watermelon, Max screams in anguish. She spins while firing from her hip at the unknown adversary high above that had now entered the firefight with the 30/30 slamming two shots deep into John's chest. Gasping for breath, he looks down at the holes in his chest. Incredulous that someone could be that good of a marksman, he sinks to his knees and falls face first onto the ground.

Rob, realising he is not being pinned down by gunfire anymore, spins around the boulders and fires three shots in succession, one missing Max's head by centimetres, the second smashing into her collarbone and flinging the 30/30 out of her grasp, and the third shot whistled by harmlessly. She dives to one side and lands on the ground heavily, jarring the wound in her shoulder that had shattered the bone, which now protruded through the skin. Her right arm hung limply by her side. Rob moves forward quickly with the 223 aimed at Max while she tries to drag herself towards her rifle. Failing at the task, she rolls flat onto her back. Max reaches across her body with her left hand and flicks the clip off the knife sheath. Rob had already passed by the wounded station owner, picking up her 30/30 and flinging it further out of reach.

Rick groggily picks himself up off the ground and looks behind to see Scrubber's body sprawled across the rocks with just a bloody pulp remaining of his head. He rubs the palm of his hands across both eyes, trying to clear his vision. Rob has turned around after throwing the 30/30 a considerable distance to see his brother emerge from the boulders into the clearing. "You OK, bro?"

"Yeah, bud, feels like I've been hit by a train. Looks like you drilled him well and truly," Rob replies.

"Wasn't me; must have been John," Rick says, turning his attention to Max's burnt face, not wasting any time. "Where is my father?" They can hear Tim's approach in the old 4x4 below, smashing over saplings and climbing as high as possible up the incline. Max's reply is barely audible through her burnt lips, the brothers both move in closer to try and decipher what she is saying.

"Not too close," cautions Rob, as Rick had moved into striking distance, eager to hear news of his father.

With the speed of a taipan, Max's left arm moves from her side where she had been holding the knife concealed under her torso and, with all her force, plunges the blade clean through Rick's left boot. He yells in pain. She withdraws the knife quickly to take aim at Rob, changing her hand position to a throwing knife. Rob, also taken by surprise at the speed of the attack, goes to lift his rifle. Two pistol shots sound out from behind Rob, with the hot lead finding its mark in Max's soft neck tissue as the knife sails dangerously close to her target, slightly off course because of the impact of the bullets milliseconds before. "That's one tough bitch," says Rob, turning to see where the shots had originated from.

Tim is only 10 meters behind him, holding the Glock in his hand stating, "She's not so tough anymore." Rob drops the rifle and moves over to inspect his brother's wound, with blood emerging from the top and the sole of his boot. Tim asks, "You fellas right?"

"Yeah," replies Rick, "just a knife wound," looking down at his foot.

"John's got pressure bandages in his backpack that will stem the flow of blood. By the way, where is he?" asks Tim, looking around for his prospecting partner.

Rob replies, "Not sure. He hasn't come down from the top since taking out Scrubber."

Tim's facial expression changes to concern as he looks above the cave for any sign of John. Shoving the Glock into his waistband, he immediately climbs straight up the face of the sandstones, cutting down considerable time from walking around the easier path.

Getting to the top, sweat glistening off his brow, he can see John slumped over and leaning up against the small ironbark tree he had managed to crawl back to after taking the shot. Moving to his side, Tim bends down, slowly pushing John's shoulders backwards to straighten him up. His whole shirt front is soaked in blood and there are two gaping bullet holes in his chest. John gasps in pain with the movement, his colour an ashen grey. "Shit," yells Tim then lowers his voice while inspecting the fatal wounds. "Hang on, bud, we will get you out of here." Moving swiftly to the edge of the escarpment, he yells to Rob, "He's been shot. Give me a hand."

Rob makes it to the top quickly. "Bloody hell," he says.

Lifting John upright, they stumble the long way round, with the wounded prospector's arms over each of the men's shoulders as he lapses in and out of consciousness. Rick has also started to make his way back down the cattle pad, limping towards the old cruiser.

All three able men arrive at the truck within minutes of each other and carefully lift John into the back. "Shit, he doesn't look good," says Rick.

Tim bounds into the back in one leap. "Let's get out of here. Where's that bloody sate phone?" Both brothers shrug as they climb into the cab, sending the truck bouncing over rocks with Tim propping up John as best he can. At the base, Rob spins the wheel to follow the dirt track leading back towards the homestead at top speed. John's eyes flicker open and he takes a deep wheezing breath. Opening his mouth, he speaks for the first time. Aerated blood slid down one side of his chin, and Tim knew the bullet had ruptured his lungs. Whispering deliriously, "Nearly made it without a scratch mate. Tell Meg to put my dinner in the oven I could be home late tonight. With all his remaining strength, John moves his blood-stained hand over to try and shake Tim's but falls short. With just a weak squeeze, he lets out a rattly sigh as his body goes limp and his hand flops onto the timber tray.

Tim lets out a yell that can be heard for miles. Rob hits the brakes just as they enter the station's airstrip. Jumping out, both the brothers take one look at John and can see what had just transpired. Glancing over at Tim, neither quite knows what to say. They climb back into the truck to continue at a slower pace, leaving Tim to say his goodbyes to his buddy in private. Arriving at the half burnt-out station, Rob asks Tim, "Do you want to move him into the cab, mate, to keep the scavengers away?"

He looked at them with a blank expression. Rick breaks the silence. "Bro, we all agreed before we came out that should anything happen to any of us, we would have to be left behind or we all would rot in jail. That was the deal, and I reckon John was a man of his word."

Tim snaps out of his trance. "Yeah, you're right. He was a man of his word. Help me get him in the front." Once done, the three shake hands. Tim says, "Talk to you in town, boys. I'm going to cut across the river further downstream and head back to town the other way." Rob waves with his spare hand and helps Rick keep the weight off his left foot as they make a start back to their camp, following the road as daylight starts to fade, with Tim disappearing in the opposite direction towards John's 4x4.

Just before dawn, the young men pull up in front of their parents' place. The lights flicker on inside and Sue meets her two sons at the door, tears of relief rolling down her face as she hugs them tightly. "Let's get you cleaned up," she says, mothering her sons and shutting the door as soon as the two boys step inside the house.

Tim arrives in town a couple of hours after Jack's boys, having had trouble finding an old river crossing in the dark that he had been told about years previously. He turns the corner leading into John's street with a slight tremor in the hand holding the steering wheel. Meg is washing up her breakfast dishes. Recognising the noise of the three- inch exhaust on her husband's truck, she frowns as it does not drive through the gate. Wiping her hands on the tea towel, she moves to the front door to be met by Tim. Happy to see him alive, she hugs him, her face lit up with excitement. "John must be ecstatic, where is he?" she says, leaning around Tim's shoulder, looking towards the empty truck.

Tim reaches over and touches Meg on the shoulder to get her attention. Swallowing a dry lump in his throat, he says, "Meg, he did not make it. I wanted to bring him home but it was not possible."

She looks at him quizzically. "What do you mean?" she says, confusion raining down on her as she tries to fathom what Tim is trying to tell her. He fills her in on the events that unfolded out bush, including his anonymous call to the police when he arrived in town. When the conversation gets to finding John, Meg loses the strength in her legs. As they start to buckle, he grabs her and leads Meg back inside to the lounge. "I will drop his truck back in a few days. I am so sorry, Meg. I don't know what else to say." It falls on deaf ears as she sits in shock, gazing at nothing in particular. Tim turns around and leaves the house.

Sitting in the 4x4, he is deeply saddened that his plan had gone so close to being perfect except for losing his best friend. Starting the truck, he knows he also needs to go over and see Sue but he is exhausted, both mentally and physically.

Sue's house is another hour's drive out of his way so he opts to visit over the next couple of days, reasoning that she would have her hands full, anyway, patching up the boys. He also needed to organise with the brothers to retrieve his own vehicle before they went back to work. Finally he heads for home, longing to have Danni in his arms. The reunion between them is very emotional and passionate, with even a tear forming in the tough prospector's eye.

The bikers pass through the tableland towns without incident. The ute is full of gas bottles and they have two bikes travelling an inconspicuous distance in front and behind. Arriving at their scheduled pickup point, they patiently wait for two hours for the station vehicle. The Sergeant at Arms decides to call the clubhouse to find out if there is any contact or a change of schedule. Finding no changes had been made, and having been around the traps long enough, he has a gut feeling that something has gone wrong. Turning to his crew, he says, "Come on, let's ride until this shit gets sorted."

Two weeks later an unmarked police car pulls up out the front of Tim and Danni's house and the detective knocks on the door. Danni finally answers. "Oh, hi Grace." This time she does not invite her in for a cuppa.

"Hi. Danni, just thought I would drop by and give you an update on the case." Glancing around, she notices a pair of large male thongs beside the bottom step of the house.

Danni follows her gaze and colours slightly. "Go on," she replies, trying to take the detective's mind off from the thongs.

"Yes. We had an anonymous call two weeks ago about more gun fire out at Hatchet River Station. Our team was first onsite; what a mess, bodies everywhere." Danni holds her gaze, not responding. "We found your husband's prospecting buddy, he'd been shot multiple times, in one of the station's vehicles, along with a burnt-out chopper, station buildings, even a burnt-out drug lab full of dead bikies and the station owners."

Grace continues on in a dubious tone, "This John must have been one hell of a tough nut to achieve all this on his own; some would say it's impossible. We might never know exactly what happened out there. At the moment it's in fate's hand, but what we have pieced together so far is a major drug ring has been crushed. Only four survivors were found; two backpackers near the river, they identified John as the man who saved them. Also a man found 4km from the station homestead, barely alive with severe dehydration, both leg tendons cut and one side of his face nearly totally void of flesh, including the loss of one eye from the crows. That's the only reason he was found – the unusual number of scavenger birds circling the area. Looks like he had dragged himself on his stomach for miles, sure is one tough fella. Hopefully we will get to question the man, he is still critical in intensive care."

Grace starts walking to her car. As Danni follows, she says, relaxing a little after the last comment, "Yes, John was one hell of a man, as was my husband, as was Jack," in a subdued tone.

The detective, now seated in her vehicle, smiles slightly. "Oh, nearly forgot. I found this in John's shirt pocket before the emergency chopper took him to hospital." She passes the blood-soaked letter from Tim through the window. As Danni reaches out, Grace adds, "It makes for interesting reading."

Danni cuts in. "You must be mistaken; you mean before they flew John to the morgue, not the hospital."

"No, like I said earlier, he must be a tough nut. I personally checked his pulse while he was still in the vehicle and there was not one. I instructed some of the younger officers to remove the body then bag and tag him. When they opened the door, he fell heavily to the ground, projecting a lump of congealed blood the size of my fist out of his mouth. One of the officers, inspecting closer, noticed a slight eyelid movement and yelled, 'He's alive.' I rechecked for a pulse, there was a faint one that definitely was not there before. He was dead. The surgeons have put him in an induced coma. They are worried that even if he does survive, the bullet wounds and the extreme heat from sitting in the vehicle without fluids could have fried his brain; there is a high probability of permanent brain damage."

"So he's alive." Danni smiles.

"Yes," answers Grace, "but as it stands with the evidence so far he is our prime suspect, up on multiple counts of murder including arson and depravation of liberty to name a few. If he survives and is proven guilty in a court of law, he will spend the rest of his life in jail. Both men are under heavy guard, 24 hours a day, 7 days a week."

Danni is still smiling as she says goodbye to Grace. She is bursting to tell her husband the good news but there was to be no contact till he arrived home.

Looking out over the Hatchet River in the distance, old Mac sits down to watch the sun set over his tranquil, massive backyard bush setting. In the distance he can hear the noise of a motor approaching. Rising up off the chair, old Mac goes to his hut and retrieves his shot gun. Checking it is loaded, he returns to his chair. The noise grows more distinct as it draws closer until it finally appears below. Peering down, Mac can make out it is a quad.

Arriving at the top of the ridge, Tim is met by Mac's shotgun pointed in his direction. "Whoa up there, old timer, you wouldn't shoot an old mate, would ya?"

Mac squints in the dying light. "What the hell, is that you, Tim?" he says, recognising the voice.

Tim replies in a louder voice, "Yeah, bud. Had to come and pick up John's quad and trailer so I thought while out this far I may as well call in. A whimper starts from the plastic cage well tied down on the back of John's quad.

"What the?" questions Mac. Tim smiles. "Brought you a new friend," he says, opening the door of the cage and the wolfhound ridgeback pup bounds off the quad." He might need a drink." Mac puts the shotgun up against his old hut, smiling. "Of course. Here, boy." He shuffles off to fill a bowl of water for his pup, fussing over the dog instantly. "Are you staying for a while?" he asks with hope in his voice.

Tim replies, "No, my old friend, I will be leaving to-night. I have unfinished business to deal with, but I will be back when I'm done to take you up on that offer." They talk briefly then shakes the old timer's hand and loads on a hessian sack before starting the motor, drops off the steep bank into the darkness. Mac follows as the headlights swerve through the bush down below. With the pup having had its fill of water, it stands beside Mac, ears pricked up inquisitively, watching the light also beside his new master.

A nice 5' ounce gol d nugget

One of Tim's intri cate craved statues of a Chinese miner standiruz 9 foot tall.